RATS

A ROSS SIEGAL PSYCHOLOGICAL THRILLER

To Marv Goss
a great Goss
Read & Enjoy
Herb P
6/17

Herb Padzensky

RATS: A Ross Siegal Psychological Thriller
Published by HERO Publishing LLC
Denver, Colorado

Library of Congress Control Number: 2017906305
PADZENSKY, HERB, Author
RATS: A Ross Siegal Psychological Thriller
Herb Padzensky

ISBN: 978-0-9985034-0-0

FIC031080   **FICTION** / Thrillers / Psychological
FIC031090   **FICTION** / Thrillers / Terrorism

QUANTITY PURCHASES: Schools, companies, professional groups, clubs, and other organizations may qualify for special terms when ordering quantities of this title. For information, email herobookpublishing@gmail.com.

HERO

PUBLISHING

I dedicate this book to my wife Ro who has nursed me through my learning disabilities and listened to countless rewrites with the patience of Job.

My appreciation goes to those skilled team members who have made this novel a better read. Thank you; Polly, Susie, Bobby, Pam, Andrea, Micah, and my granddaughter Jamie.

PART ONE

IN THE BEGINNING, GOD CREATED heaven and earth. Then He created the firmament and animals. Feeling proud of His accomplishments, He created humans. All was wonderful, but this is where He should have stopped. In His great wisdom to create all things wonderful, God made one mistake. He created animal behavior and allowed humans to possess it.

ONE

A WHITE, UNMARKED NISSAN MINIVAN slowed as it approached the entrance of the Second International Bank of Harbin, China. It came to a stop in the bank's customer loading space. Its windows, tinted by silver Mylar, hid the driver and riders inside.

The right-side door slid open. Five men wearing long coats stepped out. They approached the bank in a deliberate, well-rehearsed formation. They wore no masks or disguises to distinguish themselves from other banking customers. Nothing unusual. Nothing to forewarn their arrival. Nothing.

The bright sun, sinking in the late day sky, glared through the bank's large front windows. It obscured the men's faces, making it impossible for surveillance cameras to capture facial recognition images as they walked through the double doors into the lobby. No one paid them any special attention. No need. They were just five people, non-Chinese tourists, visiting this Liaoning Province city to carry out financial business.

A nod by the leader changed the peaceful afternoon scene in an instant. The long coats of the five opened in unison, exposing AK-47s. Bullets shattered the calm. The four tellers were knocked over like bowling pins. Blood and viscera splattered against the wall behind them. It happened so fast. There was no time for any of them to set off an alarm. Customers standing in the lobby froze in shock.

Another head nod and a second hail of bullets sent the helpless guard, a customer he was assisting, and two bank officers still seated at their desks reeling backwards into pools of their own blood. A pair of assailants hurdled the teller counter and emptied every cash drawer, throwing the paper money into the air while laughing at their prank. A bank robbery? Hardly.

Pleading customers, still alive, were herded to the far wall that displayed a larger-than-life portrait of Yi Cho-Se, premier of the People's Republic. They huddled together beneath the portrait as a third round of bullets shredded their bodies, spattered blood defacing the premier's image.

No witnesses survived the holocaust.

A bank desecrated but not robbed. Bodies of men, women, and children, all innocent victims, lay across each other like freshly thrown Chinese pickup sticks.

Police discovered a handwritten letter adhered to the teller's counter. It was pasted there by blood from the victims. It read:

You have been warned to pay tribute and you chose to ignore me. I grow impatient. I demand 100 million American dollars. Disobey and I will slaughter more of your citizens. I will contact your Central Government in three days with specific instructions on where to send the money.
REBUS

It was over in three minutes. This was the fifth successful attack across Europe and Asia in less than two months. More attacks were sure to happen unless Rebus could be stopped.

TWO

HALFWAY AROUND THE WORLD AT City University in Denver, Dr. Ross Siegal sat at his office desk in the behavioral studies lab, pondering what the coming year would offer. He held the dubious title of Chairman of Behavioral Science, a one-man island in a psychology department whose other professors were staunch Freudian theorists.

Intent on making this new fall term more exciting, he studied his lecture notes and new rat lab experiments. In the past, his grant requests for experimentation were often met with quagmires of red tape. This year he hoped it would be different.

The alarm on his watch, one of the few modern technologies he allowed in his life, rang. *Time to meet Simi.*

A YOUNG MAN brandishing a "JESUS SAVES" sign like a broadsword stood on a wooden crate in front of Quandary's, the favorite watering hole and haven of professors and graduate students. "Are we all like the people of Sodom and Gomorrah?" he said. "Must we all, innocent and guilty alike, die before God preaches his final sermon to love each other?" A few people stopped to listen; most did not.

Siegal gave a quick glance at the man as he hurried by. Simi would be inside waiting, a warm pleasure he anticipated.

Siegal rubbed his eyes as he exchanged the bright sunshine for the dimly lit bar. The smell of stale beer and greasy food from this 30-something-year-old grill permeated every cranny. Most of the two dozen red vinyl-covered tables were empty, normal for early August. Here and there, locals mixed with a few college drop-outs—nicknamed slummers by the valid university students—who pretended to brush elbows with the intellectuals in the hopes their parents would continue sending phantom tuition checks.

Siegal smiled, spotting Simi Block, one of two graduate research assistants he mentored, sitting at their regular table near the rear of the room where they could survey all without being the center of attention. They traded kisses. He then joined her in noshing the house specialty, chile con queso. They cut the heat with a popular local brewery's quaff, Old Dog's Leg Lager.

A forty-five-year-old bachelor, Ross Siegal stood almost five foot six, muscular, a full head of curly black hair with hints of grey around the sideburns and balding at its crown. He cared little for fashion, politics, or the world around him. Avoiding most radio or television news programs, he would not have known about any of the raids by Rebus, especially the latest one in China that would forever change his life. His modest apartment had one old-school small screen in dire need of an upgrade.

Few among Siegal's contemporaries appreciated his creative and innovative psychological theories. Neither did they care to have him as a friend. In turn, he prided himself in offering persistent criticism of what he considered mistakes in their thinking and research design flaws.

Simi Block, five-foot-two and just recently turned thirty, was a little fleshy in the places men seemed to enjoy. She described herself as the type an aunt wanted you to date because of her great personality. Two years prior, she survived a difficult divorce after her husband took off with the male doorman of their luxury high-rise apartment. It was this event that caused her to gain twenty pounds and commit to finishing her degree. When she became Siegal's research assistant and lover, she discovered the joy of becoming one of the beautiful women with a mind and will of her own—not a trophy as her husband saw her.

They soon were joined by BF, a young associate professor in the psychology department, and Sally Ryan, Siegal's other graduate research assistant.

The table was now, once again, filled with fearless free spirits, pathfinders on their own roads less traveled. They made a perfect band of malcontents, challenging the world's conservative dogmas. They vehemently argued among themselves but always united against the ideas of others.

Never at a loss for words, there was always a topic to discuss. Tonight's conversation was about world politics, a rarity, especially for the anti-political Siegal. BF observed they needed reinforcement. He motioned for Mary the waitress to bring an order of house specials and two pitchers of ODL to fortify their thoughts.

"Horseshit," blurted Sally, whose use of the King's English did not reflect a child of religious parents, her father a priest of their Christian church. "Those do-nothing bastards and bitches at the UN need to get laid. Hey, Secretary Segurian, you need some. Here I am." Her hands moved seductively up and down her body.

She rocked slowly, pausing around her twenty-two-year-old pointed breasts.

Simi blushed at the action and asked, "Ross, honey, would you like me to give you some of Sally's politics in bed tonight?"

Siegal blushed back.

It could have been the beer talking which made Siegal smile in anticipation of Simi's suggestion, or maybe his smile came from BF's attempt to balance while standing on his chair to prove some ambiguous point.

Sitting back down, BF bent over the table and banged his glass. "Ahem. I have something very important to say." He wobbled, acting slightly drunk and pretending to slur his words. "It's all right to have a formal place like the U-u-u…"

"United," the other three chimed in, laughing at BF's lame pretense.

It only spurred him on to continue. "Yes. The UN is a perfect symposium to express problems and to ask for support." He paused for effect. "But it is not our salvation. What we really need is a new invention of the wheel. Instead of thinking to change the U-u-u…"

"United," chimed the choir.

"We must create an NT: a New Thing."

The group applauded. They knew of his track record for stating the predictable future and for viewing such philosophical statements as some fantastic insight.

"You're talking like Orwell," said Simi.

They talked, drank and scarfed two more orders of house specials till they ran up against Quandary's summer closing hour. All shared the tab. Siegal, with the highest income, paid the tip as usual. Sally and BF, both living with parents, had satisfied themselves earlier in BF's back seat and went straight home. Simi and Siegal chose her apartment.

FIGHTING THE MORNING light, Siegal remained in a semi-dream state. For the first time in his life he was in love. His first meeting with Simi played out in his mind. It was the initial class day of the last fall term.

"Ladies and gentlemen, welcome to Psychology 520, Advanced Research Design." One person, older than the mostly twenty-year olds, entered late, walked down the steps and sat in the front row. Siegal checked his computer-generated roster. "Ms. S. Block, so nice of you to finally join us. I trust an eight o'clock class is not too early a start for you."

The class let out supportive murmurs.

Unfazed and smiling, Ms. Block nodded, acknowledging Siegal's attempt at professorial humor, and crossed her legs as she settled in her seat. Her short skirt, one of many she wore, did not quite cover her lower body parts. And whenever she raised her hand to ask a question, her form-fitted sweaters raised to her bra line.

This mature and very sexy woman caught Siegal's immediate attention. Her demeanor forced him to remain behind the podium in order to avoid revealing his physical reaction to her. This game played out every class day. Often she remained after class to argue a theoretical point he made during a lecture. This led to sharing coffee at the university cafeteria, dinners at local restaurants, and their first physical encounter four months later.

On this morning, he felt blood swelling in his groin and reached over searching for his lover. An empty pillow greeted him. He wanted more.

Simi's call from the kitchen, "Breakfast is ready," roused him out of his reverie.

Siegal reached for the sweatshirt he kept on a chair by the bedside. Simi had already claimed it. He found a pair of boxer shorts in the bottom drawer of the dresser, kept there for such emergencies.

Simi stood, facing the stove, wearing the sweatshirt, nothing else. Siegal caressed her bottom and kissed her ear. "I am the evil lord and you are my maidservant."

"I am your slave, master. But not today."

Siegal frowned at the rejection.

"I have to work on my dissertation at the library. And you have to go downtown. Save it for tonight."

THREE

TWO TIME ZONES TO THE east, in the Oval Office, sat President Elwin Russell and his trusted Chief of Staff, Tom Danielson. Each morning, the two reviewed events from the previous day and planned strategies for the days ahead. Most often these meetings were held long-distance by messenger, phone, or secured email. Sitting face-to-face this morning was a rare exception.

A flat-screen monitor tuned to MSNBC replayed news anchor Robert Gallow's interview with United Nations Secretary General Andre Segurian.

Secretary Segurian spoke fluent English with an accent common to his country. "The world is in a state of constant turmoil led by new generations of radicals attacking countries with impunity and little fear of reprisal. We of the United Nations are attempting to resolve these issues but the leaders remain either unknown, or unwilling to negotiate."

Gallow responded, "I understand. The diplomatic process is slow and arduous. Mr. Secretary, we at MSNBC received frightening reports of what appears to be continued gangster activity across Europe and Asia, in particular mainland China. Can you elaborate?"

President Russell and Danielson watched the 10-second grainy footage of the carnage at a bank in Harbin provided by the MSNBC news staff.

Segurian avoided a response, but his facial grimace indicated he was aware of the event.

Danielson slathered a half piece of bagel with some cream cheese and put a slice of lox on it. Before becoming the President's chief of staff, Danielson was a colonel, now retired, in a crack Navy SEALS team. He never got used to the plodding ways of world politics.

"El, the UN is helpless in these instances. They have the strongest nations of the world as members and they show little authority to do anything of meaning. As I've said many times before, we need some form of world organization that is lean and mean. One that moves without all the fancy rhetoric."

Biting into his own bagel, Russell nodded in half agreement. "I'd like to agree. But no can do, Tom. The UN does many good things. Aside from cutting off the only major international forum for smaller nations, give me a better suggestion. There's got to be a better way. I need good an idea from you."

Both men enjoyed their daily repartees. It was through these interactions that many important policies came out of the Oval Office.

Danielson took a sip of coffee. A smile crossed his lips.

"I can see some wheels turning in that head of yours," said Russell, pointing his finger at Danielson.

"Don't you think there is something odd about that release, El? That clip came from the bank's security camera. Right? China would never let it become public, especially when it puts them in a bad light. What if the leak was on purpose?"

"Good point," said Russell, slapping his fist on the table. "I recall most of the Chinese people never saw anything about the riot in Tiananmen Square, even though most of the world witnessed it. You're thinking that their leaders had something to do with the leak?"

"It makes sense," said Danielson. "Those guys never want to lose face in the eyes of the world. They would normally keep this event out of the press. I think they're masking something. Something they want to hide."

President Russell learned many years ago to trust Danielson's intuition. As his campaign manager, he helped Russell win an upset election to Congress, and successfully orchestrated two terms in the White House. His genius for solving myriad problems at every level made him an indispensable confidant.

The television interview concluded. As Russell and Danielson returned their attention to the notes on the coffee table, the President's red desk phone rang. They both looked toward the phone, originally installed during the Cold War with the Soviet Union. Russell chose to maintain its use for selected individuals who needed to talk with him directly without lower-echelon staff determining the call's priority. "That damn phone seems to be ringing too much lately."

Russell answered, "Good morning, Mr. Secretary." He whispered to Danielson. "It's Andre Segurian."

Danielson took his cue and left the room.

PRESIDENT RUSSELL HELD no secrets from his chief of staff. It was just proper protocol. He'd find out later if and when the President chose.

Amanda Keyes, President Russell's personal secretary, looked up from her oversized desk as Danielson entered the outer office. Miss Keyes had been with the President longer than Danielson. She first worked in his law office and then as personal aide during his stint in Congress. Russell bragged he never missed an important vote because of her.

Danielson smiled as he went directly for the coffeepot. "You look very nice today, Miss Keyes. Blue is definitely your color."

"Why thank you, Mr. Danielson." Her eyes fluttered. "If I didn't know better, I would think you are trying to flirt with me."

The two had been close to each other since Danielson became part of Russell's team. But they always maintained a businesslike attitude out of respect for their boss.

Moments later, the light on Miss Keyes's intercom blinked, summoning Danielson back. He dropped the cup and the few remaining drops of coffee into the wastebasket and went back in.

"IS SEGURIAN CALLING for a lunch date?" asked Danielson, hoping to change the frown from Russell's face.

"You can put that idea on the damn back burner. There has been lots of talk about this Rebus. As we have talked before about him, his gang slaughters everyone in sight without mercy. Yesterday was the second time in so many days that Rebus hit a bank in China demanding a ransom in order to stop. So far Cho-Se has refused to pay."

"I give him credit for that. What's Segurian's take?"

"This time was the final straw. Cho-Se's daughter and granddaughter were in the bank that Rebus raided. They were slaughtered along with the rest of the innocent victims."

"Cho-Se is begging for UN help, right? And the Sec Gen is hoping you'll put our American ass in the middle."

Russell said, "We can't capitulate to every UN request. The other governments where Rebus attacked have also talked to us about doing something. If we don't step in, one of the countries not so friendly to us will. Then we'll have another enemy to deal with. I want you to check into it, under the radar of course. I know you have a unique network of connections and ways to look into sensitive issues in a manner I can't condone publicly as President and I'm not asking you to tell me about them now. But we can certainly use some of your magic."

"When I commanded a SEALS outfit, I would just let the two men who had a problem duke it out. The matter was quickly settled and everyone parted with bruised eyes and egos, but they parted as friends."

"I can't do that here. America is a country that believes in rights for every human being. We work to resolve conflicts in a peaceful manner if at all possible."

Danielson asked, "What exactly did Secretary Segurian say?"

"He said Chairman Cho-Se thought a young Chinese gang was doing this. But the last attack, the one we saw from the bank's security camera, showed all the combatants involved were definitely not Asian. That makes it more than an internal issue for China. Segurian added that each time there was a ransom note left at the scene. Signed by Rebus."

"And this ransom note was signed?" asked Danielson.

"Rebus."

"El, I know the name. He's a notorious bandit in South America, bullying schools and churches for pocket change." Danielson paused. "Odd, he seldom killed anyone. Rebus seems to have morphed from attacking helpless third-world countries in South America to becoming a heartless international killer."

President Russell walked over to his desk and opened his planner, where he kept records of every call to his office in preparation for his memoirs following retirement. He copied several names on a piece of stationery and handed the list to Danielson. "Here are names of the leaders from the countries attacked by a gang using the same MO as Rebus."

Danielson scanned the names. "I know these guys very well."

"We need to put an end to this before we have another Osama to deal with. I want a secret meeting with them. Can you set it up and keep it under the radar?"

"Shouldn't be too difficult. I'm guessing they all have dedicated phones like your red phone so we can communicate without political fuss. What kind of timeline do I have?"

"These men are all interested to get it done. How about a week?"

"Make it a week and a half."

"Done. Ten days. Use my red phone to make arrangements. Any travel must be done in your personal car and on commercial air travel. No Federal involvement. Not even Amanda can know about this." Russell took the last bite of bagel. "Use our safe house in the Colorado Rockies as a meeting place. If the press catches wind, spin something like a short meeting on renewable energy."

FOUR

GOING DOWNTOWN MEANT GOING TO his second job. Like most university professors, Siegal needed an additional paycheck to supplement his anemic salary. He landed this position a little over a year ago as a part-time consultant for Interaction Dynamics, a personnel development firm.

ID specialized in team building, time management, conflict resolution, and often did headhunting searches for corporations seeking individuals to fill specialized skill positions. Jerry Ravid, ID's CEO, maintained a staff of three full-time psychologists and a cadre of part-time Ph.D. professors from the nearby universities. Everyone respected each other's degrees and seniority, but maintained a family atmosphere by using first names except when meeting with clients.

Siegal had barely settled in his small office when his intercom buzzed. It was Ravid's secretary. "Jerry is requesting your presence in the big office as soon as you're free."

Siegal knew this was a command request and all other activity ceased. "Thank you. Tell Jerry I'll be right there."

Ravid's secretary acknowledged Siegal and nodded for him to go in.

"Good morning, Ross. Please sit down." Ravid didn't mince words. "I've got an ugly job for you. It's that time of year to publish our annual activity report. And as low man on the seniority office totem pole, you are automatically nominated to write it."

Siegal had heard about these reports but never had read one in detail.

Ravid continued, "These reports are very important. They tell prospective clients the kind and quality of work we do."

Ravid winked. "I know you'll do your best."

Siegal thought, *Dreary as this responsibility seems, it is still a welcome change from the intellectual foreplay of academia to the real world of profit and loss balance sheets.*

Siegal forced a smile. "Thank you for the responsibility. I'm on it."

He left Ravid's office and proceeded directly to ID's library, which was more of an archival closet for rarely-used documents. Selecting one each of the last ten years of blue-covered, hard-copy annual reports, he retreated to his office, stopping first in the break room for a coffee bracer.

Siegal stacked the reports on his desk in yearly order. He opened last year's report. "Ninety-nine pages," he mumbled aloud. "All these other nine reports, they're the same, exactly ninety-nine pages. Even the table of contents are exactly the same.

"Odd."

Siegal's rebellious nature kicked into high gear.

I wonder how Ravid and the staff would feel if my report this year was one hundred pages long? Or more forbidding, if I filed a report only eighty-four pages in length. And what would the world think if I put the report in a red cover instead of blue? He smiled to himself. *And who would ever give a shit?*

He located a two-wheel dolly in the archive closet and lugged eight cartons of hard-copy data from the past year into his office and started reading. He found that ID focused on five areas: conflict resolution, staff productivity, headhunting, fat-trimming, and redefining job descriptions based on skills and decision-making risk. All familiar skills in Siegal's background.

Using his office walls, he taped up a large flip-chart sheet and with a felt marker outlined what each consultation included: "Client Name," "Focus Problem," "Strategy," "Time," "Staff and Material Cost," "Results" and "Conclusions."

On a second sheet taped to the wall, he wrote "Interviews," "Standardized Tools," "OD-developed Tools," and "Follow-up Reports."

What's this? Every report shows the same success rate of eighty percent, give or take a couple of points. The data is following the Italian economist Pareto's 80:20 principal. I'm new to the consultancy game but this must be the norm for personal development consulting firms like ID. I think we're better than other firms. I wonder if I can work the data to indicate this.

Siegal had a lightbulb moment. Flipping off the cap on his felt pen, he wrote down some design changes. Lecturing to his wall notes like students in one of his classes, he said, "The mistake is not what we do, but how we report our results. An eighty percent success means a twenty percent error level. As an expert researcher in behavioral studies, I can manipulate the data to indicate a lower error level and make ID look better to its clients. And I don't mean by cheating the data."

He added a third sheet and wrote a mission statement. "Why information does not produce better than eighty percent positive results," and "Suggested modifications to improve results in the future."

Gulping the last of the coffee, which was now cold and bitter, he muttered, "When I'm finished, my report will have meaning to anyone who reads it."

Siegal's stomach growled. He had not moved out of his office, not even for a bathroom break. He looked at his computer. Ten minutes after five. He called Simi's cell to tell her he was leaving.

My report will not be trite. He turned off the light and closed the door.

IT WAS ALMOST five thirty when he spotted Simi on the library steps.

"You're late."

"Sorry. I really got involved today. Kiss?"

"Not now, mister."

Silently, they drove to Quandary's. BF and Sally were already sitting at their regular table.

BF looked up from his beer, "You look frustrated, boss. Try my couch."

"Even worse," Siegal said. "I'm disappointed." He explained the ninety-nine page compilations of the past ten years. "As long as I have to write this shit, I want it useful. I want my report read."

"No big fucking deal," said Sally. "I bet you can do that in your sleep."

"Hell, boss, just type it in twenty-four-point font to make it easier to read," suggested BF.

Siegal let the sarcasm pass.

"What is the real reason you were late tonight?" asked BF.

"It's weird. I just somehow got energized about the report I'm supposed to write for ID. You see, the real meat of the data is the unexplained twenty percent. In good research, everything must have an answer. You all know I believe there is no chaos. Every piece of data must be explained. I intend to write a compelling document; one that somebody will find and read…maybe even somebody important.

"One thing we know," said BF, "You have uncanny intuition. I say follow your instincts. I predict this report will make you famous… maybe even save the world."

Sally added, "As my Methodist preacher daddy would say, and I believe he stole this from some Jewish friend, 'From your mouth to God's ears'."

FIVE

A RED BRICK BUILDING AT the edge of City University's campus housed the psychology research laboratory. Siegal enjoyed an isolated single room at the rear away from the prying eyes of the other, Freudian-oriented psychologists. It doubled as his office and research lab. In one corner was his desk, piled high with books and papers that should have been filed in two green metal file cabinets or on an old wooden bookcase, all scavenged from the University's used furniture storage area. Simi and Sally, the two finest graduate assistants he'd ever had, used the large table in the center for studying and to construct research projects. A large storage closet, almost as large as the main room, housed their experimental rats and other paraphernalia.

The fall term start was still a week away, but the three residents of the rat lab were busy preparing for it. A man wearing a Silver Streak Courier cap rang the bell to the behavior lab.

"Come in, whoever you are," called Siegal, without bothering to look up.

The man wheeled in six cages, each containing a white rat. He handed the delivery invoice to Siegal. Squeaks from the cages made Siegal look twice. He scratched the thinning bald spot on the back of his head.

"Simi! Sally! Front and center," he barked.

The two ladies looked up from their work tables.

"I just accepted our fresh supply of experimental animals. I should have made an appointment with my ophthalmologist instead. Unless my eyes deceive me, we still have our experimental rats from the spring quarter. You were told to get rid of our previously trained rats so they won't contaminate our new test trials. We need to follow certain rules of quality research."

Sally stammered, "It's Tigger. Do we have to destroy him?"

"I know you ladies named him Tigger because of striped markings down his back instead of the usual all-white or mottled fur patterns. But he's still part of last spring's test animals."

Simi added, "It's not because of his unusual fur pattern that we want to keep him. He holds the record for the least number of trials to learn every one of our experiments this past year. There is something special about him."

"I suppose you can keep him as a pet if you house him apart from the newbies to avoid contamination," said Siegal.

Simi added, "You're the boss. But then why kill any of them? Comparing results of two generations side-by-side can be important, scientifically speaking. You said it many times, Ross. More accurate behavioral information reduces the amount of untestable results. Your words, 'less chaos'."

Sally broke in. "I've...I mean Simi and I, have already started some preliminary research designs combining the two groups, hoping you would like the idea. We would be extra careful keeping the two groups separate."

Simi gave Siegal a kiss on the neck. "Just expanding our research a little."

Siegal shook his head in disagreement, but it was Simi's dimpled pout that stopped his argument.

Sally said, "I know I only became a research assistant at the beginning of the spring quarter, so I'll go along with what's right. But it sure sounds like a good idea to me."

Siegal knew Sally, a true animal lover, disliked killing even the smallest bug. Siegal also had a history of walking the edge of accepted research methodology when it meant gathering groundbreaking knowledge.

"Looks like I'm outnumbered. Those Freudian guys down the hall will have a field day when they find out. Granting agencies are already reticent to support what they call my harebrained ideas. I'm surprised the university even keeps me."

Sally rebutted, "We know why they keep you. Your students love you. Every year your classes have long waiting lists."

He nodded. "Okay, you made your point. Combining smart rats with naive ones can be a new way to explore complex social interactions. I like it. Now I'll see if any national granting office will give us a flyer. The odds are slim. If not, I'll use some of my income from ID to supplement what the university gives me to cover our additional costs."

"Holy shit! Tigger stays," said an ecstatic Sally. "By the way, last night you were pretty discouraged with your project at Interaction Dynamics."

"I've about licked it. Using more sophisticated formulas, I can increase prediction ability by at least ten percent. That would put ID well ahead of any other management consulting firms."

Simi added, "You know, maybe we can translate our rat results here at the lab into human terms to help you at ID. You love making conclusions from obscure facts."

"BF said it last night: Our conclusions can even save the world."

SIX

DANIELSON DID HIS JOB WELL. The private invitation of leaders from the president's list went off without a hitch. Not a single news pundit discovered the real purpose of the trip.

The meeting site, a secluded lodgepole chalet near Central City, Colorado, nestled at the end of an old logging trail, was originally built in the 1950s as a hunting lodge for a rich recluse. It later became a bed and breakfast retreat for well-healed tourists. The FBI bought it for a safe house in the 1990s. They gutted and totally modernized it, including the latest electronic technologies.

The inside was much larger than it appeared from the front. A great room with a moss rock fireplace covering most of one wall, a conference room-sized dining area, and a kitchen completed the main floor. Outside, the double doors of the dining room led to a redwood deck. Upstairs were six bedrooms, each equipped with a full bath, Wi-Fi connection, and a secure phone.

Security was a simple matter. Sensors were embedded along the single gravel road, which led off the highway for almost a mile. The surrounding woods were thick with pine, aspen, and scrub oak underbrush. It was a difficult walk for even an accomplished mountain hiker. A grassy clearing surrounded two-thirds of the lodge and could be easily observed from the redwood deck. The chalet was both serene and safe.

President Russell and Tom Danielson arrived a day early to make sure everything stood ready for their guests.

"First things first," said Danielson as he lit the moss rock fireplace in the great room to remove the chill. Crackly logs of collected beetle-kill pine soon filled the room with a smell of fresh outdoors.

"And now it's time for a drink." Russell retreated to the dining room and returned with a bottle of fifty-year-old, single-malt Glenfiddich. He also carried two glasses. The men settled into the pair of overstuffed leather chairs fronting the fireplace and toasted to a successful meeting.

"So, El, what's your master plan to get our guests to cooperate? They'll have little love for working together. Odds are against you."

"One step at a time, Tom."

"Their nations have been at loggerheads for generations. What's your hook?"

"I'm betting none want to upset the delicate détente between all of us. An outsider like Rebus could do this. I have to play to their egos. If they all see themselves as keeping their international sovereignty, they will come together. My master plan is...well, to keep them talking."

THE BRIGHT ORANGE sunrise creeping over the mountain peaks woke Danielson. Wrapped in a terry bathrobe to guard against the morning nip, he went downstairs and stepped out onto the dining room patio to breathe the fresh air so often missing in D.C. He gazed across the open meadow, wondering how nature could provide such beauty. A breeze caused him to tighten his robe.

It was the beginning of fall. Aspen leaves displayed their rich golden yellow intermixed with ground-hugging red scrub oak. Three does and their fawns grazed on the last green of summer near the clearing edge. An eagle ruled a bright blue sky overhead, searching for an unwary field mouse or vole. A scene of serenity, almost surreal, challenged the event soon to transpire. Only a lonely whip-poorwill's call broke the tranquility.

"Is that you out there, Tom?" came a voice from the dining room.

The sound of Russell's voice startled Danielson. "Just checking things out. In a couple of hours this place will be hopping." He signaled to the two Secret Service agents standing at the clearing edge to begin laying out landing pad flags for their visitors arriving by helicopter from Buckley Air Force Base. "I can use some coffee. How about you?"

They returned to the warmth of the dining room and filled two mugs, prepared by unseen security people.

BY ELEVEN O'CLOCK, four Blackhawk helicopters arrived and dropped off their passengers. Russell greeted each of them with a formal salute and handshake. They smiled and nodded their heads. Whirring chopper blades shielded whatever conversations took place. Secret service agents guided each guest to their rooms on the second floor.

At noon, they all met in the great room. A Secret Service agent had lit the fireplace. Danielson wheeled in a food cart and served a light lunch.

The mien of Russell and his guests appeared relaxed as they ate, but Danielson could read their cautious facial expressions and hear their guarded conversations.

AT JUST THE proper moment, Chief of Staff Danielson guided them to the dining room and directed them to their chairs around the large dining table. Nameplates were not needed; everybody there knew each other very well. President Russell sat at the head of the oblong dining table. Starting from his left and continuing around the table sat President Mikale Sokoloven of Russia, King Ahmed Ishmere of the United Arab Emirates, and President Henri Galdet of France. Chairman Yi Cho-Se of the People's Republic of China sat on the president's immediate right.

President Russell remained seated as he spoke to his peers. "Thank you all for adjusting your schedules to be here. We have a problem: how to deal with Rebus." He acknowledged each with a thoughtful and protracted nod as he stated their names, keeping eye contact around the table. They returned the gesture.

President Sokoloven said, "Before commencing talks about this menace, let me say I hear this part of the world holds the best trout fishing. We have fine trout streams ourselves. Mr. President, do you think your American trout can be fooled by my Russian fishing lures?"

"I certainly invite you to try your luck."

Danielson heard Sokoloven's words as sounding a challenge of power between the two nations. He breathed a sigh of relief that Russell did not take the bait.

"A little over one week ago I received a concerned call from Andre Segurian, which crystallized the need for this meeting," said Russell. "I also have phone dispatches from each of you on this same point. It is important that the five of us should solve this problem outside the aegis of the UN. This is not a diplomatic matter between nations."

"I do not understand why the United States is here, President Russell. You, I am told by my informants, have not had such attacks," said Sokoloven.

"I believe that you, Mr. Sokoloven, and all of you here will agree that getting rid of this Rebus is a topic of mutual concern. And that does include the United States," rebutted Russell.

"Then continue for now," said Sokoloven.

"Rebus's diet of smaller South American nations no longer fills his belly. If he continues unabated, he threatens to destroy the delicate balance between our five nations, pitting us against each other. Is there anyone here who wants to change this calm between our nations?"

The meeting room was silent except for sounds of briefcases clicking open and recorders turning on.

"Like Godzilla, Rebus has risen from across the sea. We are not here to argue our differences, but to create a means to eliminate Rebus," said Galdet. "I want to hear from Chairman Cho-Se."

Cho-Se, using his finest English acquired while attending UCLA, wasted no words. "Rebus's power is extraordinary. I am told that many followers join him without question. He is antigovernment, any government. We attack his latest-known bases with futility. Each time he manages to learn of our plans in advance and escape. He brazenly attacks our financial institutions and kills without provocation. We believe, regardless of his target, his goal is the attack of our nation itself." Cho-Se looked down at his hands for just a moment. "His last raid killed my daughter and granddaughter." He paused and drank some tea from his cup. "I believe he may soon start competing in the international drug market."

President Sokoloven spoke. "This Rebus is a bug, no more important than fish bait. And like a bug, we will find him and squash him."

Galdet spoke up, "I agree with President Sokoloven. Monsieur Cho-Se, why not just let our intelligence agencies handle this hoodlum? I believe it is only a matter of time until we get him and his gang." Then with a nod of the head to punctuate his point, he said "I, like Mr. Sokoloven, am not sure I feel the graveness of this issue that requires us all to be here. I, for one, am here out of respect for President Russell."

"Rebus does not just attack our banking institutions. He slaughters everyone in his wake. And he is becoming more brazen over time," Russell argued.

Galdet questioned Russell's logic. "President Russell, do you predict he can rupture the détente we have worked so hard to establish?"

Russell paused and then spoke in a soft tone to emphasize the gravity of the problem. "Once he has disrupted a country, he then can turn the tables and offer peace if that nation agrees to work side-by-side with him against the rest of us. At this time I believe he is still a gangster with a den of thieves. But, if he unsettles even one nation, this madman can morph from a hardened gangster into an international terrorist. Not just a few lives will be lost at each of his attacks, but thousands at a time."

Finally, the silent King Ishmere stood up. Stroking his short goatee, he said, "Your point is well taken. In my country, we have a saying: One who only looks to the West can never find the oasis just to the East."

They all nodded in agreement.

"I think we can no longer depend upon the alternatives in the West, such as the United Nations, to control every miscreant. We must look to the East, each other, for that support."

"No," argued Galdet. "I think your Allah would never suggest going outside the providence of the United Nations. We need the United Nations and must continue to support it. What I am hearing is we here today form our own world organization. We already have NATO, the European Bloc, and other coalitions almost too numerous to list. I am not sure I want to be a part of a plan that forms another political layer of world governments."

Danielson could see that each leader let his ego get in the way of any progress. Yet, they were talking, as Russell wished.

After more than three hours of discussion, Danielson, standing near the buffet, said, "Gentlemen, excuse me for entering this discussion. This meeting was intended to last just this one day. You may choose to continue talks in the morning. I can manage the travel logistics."

President Sokoloven argued, "You requested my presence. I think it is a waste of my time. There is much to do in my own country." He looked directly at Danielson. "Call for my helicopter. I demand to leave now."

"I'm sorry, sir," said Danielson. "We are in the mountains and I am in constant communication with the weather bureau. I have been told to expect very serious wind shears off our front range. It is impossible to safely fly any aircraft in or out of this location earlier than noon tomorrow."

Danielson lied to bide time for his president to change the mood in the room.

"Nyet. Nyet. Maybe I should pound my shoe on the table like Comrade Khrushchev to gain the attention of the room. If you think this Rebus is so vile, then you, President Russell, should dispose of him like the pig he is." Sokoloven emphasized his point with his fingers making a slash across his throat.

Danielson could see that matters were getting worse. *Sokoloven remains aloof. France not far behind.*

Cho-Se said, "My Zen tells me we came together for a purpose. It is not so clear at this time. Tomorrow, with new light to show the way, I am sure that purpose will show itself."

Russell stood for the first time. "It is late, and all of us are tired from our long trip. I say we take Cho-Se's advice and begin afresh in the morning."

Danielson spoke, "Gentlemen, it is almost five o'clock. I have prepared dinner on the patio." He opened the doors and led them outside.

Recorders turned off and briefcases snapped shut.

Russell whispered to Danielson, "Not a good start."

Danielson turned to Russell as they followed their guests out to the expansive deck. "It could have gone worse."

SEVEN

"YOU STILL AWAKE?"

Danielson focused his eyes on the bedside clock. "It's two a.m."

"I know," Russell whispered.

President Russell seldom slept more than three hours a night, choosing instead to take short power naps throughout the day as his schedule permitted. It did not matter if his chief of staff was asleep or not, he always answered.

Danielson grabbed a robe and opened the door.

"I was hungry and made myself a sandwich. Then I thought you might want one, too. I hope you like peanut butter and jelly." He smiled and set a tray of sandwiches and two glasses of milk on the table near the window.

Danielson knew his boss didn't make food deliveries on a whim. "What's on your mind?"

Russell's smile changed to a sober look. "The good news is we got our miracle to keep this group on message. The bad news is this." He pulled a thumb drive from his pocket. "This just came from Amanda. Do you remember when the CIA sent two undercover agents to Australia following some credible intel that something was about to happen down under?"

Danielson nodded.

"One of them was accepted into a known group we thought maybe belonged to Rebus's gang. It seemed luck was on our side until Amanda's call, which flushed all that down the fucking toilet." He plugged the thumb drive into Danielson's computer.

Amanda Keyes came online first. "I just received a call from General Walters at the Pentagon. A Qantas jet, originating at Brampton Island near the Great Barrier Reef with a stop in Alice Springs and heading for Melbourne, was hijacked one hour and fifteen minutes ago. Information is sketchy, but this is what we know now from radio messages inside the cockpit."

"Mr. President, this is General Walters. A Qantas jet was commandeered on the ground at Alice Springs. Nothing seemed unusual at first. And then…"

"Alice Springs control tower, this is the pilot of Qantas Flight 234 requesting permission for takeoff to Melbourne."

"This is Alice Springs control, Qantas 234. You are third in line for takeoff on runway two-south."

Several screams were heard from the passenger area as the door to the cockpit exploded open.

"What the hell?" came the pilot's voice.

A male voice with a European accent spoke next. "Do as I instruct. We have taken over your fucking airplane. We have just killed two of your cabin crew and you will be next if you do not follow my instructions. Tell control tower to grant immediate clearance to Melbourne or we will start killing your passengers."

"Jesus, El. This just happened?"

"There's more."

"Tell Alice Springs to radio ahead to Melbourne to hold their United Airlines plane. We intend to use it next. And if there is any interference either in the air or on the ground, we will kill everyone on board. We are not afraid to die for our cause. We mean business. You two, throw the dead crew out the door and secure the latch."

General Walters said, "Melbourne airport security was preparing for their arrival and a possible boarding by having attack agents dressed in refueling and food delivery uniforms. Then the bastards fooled us.

"Fifteen minutes in the air, Flight 234 changed course and flew to Cairo. Our satellites tracked them and with the help of Cairo security prepared for their arrival with snipers. Mr. President, they again outsmarted us by landing behind some trees on the far runway. Everything was quiet for a couple of minutes. Then all hell broke loose. Listen to the message."

"Control tower," said the hijacker, "I want six SUVs with full tanks of gas for our escape. Place one loaded assault rifle in each van. We will want a four-hour head start out of the airport. We have people in the terminal who will let us know that you have kept your bargain. Now have drivers wearing only speedos deliver the vans to the plane. After we commandeer the vans, you can have your fucking airplane back and all the people on board. We will keep the van drivers as hostages. You have exactly twenty minutes to comply or we will start killing innocent passengers."

President Russell dialed Amanda Keys. "Get General Walters on the phone." He looked at Danielson. "What are you thinking?"

"It's not like Rebus. He always makes demands right after his attacks. I've got a gut feeling this is a new menace."

Russell's cell rang. "General Walters here."

"Thank you for calling back. What else have you learned?"

"We are certain they boarded in Alice Springs but weapons may have been planted there for them beforehand."

"Tom Danielson here. We're on speakerphone. Were any of the hijackers caught?"

"Two of the SUVs got away and into the desert. A third van was overtaken but the insurgents committed suicide by ramming into a bridge abutment, killing the hostage as well. One mysterious turn: three hijackers were shot in the head by their own pack and thrown out of one vehicle. I checked the identities with CIA. Two were Australian nationals...but one of the victims was a CIA agent. Over and out, Mr. President."

"Are you going to tell our friends at the chalet?"

Russell thought for a moment. "This may be the glue that keeps this summit together. As my super-strategist, I was hoping you..."

"We have two assholes now. Rebus is a single person with a finite gang. I've got men out there that can track down Rebus and deal with him. This new problem indicates a much smarter leader with fingers in many directions. A much harder enemy to combat. This international crisis trumps Rebus. This new menace should give our leaders a better reason to work together, El."

SOMEWHERE JUST OUTSIDE of Cairo, the man with the European accent dialed his cell phone. "Mission accomplished. Your plan worked to perfection."

"And those that did not fit our group?" asked the faceless voice.

"They were managed exactly as directed."

EIGHT

MOVEMENT ON THE SECOND FLOOR at the chalet meant the visitors were rousing and preparing for the morning.

President Russell refilled his coffee mug and reached for another roll. "I need you to have a plan for today's session, Tom. And, I hope to hell you have one.

Danielson poured tea and coffee for their guests as they entered the dining room. "Toast, bagels, and Danish are on the buffet. I've ordered eggs and breakfast meats. They'll be out in a moment."

The leaders carried their food trays back to their assigned seats and waited for President Russell to begin the session.

"I will not start today with such words as good morning or good day. No doubt each of you received much the same communiqué last night as I did about an airplane hijacking. And, some of you had your own citizens aboard that flight."

Nods indicated they had.

"Gentlemen, our intelligence believes it is not Rebus. Comparing the assaults in China and your nations, the hijacking of Flight 234 may end up being more ruthless, more diabolical, and more cunning than that of the Rebus gang. We need to combat this new menace."

"President Russell," broke in an agitated Sokoloven, "it is you who brought us here with Rebus in mind. You are now suggesting we drop this Rebus maniac and go after still another flea? I believe you must have a plan to get rid of this Latin American jackal even before you invited all of us. Rebus or someone else, it makes little difference to me. But does it take the highest leaders from each of our nations to put all this energy into a single criminal act? I, for one, know what to do once we corner either hoodlum.

"We would all have the same solution at that point," responded Cho-Se.

"I disagree. If we kill off this new menace, they become martyrs for others to follow," argued King Ishmere. "Each of us should end this scourge in our own way."

Each leader spoke in turn of both Rebus and the hijacking, but offered no solutions.

Russell waited, then summarized. "I hear, by consensus, we are in agreement to handle Rebus independently. But this new terror becomes our new united threat. We don't know who it is or who leads them. We must discover their motives. I don't need to remind you, it is imperative we must move forward without delay."

"So, friend, do you have a plan or not?" said President Sokoloven, sounding even more impatient than before. "My helicopter should be here shortly. I am packed and ready to go."

"All of you know our host, here, Tom Danielson, is also my chief of staff." Standing, President Russell pointed to Danielson. "He has been suggesting a course of action. I am committed to having Mr.

Danielson spearhead the effort for the United States. But we do not wish to go it alone. I need approval from all of you here."

Cho-Se said, "I first wish to hear what Mr. Danielson has to offer."

"I do not like this so much," said Sokoloven. "You invite us to your country to catch Rebus. I feel I am the fish waiting to be caught. Now you add one more American to your side. You asked us to trust each other. But can we trust you?"

Danielson had not wished to give the appearance of a meeting of two Americans versus four visiting dignitaries. Now he felt there was no choice. "Just about two weeks ago, President Russell and I became aware of the latest incursions by Rebus, a most appropriate name for such a puzzling enemy. This thug caused mayhem in several South American countries. Now he has launched attacks on each of your soils."

President Galdet interrupted, "I see no difference whether we call him a thug, as you say, or a terrorist."

Danielson answered. "Excuse my impertinence. If he is a terrorist, then he must be treated as a political enemy who has international support and sleeper cells positioned about the globe. A common criminal such as Rebus is not a terrorist. He directly leads his gang on any assault. Cut off his head and the onerous animal is dead. The tapes collected on Flight 234 indicate this new terrorist conducted this operation from afar. Stop the leader on the airplane and you haven't accomplished anything at all."

President Galdet agreed. "You make good points."

Danielson temporarily won over the French. *One down and Russia to go.* "We must pool our intelligence and together rid ourselves of him."

President Sokoloven was not so easily won. "All this is rhetoric. Terrorist, thug, brute...whatever. We do not know who he is, how many supporters he has, nor do we know his intent. Mr. Danielson, you still have not told us your plan."

"It is not complicated," said Danielson. "Bear with me. They didn't kill all the crew, make demands, or seek any reward. Yet three of their own people were slain in cold blood. One thing we can determine for sure is the great amount of detail with which this complicated assault was carried out. We are dealing with an uncommon enemy. He is not done attacking. I believe our unknown subversive's reign of terror just may be the beginning. And if he continues to have success, he will get stronger and more dangerous. Others will blindly follow his path."

Russell acted impatient, "Come, Mr. Danielson, what is your plan?"

"I apologize, Mr. President. I stress this point: we have to understand and not underestimate him. We must understand how he thinks before he thinks and predict how he will act even before he acts. We need a new anti-terrorist specialist, a human behavioral specialist. He must be above reproach, be his own person and hold no political ties or loyalties to any individual or government."

Russell asked, "Do you mean a psychologist, a profiler? Excuse me for doubting your thinking. But I have an agency full of such people."

Thanks for the setup, El. I couldn't ask for a better lead.

"This person must be more responsive than any profiler we have ever known. Our best profilers make guesses based on past information. The best guesses are only accurate about eight out of ten times. This error factor, gentlemen, is far too great if we are to stop him. We need a person who sets his own standards."

Sokoloven acknowledged agreement. "An interesting conjecture."

Russell eased back in his chair. "How do you propose to find this person? You do have a first step, I presume."

"Yes, sir, I do. In the past I have used a team of, for lack of a better term, headhunters, to identify just such a person. I called them early this morning. They are on the job now as we speak."

"How much time will you need?" asked Russell.

"I believe we can have this person identified in no later than two weeks."

King Ishmere said, "Even with this super person, we still need someone to direct this operation for us—someone all of us can trust. I am far too busy managing Arab uprisings to guide such an effort."

Cho-Se said, "It is my nation who originally brought this Rebus to the world's attention. It is logical for me to lead in the discovery and demise of whoever is leading this new enemy."

"Nyet," said Sokoloven. "You cannot manage Rebus. I don't think you can lead this hunt."

"Gentlemen," said President Galdet, "I doubt we can reach consensus. Our alternative is not to select any of us. I believe we already know a man who can do this…under our close supervision, of course." He stood to emphasize his point. "As much as I respect all of you as your country's leaders we must remember why we are here. We must solve our problems, not argue our differences." Galdet remained standing. "President Russell, you called us here to solve a grave problem and now we have a problem even more grave. It seems we have the person to guide us in our own midst. I suggest that we select Mr. Tom Danielson to chair our future direction. I have known him for a long time and have had many high-level dealings with him. His experience as a warrior and leader make him well qualified."

King Ishmere said, "A wise suggestion. I also have confidence in him. If we think Mr. Danielson is no more than a person who serves us coffee and tea, then we are pouring out of the wrong pot. If, at any time, this is the wrong decision, we can always negotiate another action. We as leaders delegate heavy responsibilities every day. I suggest we delegate this action to Mr. Danielson."

The group grew from five to six, and Tom Danielson became lead person to some of the world's most powerful individuals. President Russell vacated his seat for Danielson at the head and pulled up a chair at the opposite end of the table.

"Thank you, gentlemen, for your confidence." Danielson paused and let his literary license sneak out. "From now on we shall call our group the Summit of Six, or codename SOS."

"Mr. Danielson, you are now in control," acquiesced Sokoloven, who remained only partially convinced.

Danielson recognized his tremendous responsibility. "We have accomplished a great deal this past day and a half. Gentlemen, the weather is closing in. I suggest we break now and prepare to leave. Your transportation will be here by noon."

Five helicopters landed and loaded their passengers. The small-ish looking chalet was again left to the remaining Secret Service personnel and to nature.

NINE

DANIELSON LOOKED SURPRISED AS HE entered the reception area of the Oval Office for his morning strategy session with the president. Amanda Keyes, the president's secretary, was not at her usual place behind her oversized desk. The door to the Oval Office, usually closed, stood open.

Odd.

"Come in, Tom."

Danielson complied, sensing a seriousness in his good friend's voice. He saw Miss Keyes, notepad in hand, sitting across from the president's desk.

Russell paused, frowned, then place his open hand on his desk. "No sense beating around the bush, Tom. I'm having Miss Keyes draft," he hesitated another moment, "your letter of resignation."

Danielson gasped. "My letter of…? What have I done to force such an action?" He and the president often disagreed on issues, but he never imagined he would be cut loose. Definitely not on such short notice. He felt sweat forming on his forehead.

"Holy shit. Excuse my profanity, Miss Keyes." Danielson fumbled to pick up a cup of coffee she prepared for the occasion.

"All right, it's settled. Miss Keyes, draft a letter. Have it say that Mr. Thomas Danielson, Colonel Retired, has been told by his doctor that his position as White House Chief of Staff has become too stressful. He needs a change of venue. Include all the platitudes appropriate for the occasion. Use all the 'with great regrets' phrases you can imagine. I'm sure the media, no matter what is said, will have a field day. Be sure his reason for leaving is personal and sincere sounding. Copy Segurian and, of course, the Senate and House leaders."

Russell waited until his secretary left the room to type Danielson's letter of resignation. "It's not what it appears," said Russell. "You can't work for me and the Summit, too. I can't be your boss at the White House and one of your subordinates with SOS."

"Give me a minute to restart my heart. We could have talked about this first. You just knocked ten years off my life."

"No choice, Tom. You need freedom to act independently."

"You're the boss...I mean were my boss. That is, if it's something permanent."

"For the moment, anyway. Finish your coffee. It's still free for guests." Russell's comment eased the tension.

"You know, as chairman of SOS you have to divorce yourself from me to ensure there is no conflict of interest. The Summit must remain successful and we want no possible excuses from Sokoloven or any of the others to disassemble what needs to be done."

"I'll be out of here by the end of the day, El."

"Oh, I've arranged for a small private office near the Capitol so you won't be homeless. Take up the title of consultant, something obscure so it can't be checked. Everyone here in Washington who doesn't have a regular job does the same thing."

"Either that or a lobbyist," said Danielson, making an empty joke while knowing this was no laughing matter.

"It'll be a natural for you to be in the mix. Your expenses will be managed from the presidential discretionary fund Congress gives me. The good thing is, it can't be audited. I'm on your side, you know that. But you'll have to act on your own for now. No one will be watching your back. And, by the way, all your decisions have to be right. There is no strike three, you're out. You have to jack a home run every time."

"What a plan. It can't miss."

"Back out now and we have to kill you."

He knew it was an empty threat, but for Danielson, there was no backing out. In truth, he secretly began his plan that night in the mountains without the approval of anyone, including the president. Before leaving the chalet, he called his team of headhunters to begin searching for someone who could find this super behavioral profiler. He also set in motion his plan to end Rebus's cruel actions.

A handshake closed the proceedings. Danielson walked outside, signed his letter of resignation at Keyes's desk, and left.

He waved a goodbye to her. He wasn't sad. Being involved in an active mission renewed the energy within the retired combat veteran.

ONE DAY LATER, stopping only to look over his new office digs, the newest of Washington's consultants drove north out of the city.

"Damn," Danielson muttered. A traffic accident closed the freeway from downtown D.C. to the Smoking Musket Restaurant, which was just inside the Maryland border. The former White House Chief of Staff looked at his watch as he pulled into the parking area. "Thirty-two minutes late." Being late was something he never allowed anyone working for him. *I should have given myself more leeway.*

A parking valet at the Smoking Musket took his car. No claim check was necessary. In the Washington, D.C. political arena, every waiter, bellhop, taxi driver, uniformed patrol, and even parking valet knew all the VIPs. Tom Danielson was one of those entities. His face was on television almost every week, sending out the president's message.

Built as a wayside inn more than one hundred and fifty years ago, the Smoking Musket property was originally a popular overnight stop for people traveling from the north to the Capitol. The outbuildings, used as sleeping quarters and horse barns, were long since torn down. Only the single brick-and-rock structure housing the restaurant remained. The honeycombed interior provided a perfect setting for keeping conversations private. Clandestine meetings were commonplace, with allies and enemies often seated in adjacent nooks.

The hostess greeted Danielson at the door. "Good morning, sir." She immediately recognized him with a slight nod but avoided using his name. "Your guests have already arrived and are seated at your table."

He walked directly to where four smartly-attired individuals in business causal waited. "Sorry I'm late. Traffic accident." The apology passed without comment. No one minded. He continued, "What have you to report?"

The lady in her early forties, striking in her conservative suit, spoke first. "You haven't exactly given us a yellow brick road to follow, so I don't know what you would expect from us. You said, 'Go out there and find a person or persons who can be trusted to never give up discreet information even at the risk of life.' Only that was not enough. This person or persons has to make decisions that could be very unpopular with almost everyone. And finally, this person or persons must be the best judge of human behavior of anyone else in the world. You emphasized the best, so I'm guessing second choice was not good enough."

"Funny. Only you got it exactly right, Jamie," said Danielson, using first names only, should anyone overhear the conversation.

One of the men, Doug, athletic with short, kinky-tight red hair, added, "And then you expected us to do this little task without letting on why we are carrying on this search."

"Those are the rules of the hunt," said Danielson. "How have you been doing? You've had almost week. A lot is at stake." Danielson knew that in front of him was the finest group of people-finders anywhere, even when given almost nothing with which to work. It was not the first time he had used this quartet for unusual tasks. He knew they couldn't fail, not this time, not with so much at stake.

Jamie continued, "I feel we found what you want. We whittled our choices down to two companies, both American. One is in Cleveland, the other in Denver. Both have excellent reputations achieving superior results. You can have your pick."

"Too many choices. I asked for a single name. I don't want a group. Find that individual who consistently gives us a low error factor. One hundred percent perfection is your benchmark. Let me know the moment you find this person. Team, this meeting is over. There's still work to be done."

Then, changing his voice to a less businesslike tone, Danielson said, "As long as you're here, order brunch. They have fantastic omelets. It's on me." Danielson repeated, "I need one answer. One person. Stat." He finished his coffee and left.

TIM, THE YOUNGEST member and a math wizard, said, "We limited our choices from over a hundred firms. Picking the single person should be an easy reduction problem. Get out your calculators, guys. We still have work to do."

The red-headed Doug asked, "Does anyone have the slightest idea why we are doing this?" No one did. "Sailing on uncharted waters without a compass. Sounds like fun."

"Yes, but on what planet or even solar system are we on?" asked Tim, whose face usually required an ID to order a drink.

Jamie, the team leader, answered, "It's obvious we are on a need-to-know basis. Mr. Danielson will tell us if and when it's appropriate. Until then, it's none of our business."

The fourth headhunter, Kevin, about thirty, muscular with dark brown hair looking a month overdo for a trim, said, "We were asked to find the top expert in determining and predicting how human behavior works. We found the best companies. Our next step is to come up with the one best person suited to Danielson's needs. Seems straightforward enough."

Jamie said, "To save time we need to split into groups." She pointed to Kevin and Tim. "You look into the Cleveland consulting company. Doug and I will head to Denver. Look into everything. We have to be prepared to tell Danielson what hand he wipes his butt with if he asks."

"One last word, gang," said Jamie. "There are no second choices. Right after I have my omelet."

TEN

SIEGAL SHOT A FRUSTRATED LOOK toward the calendar. Only four days remained to submit a research proposal. Simi and Sally sat at the work table. BF, preferring his friends here over the people in his own office in the General Psych building, sat at the same worktable.

"Does anyone have a good idea how to break my track record of two straight years without a major funding grant? My longevity here concerns me. I've already received vibes from the university suggesting that I either produce a grant or expect problems with my continuing employment."

"You said pairing your new rats with last year's group, that the new rats learned faster," said BF. "Maybe you could study that phenomenon. Maybe they're communicating in some way."

"Another profound insight," said Simi, waving a victory pose.

"And some rats are better communicators. The naive rats learned faster with Tigger in their presence than with any of the other second-year rats," added Sally, elated because her favorite rat showed off best.

BF concluded, "Multiple pairings between two rat generations can help you understand some chaotic behaviors through controlled laboratory research."

"Intriguing," said Siegal.

"It may be just the thing that can change the eighty-twenty ratio of prediction of natural behavior into something better," suggested Simi.

"It's settled." said Siegal, slapping his desk. "Regardless of whether we receive grant money or not, I want to move ahead with this line of research. The knowledge we learn is far too important for a few stuffed-shirt intellectuals to stifle us."

"I may get my father's insurance company to offer some shekels," offered BF.

"My dad will offer a prayer from the pulpit if that would help," said Sally.

Simi laughed out loud at her own thought. "My ex would pay dearly for me not to make his sexual preference public."

"Get serious," said Siegal. "BF, your idea makes sense. A unique research design may do the trick."

"You guys have lots of work to do. And I'll just be in the way. Got to go," BF gave Sally a kiss. "See you all later."

THE RACE AGAINST time was on. With deadlines for grant submissions only days away, Siegal's corner of the rat lab took on an appearance of whirling dervish dancers. Each of the three scurried back and forth between their work stations and storage room as if they were the experimental rats instead of their keepers. Rats were tagged with colored markers to identify specific groupings. Two walls were cluttered with drawings of mazes and lever contrivances.

A phone call from Jerry Ravid's secretary broke the team's concentration.

"This is Ross Siegal." He paused to listen. "I'll be there." He turned to Simi and Sally. "That was ID. The boss wants me in his office at nine tomorrow. A command performance."

"Just when you're needed here. Any clue to what it's all about?" asked Sally.

"No. I can't believe he's already read my report. I wonder what I did wrong. Well, there are always other firms to work for."

Simi said, "Without your job at ID you'd starve to death on your professor's salary." She glanced at her watch, which was always at least ten minutes slow. "My stomach tells me it's time for dinner."

THE LIBERAL CITY University, AS a bastion of First Amendment rights, attracted an unending supply of naysayers. While they could orate on any subject, on this particular podium outside Quandary's it was always on government oppression. That's what Dr. Ross Siegal saw and heard as he entered the tavern.

Inside, he noticed renewed activity. Graduate students and professors filtering back from their last weekend of summer break filled most of the tables in the darkened bar. BF, Simi, and Sally found their regular table at the rear of the room. The regular slummers, those not associated with any graduate programs at City University, either found places at the bar or filled the few remaining tables. On this night, two first-time slummers visited the scene.

Simi focused on them. "Look, the new slummers are drinking wine instead of beer. They don't look like a couple. She must be at least twenty years older. But these days, cougars and their boy toys are coming out of the woodwork."

"Or maybe a mother escorting her son to college," added Sally.

"Skip them. If I do your shimmy they'd regurgitate," said a laughing Simi.

For the next several hours, now accompanied by BF, the group drank Old Dog's Leg Lager, ate sausage sandwiches with French fries, and talked about grant ideas.

The evening passed quickly and the bartender called for last drink orders. The odd couple stayed to the end, leaving just ahead of the foursome.

AT EIGHT A.M., the new hard copy of Interaction Dynamics' year-end report lay on Siegal's office desk. It was an hour before his meeting with Ravid. He appreciated the opportunity to scribble notes on the newly-printed pages and prepare for any rebuttal questions from the rest of the staff.

Two people, a man and a woman, walked past his open door, interrupting his concentration. The woman carried a large report. Its thickness and red cover gave it away as his annual write-up.

Strange. I've seen them before. They seem familiar. But where?

Siegal shrugged off the feeling. He had more important matters, such as his nine-o'clock meeting with Ravid.

His intercom buzzed to life exactly at nine. He pushed the answer button. "Dr. Ravid will see you now."

"Dr. Ravid? Not Jerry?" Siegal pondered the seriousness and formality of the message. He played scenarios in his mind of the worst things that could happen.

Dr. Jerry Ravid's corner office suite was larger than any other and the only one with windows on two adjacent walls. Eight chairs sat around an oval conference table in the center. To Siegal's surprise, none of the other consultants were present. Instead, Ravid sat at one end of the oval; the woman and man Siegal saw walking down the corridor were seated on one side.

Odd. I think I saw them last night at Quandary's.

"Good morning, Ross, please take a seat there," said Ravid, pointing to a chair opposite the two visitors. The casualness of the salutation unnerved him. Before, it was always, 'Dr. Ravid will see you, Dr. Siegal.' Now it's 'Good morning, Ross.' On the table were a pitcher of ice water, four glasses, and a single copy of his report. Nothing else. Not even writing pads and pens.

Ravid introduced the two guests. Their names blurred past Siegal, who was still wondering why he was there. "And this is Dr. Ross Siegal, whom I believe you may already know."

Siegal stood up, almost upending his chair, shook their hands then sat back down.

Ravid continued, "Ross, I have been meeting with these people as possible clients for ID."

"Have we met?" asked Siegal.

The question passed unanswered.

"It seems our guests have a strange problem, one that does not ordinarily fit our range of interests. But their desire to meet with us, and more specifically with you, caused me to pursue their request for this meeting," explained Ravid. Then, turning toward Siegal, he said, "Tell me how you would go about finding an unknown super-sleuth to answer a problem that has not been established?"

Siegal paused to collect his thoughts. He was in the hot seat. "Interesting conjecture. Solve a problem that has not even been established. I'm accepting this is not a trick question. I suppose I would go to a headhunting firm or, better yet, a swami." Siegal smiled at his attempt at humor. No one else smiled. "Dr. Ravid, I hope your accountant had you collect their fees in advance." His second attempt, also futile.

The woman spoke. "The question is sincere. Our company has a large problem. We prefer to seek advice from a personnel consulting firm such as Interaction Dynamics, rather than seek a swami. At this moment, we aren't sure of the better route."

Was this the woman's response to my humor?

"Your company?" Siegal asked, hoping to learn more.

"Yes," answered the man. "We represent a large entity. We can't tell you who. It's a matter of security."

"Then at least tell us why you have chosen our human relations firm. Are you attached to some government agency?" Siegal distrusted anything that smelled of politics. *Their clothes fit midlevel politicos, maybe G-men types trying to cover as business executives.* His mind churned; no answers came.

The woman answered this time. "Interaction Dynamics has a reputation for being one of the nation's two finest personnel consulting firms. Your style, Dr. Siegal, is behavioristic in nature. Is that the correct terminology?"

Siegal sensed they were not as naïve as they pretended. "It sounds as if you two have done some homework." He decided to stop being the inquirer and see where this conversation headed.

She continued, "The second part of your question is more complicated. Using a consulting firm such as Interaction Dynamics is only one of our considerations. We may not even be looking at a firm but possibly a single individual."

"Interesting, an individual," responded Siegal. "Then the only person in this office with the knowledge you seek must be sitting there—Jerry Ravid. I have worked here for over a year and know from experience you cannot have made a better choice."

The man held up his hand, stopping further conversation. He picked up the red report and extended his arm to shake the hands of Siegal and Ravid, concluding the meeting. "I'm sorry. We have other obligations this morning and must call this meeting to a close." Before he reached the door, he turned and asked, "Oh by the way, Dr. Siegal, being a strict behaviorist, what is your position on chaos theory?"

Before Siegal could answer, the pair thanked Ravid for his time and left.

The meeting lasted eleven minutes. Frustrated with only questions, Siegal looked at Ravid for some answers. "What just happened?"

"I don't know. I'm as much in the dark as you. I have meetings the rest of the day. Sometimes ruminating for a while will help bring clarity. We'll talk about it tomorrow."

ELEVEN

"HAVE YOU EVER FELT YOU were being watched?" Siegal asked as he and BF walked across City University quadrangle to the psychology building. The flagstone pathway was beautiful this time of year in its adornment of stately elms and maples dressed in fringes of yellows and reds. The air held a slight morning chill. It was the first day of the fall term. It was a time of new beginnings, an omen of change.

"Can't say I have," answered BF. "Do you mean like being spied on? Or the normal administration activity of keeping tabs on its non-tenured instructional flock?"

"I mean the undercover variety, men in raincoats and wide-brimmed hats peeking out from behind trees."

"Are you munching rat pellets laced with some of your students' special harvest?"

"Hear me out. See what you make of it. You know, Ravid called me into his office yesterday. I figured it was to discuss my year-end report with the other consultants. Instead, two people were sitting there with my report in front of them. I believe they got the final draft before I did."

"Ravid probably gave them a pre-release edition to help sell them on ID. He just had you there to answer any questions about the results. You're becoming paranoid in your old age, friend."

Siegal rubbed the thinning spot on top of his head. "Maybe, but my gut tells me something else. On the surface, they appeared to be searching for consulting help from ID. But whenever I asked a direct question about who they represented, they beat around the bush. Not really lying, just being evasive. As we finished, one of them asked me if I had views on chaos theory. And then didn't wait for an answer. How did they know I've been batting the idea around? I've never discussed it to anyone but you and the girls. Not even Ravid. I think my mind's been bugged."

"Or just fall-term paranoia?"

"I don't think so. It's against all odds that they said it without purpose. Everything they said in that meeting was with purpose. They gave me the sense of being government types and yet, not really. My report lay on the table, and it was never mentioned. Another thing. Why only have me, the newest consultant on staff, without any of the others? I was, for some reason, their focus. It was like I was being interviewed and I don't have an inkling why."

They passed the Quadrangle, where crowds of students explored a large display board to determine which building housed their classes. Two people, a man and a woman, stood near one of the old elm trees behind a group of students.

"Look over there," Siegal stiffened, not pointing but tilting his head so as not to attract attention. "Those are the two I met in Ravid's office."

"Maybe they're just sightseers with a little extra time on their hands and are enjoying the campus atmosphere."

"They just know too much about me. I'd like to know more about them.

"You're working too hard. You've taken on an extra class to satisfy the administration, ID is giving you more responsibility, and Simi is busy getting her dissertation on track, cutting you out of private time."

"You're right, as usual," Siegal said. "If it is anything I should worry about, it will show up in due time."

"WHAT THE HELL?" said Simi, opening the storage room door in preparation for feeding their lab rats.

Every cage stood open and empty. Newbies and old pros, the team's nicknames for their two generations of experimental pets, scurried about on the floor and tables. Food pellet bags had large holes chewed open by feasting rats.

Shocked by the discovery, Simi managed enough sense to close the storage room door, leaving the rats trapped. Then she ran to the psychology classroom's building, looking for Siegal. Instead, she found Sally.

"Come quick, girl. There's no time for questions."

They hurried back to the lab.

Simi eased open the door to the storage room. It was a Piccadilly Circus, with both ladies chasing the rats with fishing nets and paper cups.

Sally, half winded from chasing, said, "Damn good luck. Thanks to color-coding their tails, we got them back in their proper cages." She made doubly sure this wouldn't happen again by securing the cage latches with wire twist ties.

Siegal arrived just as everything returned to normal. "What's up, ladies?"

"You don't want to know," said Simi.

Sally chimed in, speaking over Simi's words. "It's a fucking mess. We tried to keep all of them separate and now our experiments are blown."

"Contaminated is the word," corrected Siegal.

"That, too. I mean, they must have been out most of the night copulating and who knows what else. Now we'll have three groups to study. Newbies, old pros, and bastard offspring."

"Do you realize what just happened?" he asked.

"Yes, those goddamned little creatures accidentally got out and made a mess of our storage room," answered Simi.

"Nothing is an accident. One cage being opened is chance. All of them opened at one time? What are the odds?"

"How about someone coming in and opening them?" suggested Sally. "I wouldn't put it past any of your so-called psych colleagues down the hall pulling such an anus trick."

"No chance. We are the only ones who know the combination to the padlock on the storage room door."

Simi added, "Six separate cages opened. Were they totally unrelated events or did one rat open his cage and then open the others? Whichever, they combined their intelligence and did some unique communicating."

Siegal said, "The intelligence gene to escape has to be somehow coded into their brains. No direct learning had taken place. They learned this by observing us. This is one hell of a discovery. There's a lot we can learn from this event."

"This won't happen again without our knowing their movements," said Simi. "I'm setting our only video camera for night surveillance. It's obvious the rats are not going to show us anything while we're watching."

BF walked in and listened to what happened. "Who instigated it all? It's an interesting turnabout for sure. The rats are now your teachers. The three of you, their students."

"I can't do anything more here. I need to leave for the library," said Simi.

Siegal shrugged, "That leaves me with designing a three-variable research design proposal, expecting we'll have a new generation of rats to study. I'll put it out online and see if we can get some interest."

On his way out the door, BF said, "I'm the extra cog here and need to be out of the way. See you all later at Quandary's."

Siegal said, "To be sure, a quandary we are already in."

TWELVE

RAVID STEPPED INTO SIEGAL'S OFFICE. "Good morning, Ross."

"Good, we're on an informal basis again."

"How's it going?"

Siegal shrugged. He knew not to start a conversation without waiting for Ravid to initiate it. His patience was rewarded.

"Thinking about the meeting, aren't you?" asked Ravid. "What's your take? Will we get them as clients?"

"That's the point. I don't think they're clients at all. They don't fit the profile. They didn't dress exactly like ID clients. They didn't reveal enough for us to make a sales pitch. And even more, they didn't ask the right questions."

"Is that all?" asked Ravid.

"No. I first thought I was called into your office to review my report. Then these two came in carrying an advanced year-end copy of it."

"Well, Ross, they asked for it."

"How did they even know about it? It was only a couple days old."

"They've been here two—no, I think three—times before. I must have told them about our reports and they must have requested this edition as soon as it came out. My secretary probably gave it to them and forgot to tell me. No biggie."

"Maybe. It makes sense when you put it that way, but why on God's green earth did you call me to sit in and not one of the full-time staff?"

"It was by their request. During my previous meetings with them, we talked about who was with this firm. When I came to your name, they paid more attention. That woman specifically asked for you. That must have been after I told them about your year-end report."

"Do you think they'll be back?"

"Like you, I don't think so. Anything else?"

"I might as well ask how you think I'm doing here."

"I apologize for that. In the short time you've been here, you've shown me more creative talent than the rest of my staff combined. Not only do I relish your input, but your report is the best we've ever had. I especially admire your taking the risk to do something different with it. Your mind works in unique ways."

Siegal's faced reddened. He was not used to compliments from other than his students and three friends. "Just doing my job."

"I would like to be more than your CEO. If ever you need to confide in me about any problem, professionally or personally, feel free to ask me. Let's keep our office doors open to each other. And if you ever decide to part ways at City University, you have a full-time spot here on staff."

Ravid's compliments put Siegal's mind into park. He had never felt like this before. By noon, he finally gave up trying to work.

No sense wasting my time here. I might as well see how things are going on campus.

On the way back to the lab, he checked his campus mailbox. The treasure included several letters addressed to "Occupant" and four more rejection letters.

Shit.

THIRTEEN

TWO JEEPS IN CAMOUFLAGE PAINT traveled a two-rut road in a remote forest area of central Columbia. The lead jeep carried four combat-uniformed men armed with AK-47 assault rifles. They scanned the thick underbrush for danger, should any rival faction be foolish enough to attack. The second vehicle had three men in like attire, the driver and two sitting in the back seat.

"Are you having fun, amigo?"

"Si, General Rebus. We have been very successful showing our power. The peasants fear you and many wish to join your army."

"Here," said Rebus, taking three cigars from his breast pocket. He handed one to the driver, a second to his companion, and put the third between his teeth. "These are the finest Cuban cigars given me by my good friend Raul Castro. Our raids in Europe and Asia have made me very powerful. We shall unite with Cuba and form the largest drug cartel in Central and South America."

The three men laughed as Rebus passed around a bottle of rum.

"I will become even more powerful as well as very rich. And you, amigo, as my number one lieutenant will become rich a well. All of my amigos will become rich. Beautiful women will rush to be by our sides."

The three smoked, drank rum, and laughed as they continued their travel. Without warning a rocket grenade, fired from the dense underbrush, carved a crater in the road just in front of the lead jeep.

"Dios mio," shouted Rebus.

At the same moment two trees were dragged across the road from behind the rear jeep, blocking any possible retreat. Rebus stood up and shouted to the front guards. "Attack the bastards and...."

Before he finished his order, a second rocket made a direct hit onto the lead carrier, killing its passengers. The underbrush came alive with green-faced assault forces. The driver and Rebus's lieutenant attempted an escape into the jungle. A rush of well-aimed bullets killed them before they reached the green sanctuary. Rebus, the only remaining guerrilla, stood in his jeep shooting wildly into the trees, but with no success. As the target of the ambush, he was spared an unceremonious assassination and yanked from his perch.

"Do you realize who I am?" sputtered Rebus as he was trussed like a deer on a spit and carried to a small clearing about a hundred feet from the road.

A tall and muscled American barked out orders.

"Que? What is happening? Chocha, pussy, you are not the leader. You are making a very big mistake. You are only a sergeant. Let me talk with your leader. Hurt me and you are dead."

"Rebus, you did not stay in your own country. The world does not want such a man as you free to terrorize the world. We must teach you a lesson."

"You are not from another cartel. Who are you?"

"Spread his arms and legs. Peg them to the ground."

Rebus pleaded, "Please, I can pay you. I can make you a business partner. I can make you very rich. Don't kill me. Please don't kill me."

The sergeant aimed his automatic rifle between Rebus' legs and fired a single round. Blood and soft body parts splattered. Rebus screamed. But in the forest where there was no one who cared to hear, the screamer made no sound.

Rebus cried in agony. "Cut me loose."

A second attacker, showing no emotion, only determination, drew his machete from a leather scabbard at his side. "Glad to, you bastard."

Rebus felt the hot stings and crunch of his bones as two slashes severed his arms just below each elbow. With screams of tortured anguish, he cried, "Stop. Stop."

The sergeant placed a final bullet to the brain. The blackness in Rebus's eyes matched the blackness of his heart. He no longer felt pain.

"The brutality to your victims can never be fully avenged. But no one will ever have to fear you again." The sergeant spat on the mutilated body, leaving it on the ground for flesh-eating beetles and other scavengers, then walked away.

In minutes, the diminishing sound of a helicopter signaled the assault troops leaving. One world threat…gone.

FOURTEEN

IT WAS MID-AFTERNOON AND THE red Oval Office phone rang for the third time in as many days. President Russell responded, "I'm just finishing some business. I'll call you back in ten minutes or less." He punched his intercom, "Miss Keyes, get Mr. Danielson."

Danielson answered his phone from his new office on K Street, the center of Washington's consultants and lobbyists. He listened for a moment. "I'm on my way."

Danielson arrived at the guarded side door of the White House in seven minutes. A fifteen-second elevator ride brought him to the second floor. He exited and quick-stepped down the hall to the Oval Office suite. There, he greeted Amanda Keyes sitting at her desk.

"You sound winded. Take a breath." She buzzed the intercom announcing his arrival. "Yes, Mr. President." She turned to Danielson. "He says to go in."

The president's head motioned for Danielson to take the chair directly in front of his desk. Russell clicked on the speakerphone next to his collegiate archery championship trophy. "Miss Keyes, notify my last caller I'm ready."

In barely a minute, Russell's red phone rang.

The voice barked the words, "They found Rebus." It was President Cho-Se. "My informants say he was slain by members of a rival drug cartel in typical gangland fashion. I am pleased to say he will no longer be robbing banks in China and killing more of my innocent people."

"Nor anywhere else. I am happy for your good fortune," said Russell.

"And what about the other matter? Is there any progress? Or is this another American red herring?"

President Russell looked at Danielson for an answer. "I expect progress. I'm sure Mr. Danielson will be informing us when there is something concrete to discuss. In the meantime, I wish health and happiness to you and all your family from me and mine."

The President turned off the speakerphone and gave Danielson a quizzical stare. "Well?"

"Before answering, do you want me to help issue any release about Rebus?" asked Danielson.

"No, let the press manage the story. They jump at the smell of blood, especially having an international criminal slaughtered and his sex organs mutilated by a rival cartel."

"Good point."

Then President Russell displayed a rare smile. "By the way, Tom. Did we have anything to do with it? There's a rumor an American led the assault. I know I didn't order such a raid."

"I wouldn't be surprised by anything that goes on in this wild world of ours," answered Danielson. Russell smiled, appreciating the lack of a direct answer.

"How's your project proceeding? Your honeymoon with SOS is almost over. You heard Cho-Se. Galdet and Sokoloven also asked. It's been almost two weeks since we met at the chalet. Something must happen soon. I mean fucking real soon."

"What have you told them?"

"I put them off as best I could. You don't have much slack. I informed them you're no longer on staff and that you work independently from me. All messages have to come from you. I don't think they really believed me. Trust on the world stage being what it is. The clock is ticking." Russell poured each a glass of scotch. "Is there anything you can tell me?"

"This is all off the record. And, you're no longer my boss. But I relish being able to bounce my ideas off of someone."

"Then bounce away."

"I've been meeting with my headhunters. I've used them several times before. I just haven't told you about them because they did security work for you in the past without proper clearance."

Danielson outlined their investigations, narrowing the hunt to two human relations consulting firms, and finally to a single firm, Interaction Dynamics, in Denver. "The more I thought about it, the more I felt we needed a single person."

"Did you find your man with an 'S' on his chest?"

"My Superman? The hunt came down to two men, Jerry Ravid, the firm's CEO, and Ross Siegal, a consultant working there. Either one can do the job. Ravid is more experienced and a team player, but Siegal, the rebel warrior, has the best potential."

"Knowing you, your choice is the latter. Tell me about him."

"It's not a slam dunk. My headhunters found out everything about him. They put wiretaps everywhere possible. Dr. Siegal's an expert in rat behavior. His recent research looked a lot like most behavioral studies. But, as the year progressed, he came upon the idea to use rats that already performed for them and added them into the mix. Other behaviorists challenged his results. Called him a charlatan and worse. The usual grant-funding resources avoid him like a plague. He is hardly able to carry bare-bones research on the paltry budget the university allows him. That brings me to the last point. He may not survive the academic nightmare of publish or perish, but he still remains stubbornly fixed to his principles."

"If you like him, I say bring him on board."

Danielson glanced over to the archery trophy on Russell's desk. "He could be a modern-day Robin Hood who splits the center of his opponent's arrow. There is only one drawback, El. He's independent and thrives on being one of a kind. Plus, he shuns publicity and enjoys working against the system. But he sees behaviors others miss. His understanding makes him one of a kind. He could refuse my offer based on some irrelevant principle. And that includes even being asked by you. His very nature is why he's my numero uno choice, and at the same time, keeps us from landing him. He's the exact kind of person I need."

"Why would you want him if he has all those negatives?"

"It's because he has those characteristics that makes him my man of choice."

"Then offer him anything he wants. Just get him. You have my presidential account. Use it."

Danielson smiled. "Thank you! I expected you'd say that. I already have."

"What's holding you back?"

"I still need to know how much physical risk he's willing to take when more than rats are at stake. So I created a little subterfuge."

"You better let me in on this little subterfuge. You know, in case the Justice Department or Congress decides to ask."

"I created a funding source supposedly to help those special researchers explore their experimental dreams. I've called this source the Special Projects Division of the National Research Committee for the Privately Endowed Foundation."

"Sounds like a chapter of *The Millionaire*. Tom, I believe you're getting a sense of humor in your old age."

"It's no joke. Here is a copy of the letter I sent him two days ago." Danielson reached into his briefcase and handed Russell a copy.

Russell read it. "Has he accepted your proposal?"

"Not yet. And he doesn't even have to use the money, only inquire about it. If my judgment of people is as good as I think, he'll use the damn money and not worry about any strings attached. He has his own internal motivation. If he chooses to use our funds, it would only be to further science."

"When will you know?"

"Very soon, I hope. There is a letter of credit on file at the local bank at his university. If he spends even a nickel, we've got him."

"Remember, my friend," said Russell, "It's you—not we.

FIFTEEN

THE WALL CALENDAR IN SIEGAL'S rat lab told the tale. The deadline for grant submissions had passed. Rejection letters piled high on Siegal's desk, held together with large rubber bands. No letters indicated interest. None even requested a rewrite. Driven by stubborn independence, plus Siegal's meager income from the university and part-time work at ID, the team resigned to carry on their research in an academic and financial vacuum.

"Those assholes, they're so afraid to try something new. It's like we're psychedelic in a beige world," complained Sally. "They're so out of touch with opportunities for new science."

Simi shrugged. "It's an insider's game. I need some fresh air to cool down. I'll check the university mailboxes while I'm out, for whatever good that will do."

It wasn't five minutes when Simi rushed back, not even closing the door behind her. Any free lab rats could have easily escaped. "Look at this." She showed a notification card from the post office.

"It says there's a registered letter for you. They don't send rejection letters registered, do they?"

"Not that I've heard. Ladies, hold down the fort. It's probably some phony deal, but you never know. I'll go see what it is."

SIEGAL RETURNED TO the lab, awkwardly holding up a legal sized envelope.

"Well?" asked Sally.

Siegal touched his balding spot. "Could be something. Advertisements seldom come registered."

He fumbled with the flap, in part to tease his grad assistants, but he was just as anxious to find out what it contained. Whenever he did get a grant, it was often too small to be of much use. Still, any money was better than none and meant less cash from his own pocket. He searched his cluttered desk for reading glasses. Finding them under some psychology monographs, he put them on.

"Forget those," said Simi. She wrenched the letter from her mentor's hands. "I'll read it."

> Dear Ross Siegal, Ph.D.,
> Congratulations. We, The Special Projects Division of the National Research Committee, a privately-endowed foundation, have studied your proposal with great interest. Your past record of research studies show unique qualities we seek to foster.
> The preliminary results noted in your proposal indicate sophisticated language taking place among your rat subjects. We feel this direction merits further study and want to support your effort.

"This is about the flakiest—no, I should say juvenile—letter I have received since Valentine's Day in third grade," said Siegal

"Hey, boss. Don't knock it," said Sally. "It's a compliment. Someone thinks you have the great mind we always knew you had."

"You're right. This does excite me a little. But I'm so used to failure in bringing in research funds. I guess I'm protecting my emotions a little."

Simi looked affectionately at him. "You've been discovered. I think I love you." She gave him a warm hug.

"Enough of that," complained Sally. "Read on."

It is, therefore, our pleasure to inform you that a letter of credit has been filed at the Campus Union National Bank, affording you the opportunity to carry out your next generation of studies.
More information to follow.
Thomas Danielson, Chairman

Puzzled, Ross Siegal examined the letter and the envelope. The name on the letterhead was Special Projects Division, National Research Committee of the Privately Endowed. "There's no return address or phone number, only the envelope postmarked Washington, D.C. How do we communicate with this golden parachute? Smells political."

"Especially coming from Washington," added Sally.

"It sounds too good to be true." Siegal sniffed the envelope. "And it smells just as phony. I want to know what strings are attached. I've gone it alone before and was planning to do so now."

BF walked into the room, hearing the last of the letter. "Don't jump away from the gun before knowing if it's loaded. Has anyone ever heard of this foundation?"

"It's a first-timer for me," answered Siegal.

Sally suggested, "Maybe it's one of your esteemed psych colleagues playing a practical joke. They all know your shitty track record when it comes to getting grants. This has to be a joke."

Simi opened Google on her keyboard. "I'll check the *National Register of Foundations.*"

Sally added sarcastically, "Look in the envelope for tickets. We may be going to Fantasy Island." Getting on her knees while pointing toward the ceiling, and in her finest Fantasy Island imitation, she said, "Look, boss, de grant, de grant."

Deep inside, Siegal wanted the grant, but knew his team wanted it even more. Cautiously he said, "How do you suggest we proceed?"

BF said, "I say you should go about your business as if the letter never came. Still, you ought to check with the bank to see if there really is such a letter of credit."

"The Campus Union Bank is where I do all my business. I have their phone number right here on my desk somewhere."

Siegal rummaged through his desk clutter of unfiled communications, finally locating an old bank statement with a phone number on it. A few touches on his phone and a live voice answered on the other end. Siegal inquired about any letter of credit in his name.

Elevator music wafting on the line. Then an abrupt click.

"Dr. Ross Siegal? This is Bill Brown, branch manager of Campus Union Bank. You asked about a letter of credit filed in your name?"

"Yes," said Siegal, expecting the hoax to end.

"That is correct. A rather sizable credit line has been established in your name. Do you wish to act on it at this time?"

"No thank you." He paused to slow his breathing. "I mean thank you very much. I just wanted to verify." Stunned, he hung up the phone and turned toward the group. His voice trembled, "It's for real."

"How much?" asked the threesome as one voice.

"I forgot to ask."

Simi's looked up from her Google search. "There doesn't appear to be any such foundation."

"Fucking weird," said Sally.

"Okay. On one hand, this is the weirdest acceptance letter I've ever seen. And you know how I feel about this kind of secrecy. An agency with apparent deep pockets that doesn't seem to exist is ominous enough. But, the money is real. That's eerie. Do we take a flier or not?" He paused. "My first thought is no."

BF countered, "Just like you to be so stubborn. I say accept the gift but wear a life jacket in case you have to jump ship at a moment's notice."

Sally added, "Hot shit. As my father would say in one of his Sunday sermons, 'This letter is from old Satan himself. If you accept this evil money, your soul is going to hell.'"

BF moved for closure. "What have you got to lose? I say go ahead. You'll be able to add some bells and whistles to your research."

Simi agreed. "I'm not giving up my soul to the devil. But I'm not for backing off out of fear we're being used for some nefarious ends. I lost any fear after divorcing my cheating husband."

Siegal gaveled his hand on the table. "Okay. We'll only use the money as a last resort. Case closed."

Siegal's mind wandered as he gazed over at the rats in the corner, unconcerned with the research possibilities as they innocently ate their pellets. "What secrets can they reveal if given a chance? Like my mamma used to say, 'What is bashert is bashert.' Yiddish, my friends, for 'If fate wills it, then it will be so.'"

SIXTEEN

SIX DAYS HAD PASSED SINCE Danielson's mysterious letter of credit was filed in the Campus Union Bank. The normal coffee klatch in the Oval Office became an event of the past once Danielson left his chief of staff position and took up residence on K Street. Now, it could only happen by presidential invitation. And today, Danielson was invited.

"Any nibbles, Tom?" asked Russell. "SOS is growing impatient."

"I cast my bait, El. Dr. Siegal is an independent cuss, a true loner. He's not one you can lure by shiny beads and a spinner. He's not a bottom feeder like most Washington politicians. It's not going to be easy hooking and landing him."

"Just hope your bait choice is infallible. Tell me again why you are using it."

"I studied his persona in great detail. My being associated with any form of government would turn him away from me no matter how important the cause."

"Time is fleeting. We, and I'm speaking for the SOS, need him now."

"HOW'S OUR RESEARCH going, Simi?" asked Siegal.

"It's like this. Our research is going, no real surprises. We're getting great numbers that tell us there is definitely high-level communication taking place between the rats. There's a significant correlation of better problem-solving skills when paired parents and sibs are grouped together than with random parings."

"If that's the best you can do, you're wasting both my time and yours. Something's eating you ladies; out with it."

"We could really use extra equipment," said Simi. "We think much of the rat's communication is taking place when we're not here. Rats are naturally nocturnal and we only have one video camera."

"Or we can bunk in with them," added Sally. "Just kidding. More cameras can help a lot. We can observe them when they don't think we are watching. Also, with our increased population, we need more cages so we can vary our charges and put them into artificial living families."

"How much money are you talking about?"

Simi pondered the question. "Cameras, more cages, and added food supply with so many mouths to feed."

"That doesn't seem so outrageous."

"And we sure could use a couple new computers and statistical programs," added Sally.

"That's big bucks talking. You're now asking me to tap into the Foundation bank account."

Sally grimaced, in part begging and in part wondering if she and Simi were asking for too much. "Not if you don't feel ethical about it."

Siegal said, "I know there's money lying in the bank for us to spend. And suppose I don't have to sell my soul to use it. What's the worst that can happen?" He looked at his graduates' faces. Then, slapping the desk, he said, "I agree, we ought to take some of the grant money and reboot our research."

A NONDESCRIPT THREE-STORY brownstone, home of Washington's powerful non-elected, stood on K Street. It looked similar to all the other office buildings around it. And, like everything else in D.C., nothing was as it seemed. Power brokers, spies and counterspies resided side-by-side with an occasional exporter/importer sprinkled among them. No security guarded the front entrance of the building.

At the end of the second-floor hallway was a one-room office. Its privacy was protected by an opaque window with the lettering "CONSULTANT" painted in the corner, the perfect covert home of Tom Danielson.

His ten-by-twelve-foot space housed a used L-shaped desk, matching chair, a computer, and a two-drawer lateral file pushed against one wall. Long ago Danielson wore different hats, and always kept separate phones for each hat. This office was no different. A white phone for personal calls, a red phone connected to the Oval Office, and a black phone to communicate with his headhunters and the quick-strike force he had used to eradicate Rebus.

Danielson poured a mug of stale coffee from a pot that had been brewing for most of the morning. He scowled at the bitter taste that only a single man of long standing could swallow.

A pile of mail greeted him as he gathered enough courage to take another drink. One letter caught his eye. It came from the Campus Union Bank in Denver.

Dear Mr. Danielson,
The account 3644481749 09257 opened in the name of Dr. Ross Siegal has recent activity in the amount of $5238.56. Per your request, we honored the withdrawal without question.
Yours truly, William Brown, Branch Manager

Danielson smiled as he picked up the red phone and pushed the single button where normally there would be touch-tone numbers. There was a short pause and then a click.

"Tell him the fish has taken the bait."

Unexpectedly, it was not Miss Keyes who answered the phone, but President Russell's voice on the other end.

"And, maybe not a moment too soon. Can you get over here?"

"Yes, sir. First I need to send a quick communication."

Danielson turned on his computer and typed an email.

WE ARE PLEASED that you accepted our offer to assist and wish you great success in your research.
It is always difficult for a man of your high standards to receive any grant in such a secretive manner. You must understand, and accept, that our group must remain anonymous. Be assured there is nothing illegal about its source or criminal about the benefactors.
There is one stipulation.

"Here it comes, gang," blurted Sally. "Bend over, smile and take your injections like good little psychologists."

"Be quiet for a moment," urged Simi. "Finish reading."

You are required, on very short notice, to provide progress reports in exacting detail.
You will express mail any reports to the following address:

"Finally," breathed Sally in relief, "We have an address."
"Don't be too sure," responded Simi.

SPD, NRCPEF, P.O. Box 612, Washington, D.C. 20001

Simi said, "Just a P.O. box?"
"Say the word, team. I'll give back our new equipment and pay expenses from my own pocket," said Siegal.
Simi shook her head. "We need their money, Ross baby. You're such a stubborn pain in the butt sometimes."

ENTERING THE OVAL Office, Danielson saw the president's worried face. "Problems?"

"The hijacking leader of Flight 234 was spotted attempting to cross over into China. He, with the help of others, went underground and we're not sure where he is now. Our intel is sketchy, but we believe he is up to something."

"Can you put a timeframe on it?"

"No, but it means we have to get moving. What're our chances of getting this Siegal onboard post-haste?"

"It's still a crapshoot if we can even get him at all. I underestimated him and thought he would take the grant as bait right away. He's my Plan A. He's goddamn independent, that's for sure. Plan B will be iffy without him."

"Make it happen. Get your wonder man on board."

The conversation ended abruptly. It was not in the same tone of friendship the two shared in the past. This was business.

PART TWO

ONE THING SURE ABOUT LIFE is that it begins at or before birth, depending on your beliefs. And it ends at death, also according to your beliefs. Between that span in time, all one's experiences happen. Just how much anyone controls any of these existential experiences is in question. Life is often played like the field mouse that sees escape from the fox, but never quite makes it to the safety of its burrow under the rocks.

SEVENTEEN

EVENTS THAT OCCURRED JUST DAYS ago in the mountains of Colorado changed the course of Ross Siegal's life forever. Like his lab rats, he had little choice but to follow the maze and rewards set out for him. Accepting money from the mysterious letter of credit became his food-pallet release lever.

Danielson's subterfuge of hooking Siegal with financial bait too sweet to refuse was successful by the slimmest of margins. He needed to meet Siegal face-to-face. But would Siegal stay around after hearing the real reason?

Netting this rare fish would be difficult at best. If Danielson pulled the line too quickly, his quarry would snap the line and be lost forever. The lure of money was not enough for Siegal to accept anything that hinted of a bribe, especially when it would go against his moral judgment. If Siegal was asked point blank, he could refuse; and there was no second chance. Only a perfect plan would do.

Danielson looked at his reflection in the computer monitor. "I have to do better than the planning I did as campaign manager for Russell when he ran as an underdog for the presidency."

Danielson grimaced, bracing himself for another sip of the muddy liquid. "Fuck this. I'm making a fresh pot. I'll need it for what comes ahead."

Forty-eight sleepless hours had passed, and Danielson continued pawing through the stack of psychology CDs he had ordered from the Library of Congress's Behavioral Science section. It was October and the ghosts of Halloween were attacking him in full force.

He slipped the final CD into his computer. A short list of famous motivational psychologists and educators scrolled across his screen: Freud, Erickson, Jung, Maslow, Thorndike, Skinner, Atkinson, Hewett, Peters, Padzensky, and Doll. Then, not to leave out any possible clues to understanding his quarry, Danielson added historical leaders: Moses, Alexander the Great, Franklin Roosevelt, and Adolf Hitler.

The SOS chairman coveted Siegal. He instinctively knew this one-of-a-kind behaviorist was his man. His task? Motivate Siegal to pronounce three little letters—y-e-s.

He cleared his screen and typed what all his theorists agreed were human motivators: **MONEY, PRESTIGE, STATUS, FEAR, SAFETY, SURVIVAL, INCLUSION IN A GROUP, KNOWLEDGE, POWER, SELF-VALIDATION, NEW THEORY, APPROVAL, STRESS REDUCTION, SELF-ACTUALIZATION, SEX.**

Danielson mumbled to himself. "Which one will work on you, Dr. Siegal? I need just one. But two would be better." His eyes glazed from steady work and the nervous energy provided by Mr. Coffee's caffeine. He deleted one motivator after another. "What am I missing?"

He stumbled out of his chair and washed his face in the water fountain down the hall. The cold liquid revived him. A glance at his computer clock and calendar showed five a.m. It would be light in two hours. Danielson promised himself he would go out for a hot breakfast at first light.

His bloodshot eyes looked up toward the lone fluorescent fixture in the ceiling. He collapsed back into his chair, fighting the sleep his brain demanded.

Danielson's eyes brightened. **KNOWLEDGE**. The promise of new knowledge is the key to getting him out of his private research hideaway. He underlined the word.

Can I make it two? He reread his list again. He deleted every motivator that didn't fit his model. Only **NEW THEORY** remained. Danielson added it as a cherry on top of his motivation sundae. He felt proud; his research was as good as that curmudgeon Dr. Ross Siegal's.

As a top strategist colonel in the Navy SEALS, Danielson instinctively knew that just offering Siegal motivators wouldn't work. Siegal would have to discover them on his own.

Danielson blinked as the early-morning sun shone in the window. Old habits of a retired colonel caused him to follow his own orders without question. Food at first light. He donned his coat to guard against the cool morning temperature and left for breakfast.

"Dr. Ross Siegal, I've got you."

AN ODOR OF soybean food pellets and mustiness filled the claustrophobic lab area assigned to Ross Siegal. His lab was a cookie-cutter of the other animal experiment labs in the psychology department except for two differences. First, each of his experimental contraptions had parallel runways for untrained rats to be in sight of the older generation. Secondly, his rats were allowed to mate. These differences made his research unique.

The team scanned their data as it came off the new printer they bought with the research money.

"Do either of you know what the results mean?" asked Siegal, using the opportunity as a teaching moment.

Simi answered, "Maybe it means children of trained rats learned faster because of what their parents knew. And children of dumber parents learned even slower than their untrained parents."

Sally added, "I think it's more. The rats themselves decide who succeeds and who should not. They're not only communicating with each other, but also setting up a caste system, including some and excluding others. You know, my favorite rat, Tigger, seems to be the best teacher. His groups consistently do better. Is this possible?"

"Ladies, we may have just uncovered a whole area of research untouched by any experts in behavioral psychology. The mystery is here for us to solve."

Simi said, "And thanks to the National Research Committee, whoever the hell they are, we have the means to do it."

The three shared cleanup duty in the lab and feeding the animals. Simi and Siegal left for Quandary's. Sally stayed behind.

Acting coy, Sally said, "BF is coming over to discuss classwork. We'll be there in an hour. I promise." Sally took full advantage of any opportunity to be alone with BF, and the lab worktable provided a perfect platform.

"SNOWS, ESPECIALLY THESE early fall snows in Denver, are like no other place," said Siegal. "The air is so crisp and fresh."

The grassy areas and trees remained white. In contrast, the streets, warmed by the rays of the sun, were almost dry by the time

Simi and Ross finished breakfast in his apartment.

While driving Simi to the library, he said, "Something keeps bothering me. The eighty/twenty factor that keeps showing up in our statistics is the same number my predecessors got at ID. This constant brick wall means we're still missing something. Something to take chaos out of the equation."

He swerved, barely avoiding a car running a very late yellow light.

"Keep your eyes on the road or you'll never get a chance to find out. That was too close."

"It's not logical—not if one knows all the facts. It's a law of physics and holds true in behavioral sciences. No energy is ever lost. There has to be a way of increasing the predictability percentages. I know it can be done."

Simi was certain he would figure it out. After all, the man sitting next to her was Dr. Ross Siegal. They stopped in front of the library. "Pick me up at four, after you've figured it out." She gave him a perfunctory kiss on the cheek and got out.

SIEGAL'S THOUGHTS KEPT jumping back and forth between the lab and office. By the time he reached ID's parking lot, he put all rat lab activity out of his mind and began thinking only of work at ID.

On his desk was a handwritten memo from Jerry Ravid:

SEE ME AS SOON AS YOU COME IN

EIGHTEEN

RAVID'S DOOR STOOD OPEN. SIEGAL took it as an invitation, gave a single knock, and walked in.

Ravid adjusted reading glasses without looking up from his desk. "Have you ever heard of Special Projects Division, National Research Committee for the Privately Endowed Foundation?"

Siegal hesitated. "A little. How do you know about...?"

Before Siegal could finish his question, Ravid gave a knowing nod and rubbed his hands. "A little, huh? I think more. Tell me about them."

"The truth is that I don't know anything about them, except..."

"Except what?" interrupted Ravid.

"Is there something I did wrong?"

"Foundation? Sounds like you're intimately aware." Ravid pointed to the communication lying on his desk. "It's addressed to Dr. Ross Siegal in care of me, CEO of Interaction Dynamics. It was sent to me instead of contacting you straight out. I thought maybe you could fill me in. I am the boss here, or so I thought. I didn't open it. Waited for you."

Siegal looked for a smile on Ravid's face. There was none. He then scanned the return address in the lefthand corner to confirm who sent it. "Odd."

"Odd? I should say so," Ravid emphasized.

Siegal took a letter opener off Ravid's desk and slid it under the flap. The letterhead was an inconspicuous, simple block type:

Dr. Ross Siegal:

We have followed your research with great interest. That is why you received our financial offer. We would like to discuss your results at your earliest convenience. Should you care to continue our partnership, you are required to meet with us at our home office in Washington, D.C.

You are authorized to draw research funds to purchase a first-class, round-trip ticket to Dulles International Airport. Make hotel reservation at the Washington, D.C., Downtown Marriott, Room 612. We will let you know the exact time of our meeting once you arrive.

The letter ended with *Director, SPD, NCPEF.*

"Wow. I'm not a cloak-and-dagger man. How did they know I work here at ID? What do you make of all this? They are funding my research this year at the university. What kind of funding source did I buy into?"

Ravid asked, "Do you remember the two mysterious visitors who came to this office late in the summer? It seemed they were very interested in you. I think those two and the letter are connected. Are you applying for another job?"

The question surprised Siegal. "The thought never crossed my mind. I don't know any reason why anyone would be interested in me."

Ravid took the letter and examined it. "Don't be so humble. We already know your worth here at ID. Someone is doing their homework. I'd wager this National Research Committee knows more about you than you ever imagined. Just what kind of research are you doing? Developing some kind of super-rat?"

"Nothing so exotic. Most behavioral psychologists consider our studies unprofessional. Until now, we have never been able to secure any quality research grants."

"Interesting, and now they're inviting you to meet with them on their home turf. How're you going to handle it? Maybe they're after your brain and not your research. You may not be looking for a job, but someone out there is looking very hard to hire you. This could be your future. Have you examined if or how they're playing you?"

Siegal explained his unusual relationship with the Foundation. So far, he had only sent one report to them. "They've never asked any questions before. This is the first time they have asked for a face-to-face meeting. My team appreciates the funds, so I've been going along with them."

"I imagine they don't need to ask questions because they already know the answers. Are they going to kill you or make you pay back anything you spent?"

"I don't know."

"Then I think you should go see what they want. If they get too pushy..."

"I think I can always refuse any further assistance."

Ravid walked around his desk as a gesture that their meeting was over. "It's settled then. Go for it. My guess is you won't lose the funding source no matter what they demand."

Siegal walked back to his office. *My God, what cat-and-mouse game are they playing? Too much secrecy. Why does this foundation think I'm so important?*

Back in his small office, he buzzed Ravid. "I need to tell my graduate students that I will be out of town on some business. I'd like to say you need me for some oversight activity. I hope that's all right with you?"

"You get my support as long as whatever you do is legal and ethical. And so far, I can't see you violating either of these principles."

THE RESEARCH TEAM and BF agreed to an early dinner at Quandary's. It was almost six when Siegal arrived. He accepted their ribbing and complaints about how they had to wait more than fifteen minutes for their professor. The evening started on a light note. Being a lone wolf, he hoped to keep it that way.

"Wassup, Doc?" asked Sally.

Siegal, mocking a fatherly rubbing of his chin, said, "It seems my illustrious boss has given me a solo job of trust. He needs a follow-up of a consulting group in Washington, D.C. I won't be gone more than a day or two. The two of you can continue our lab experiments without my divine guidance. Oh, and BF, will you please cover my class?"

Simi frowned, pretending to be hurt. "Sure, keep us girls in the kitchen and give us the dirty work." Then her expression changed to serious. "You certainly sprung this one on us in a hurry. You always keep us in the loop about everything."

Guilt flowed through Siegal's body. He had lied to them. His instincts told him there was more to the Foundation's letter than it let on. When it came to human judgment, he was rarely wrong. "I'll let you know what happened when I get back." He hoped he could.

The mood lightened. The letter from the Foundation was successfully avoided.

Simi asked, "Did anyone read the newspapers lately? There's a hostage takeover on International Airlines flight 234 in Egypt. Our oxymoronic CIA is trying to determine who did this thing and why. They've explained the action as being done by one of three different insurgent groups they were tracking."

Sally said, "You know what? I think they're just trying to cover up for their own stupidity. If I had to depend upon their intelligence gathering as a study guide, I would have flunked out of this damn university. Any one of us could figure everything out a lot faster, and better, too."

Pretending to be involved in the linguistic exercises with his friends, Siegal's mind was steadfast on the letter. *Is my integrity being challenged? Government politics and integrity are like oil and water. They don't mix. And I won't be the catalyst for one of their schemes.*

"Your lips are moving. Did you say something?" asked BF.

"Oh. It's nothing."

NINETEEN

DANIELSON OPENED HIS OFFICE DOOR as the light flashed on the new green phone he added for business dedicated to his current responsibility: to get Dr. Ross Siegal on board.

"This is the Downtown Marriott Hotel, Mr. Danielson," spoke a woman's voice in a slight English accent. "I am the director of special relations. Room 612 has been reserved for today and Friday by a Dr. Ross Siegal. I understand he is expected shortly after three this afternoon. Is that correct?"

"Correct," responded Danielson. "Please inform him that he is to meet with the director of the National Research Committee for the Privately Endowed at seven tonight in your private dining room. I will be in the dining room shortly before. Have him ushered directly to me. Thank you."

Danielson trembled with excitement, reminiscent of how he felt the night before Operation Desert Storm. He picked up the red phone, his direct connection to the White House. Amanda answered.

"Tell the president everything is perfect. Our fish has taken the bait. I'm meeting with him tonight here in Washington."

"THURSDAY MORNING TRAFFIC in Denver is getting worse and worse. You'd think all the money they spent widening freeways would make a difference," complained Simi as she drove Siegal to the airport. "People should take rapid transit more."

"Denver drivers are in love with their cars. Nothing is going to change that."

Simi swerved to avoid a driver cutting into her lane.

"Careful. I don't want to lose you to some road idiot. Besides, there is only one decent direct flight to Washington. I don't want to miss it."

"Made it with forty-five minutes to spare." said Simi, stopping in front of the passenger drop-off at Denver International Airport. She joked, "We could have made it in bed one more time and you'd still be early. You seemed too anxious to get this trip on the road."

"I have a funny sense about it. It doesn't feel the same as other business trips to D.C." He gave Simi a parting kiss, grabbed his luggage out of the trunk, and walked into the terminal.

Bad luck happened at the first opportunity. Security decided to tag him for extra screening. He had to hurry. In a second opportunity for bad luck, the plane was delayed for one hour. No hurry now.

"I'll be in the bar," he told the gate attendant. "A beer sounds good right now." *It's about the only thing that does.*

Like Dr. Doolittle's push-me-pull-you animal with two heads, his mind kept going back and forth. This research funding meant a lot to his team and, surprisingly, even to him. His history in securing any kind of grant was poor and this one was worth a lot. It played against his personal standards, kowtowing to what he felt was some political agency and lying to his friends about the trip.

IT WAS THREE o'clock. No call from the Marriott. Danielson dialed the airport on his white phone. *Something went wrong. I should have sent a Big Brother escort to make sure he got on the plane.* A call to Dulles International gave him the answer. The flight was delayed in Denver and planned to touch down at four thirty.

He looked in his little black book and dialed a second number.

"Bill White, Homeland Security."

"Bill, it's Tom Danielson. I need your help. Can you find out if a Dr. Ross Siegal is on the United flight from Denver to Washington this afternoon?"

"I'll punch it up right now. Hold on for a minute." Danielson tapped his fingers waiting. "Here it is. He was listed on the manifest but never boarded."

Using his green phone, Danielson dialed another number he knew by heart. "Sergeant, I need you to make a little air run. How soon can you be ready to roll?"

"I'm ready now, sir."

"Be at Dulles as soon as possible. There's a Dr. Ross Siegal in Denver. I need him here in Washington. He's a loose cannon and may have his ass up in the air."

"Will I need extra muscle?"

"You're big enough to do the job yourself. Convince him any way you can, but start with gentle persuasion. I need him undamaged. A company jet will be waiting. I'll fill you in at the airport."

BACK IN DENVER, a voice piped through the terminal loudspeaker system. "United flight 4026 to Washington D.C. is now boarding for takeoff."

Siegal walked to the gate, his mind in turmoil. "I'm no activist; not even an active passivist. They can't play me. I won't let them."

He stopped. "Fuck you guys."

Fuming, he went outside, grabbed a cab and went home.

SIEGAL MOPED AROUND his apartment until about eight and started to make some salami and scrambled eggs as a late dinner.

The doorbell rang. Siegal opened the door and looked up from his five-foot-seven inch, one hundred sixty pound frame. A man towering six-foot-six and weighing over two hundred and fifty pounds stood in front of him.

"Sorry to bother you, sir. My name is Ben Goldberg."

Siegal looked up. "Yes?"

"Understand you missed your flight today. I have been asked by Mr. Danielson to help you. I have a charter flight ready. You will have to leave right away."

Outweighed and outsized, Siegal was in no position to bully the man mountain. "I would have called the Foundation, but I didn't have a phone number. I was planning to write them tomorrow. I decided not to go to Washington."

"Sorry, sir. My instructions are for you to go with me now. Mr. Danielson is concerned."

"You don't understand. I missed my flight on purpose. I'm stepping out of any agreements with the Foundation."

"I was told you have that choice, but there are some audit questions concerning your grant you must first answer."

"Audit problems?"

With his free hand, Goldberg pulled a handwritten paper from inside his coat pocket. "You purchased a large amount of surveillance equipment that needs some explanation, computer equipment for each of your graduate assistants, unusual construction of special research mazes by an outside contractor, and several meals charged at Quandary's."

"It can all be explained in a letter. I will pay back any inappropriate spending if Mr. Danielson sees fit."

Goldberg reached out and grabbed Siegal's arm with an iron-like grip. "You will have to explain that in person. Your bags are still packed, I presume. My car is waiting outside."

"Am I being kidnapped?" asked Siegal, once they were in the car.

"No sir," replied Goldberg in a voice too calming to feel sincere. "Mr. Danielson is just anxious to talk with you in person. I believe it will become clear very soon."

Goldberg remained silent for the remainder of the ride to Denver International Airport.

TWENTY

A PRIVATE JET WAITED FOR the pair outside Concourse A. Goldberg took Siegal's luggage under one arm and, to assure he would not rabbit, held Siegal with the other as they mounted the waiting jet on the tarmac. Helpless, Siegal complied like a child being led to his first day of kindergarten.

"YOU MISSED YOUR dinner, Dr. Siegal. There is lobster tail prepared in the galley. You may have steak if you prefer. I'll bring you an ODL," said Goldberg.

"Sounds like I'm being offered my last meal. Do I get a rabbi to give a final blessing?"

No answer. In minutes, they were airborne.

The cabin television was tuned to MSNBC. Showing was a voiceover with film clips of the Cairo airport:

"The United Nations met today in full debate. The subject was the mysterious hijacking of Flight 234. No single group accepted responsibility. The White House press secretary indicated this may be the action of a fugitive group based in Tunisia.

The hijackers' plane remains on the ground at Cairo airport at this moment. Their only demand for releasing their hostages is safe passage to a location of their choice. Both Iran and Syria agreed to accept the terrorists until a full investigation is complete."

"One seafood dinner, coming up." It was not the deep voice of Ben Goldberg. "Ross, my name is Tom Danielson."

Siegal forced a smile.

"May I join you? Lobster is my weakness."

"I'm supposed to meet you in Washington. Suddenly you appear on this plane instead."

Danielson's friendly smile disappeared and the look of a hard-core political debater took its place.

"I'll be totally frank with you. By now you must be wondering if there is something more to this meeting than a review of your research expenses. This is true. You have been under the microscope for some time now. The reason will become evident very soon. Let me tell you how you have been observed. And then I'll explain why. In my mind, you are a person of great interest."

The bewildered psychologist sat back. "This whole conversation sounds like a plot I don't want to be part of. You've chosen the wrong person."

"You're jumping ahead a bit. Hear me out. As a good researcher, you know how important it is to collect every fact first and then make your decision."

Siegal felt helpless in the hands of this seasoned negotiator. "So far, nothing's gone right. I can't promise I'm going to like what you say. I suppose if I refuse, your muscleman over there will make sure I do what you want."

"You do have that choice, I assure you." Danielson put an open hand on Siegal's shoulder. "For the past several weeks, you have been watched and studied. Every paper you've written has been scrutinized."

"I should be flattered, but that doesn't explain why I'm here."

"Flattered is an understatement," said Danielson, taking a large piece of lobster and dipping it into the clarified butter. "More beer?"

Siegal nodded and took some lobster himself, remembering he hadn't eaten since early morning.

A chill ran through Siegal's blood. "I still don't see what all of this has to do with my research funds. You can certainly have your funds back."

"This can go much more quickly if you let me finish. The screening has been done. You, Ross Siegal, fit all our requirements. The number of possible choices came down to two. The final decision was easy. Only you have enough balls to carry out what is needed. And your effort to challenge me proves it even more."

"I do have a question about the pair of clients I met in Jerry Ravid's office and later saw at Quandary's. Are they part of your scheme?"

"Good conclusion. I needed to observe you in every facet of your life. They are my eyes on the ground."

"Every facet? Even my se…?"

"Yes, that too," interrupted Danielson.

Siegal's scientific curiosity began to get the better of his logic. "Then it's not my research that's important. I still have the same question—why?"

"The answer is I am convinced you can do the best job. Your unique methods of viewing behavior are needed for a very special mission to succeed."

"You make me seem like Job, who was looking for the truth in the eyes of his spiritual master. When is my fitting for wings and a halo?"

"The wings and halo will never be part of your uniform. But comparing yourself to Job is accurate. As I remember the story, he continually searched for the truth. That is what I expect you to do."

"I was never a person who walked out of a movie before knowing the ending."

Danielson smiled and relaxed back into his chair. "Good to hear it. What I am about to tell you is for your ears only. No one outside a very small circle knows this information. Goldberg, bring our friend another Old Dog's Leg lager."

Pouring a second ODL in an iced glass, Siegal said, "Go on. The movie hasn't ended yet."

"You are expected to maintain a high level of secrecy."

It was Siegal's turn to sit forward in his chair. He had to hear the rest.

"The Foundation was used as a ploy to understand you better. But I expect you will need its funds to carry out some of your discoveries at the university."

Danielson kept talking, all the time studying his quarry's eyes. "This is it. We need you to identify a certain unknown terrorist rat, who is becoming more dangerous as we speak. He hijacked the airplane you saw on the television and we think he is about to come out of his rat hole again."

"I'm not a spy. I'm just a simple scientist. With all respect, this is not for me. I think I want out."

Danielson paused. He had to rework the strategy and fast. He thought through his notes and remembered key words: 'knowledge' and 'new theory'. "Any psychologist can identify such persons about eighty percent of the time. That's the best our CIA profilers can do. We don't have the luxury of accepting such a low batting average. We believe you are the best man to cut this twenty percent error down to, or at least nearly, zero. Your research in the rat lab coupled with the year-end report at Interaction Dynamics made us believe you are on the verge of accomplishing just that. I can't force you. You have to decide for yourself. I only hope I can nudge you a bit into thinking what new ground in behavioral science can come your way."

Siegal's eyes widened reflexively. He was not only hooked. He was netted and in the boat. Humility wasn't one of his strong points, but it was all he had left. "I don't believe there is any person who can do what you want."

"We know what we're looking for has not been developed to the point of practical application. You, on the other hand, have a capacity to get closer than any other known person. And, may I remind you, our search covered the world."

"You keep saying 'we.' Exactly who would I work for? And don't give me any Foundation crap." He took a last drink of ODL and swallowed. "I was really part of a worldwide search?"

"I promise you will know everything very soon. And no phony foundation crap, as you say. Finish your dinner. I have some paperwork to do before we land."

TWO NIGHTS EARLIER, a canvas-backed truck fitted with benches on each side lumbered through fresh snow in a heavily-wooded region of northern China. The headlights were covered, emitting only a slit of dim light. In back were six people, all in their late teens or early twenties. They approached an unguarded archway to a series of one- and two-story structures. A man sitting shotgun next to the driver, their leader and a little older than the others, examined a printed area layout. He pointed to one building, directing the driver to park close by it. The leader got out and motioned for everyone in back to follow and bring their equipment. Four carried small two-wheeled package carriers. The other two carried knapsacks. They entered the main lab through an unlocked door. No one spoke. Once inside, the leader pointed to a walk-in refrigerated unit. He took a bolt cutter from one knapsack and cut the lock. Four milk canister-sized containers were loaded onto the wheeled carriers and taken out. Knapsacks filled with plastic explosives and preset timed fuses were placed in separate corners of the room. The troop carrier left the scene as silently as it came. A minute later, an explosion and fireball erupted, consuming the entire lab in flames. Two of the terrorists were caught in the fire.

The leader dialed a number on his cell phone and, in an Eastern European accent, said, "Mission accomplished, just as planned."

A man on the other end laughed. "And the other part?"

"Also accomplished."

DID YOU ENJOY your dinner?" asked Goldberg. "We still have some flight time. Mr. Danielson thought you may want to see a video clip having to do with your new responsibility." He slid it into the monitor in front of Siegal.

The screen lit up, flashing a satellite image of northwestern China centering on a remote group of buildings. A voiceover offered an explanation of an event happening at that location:

An incendiary bomb exploded last night in northern China at Lijiang University. The fire and explosion destroyed a portion of the chemistry building. No group claimed responsibility. Some speculate it was a student prank targeting the chemistry department. There is also some speculation it may be linked to flight 234's hostage event only a few days earlier. The idea is not yet assumed as fact. In both instances, damage was minimal, no group claimed responsibility, and there were no ransom demands. There are questions needing answers.

THE PRIVATE JET carrying Siegal and Danielson turned north, placing the brightness of the full moon into Ross's eyes, waking him. He looked out the window to see its reflection below.

"That's not ground," he said. "Tom, are those white caps below, or just my imagination?"

"They're whitecaps."

"I don't recall this much water between Denver and the East Coast."

"Right again," said Danielson. "We're taking a little side trip to northern China to get a firsthand look at Lijiang University. The area you saw on the video. It will help you make what I hope is a decision to work with us. You may want to get a little shut-eye right now. You need to be alert for the next part of your journey."

TWENTY-ONE

A FIRM HAND ON HIS shoulder jerked Siegal from his sleep.

"Wake up, sir. The pilot is starting our descent now," said Goldberg. "We will be on the ground in about twenty minutes. You may wish to freshen up. There is a shower in the back bedroom. You'll find fresh fatigues in the closet. Also, take a parka. It is cold and snowy where you are going."

The airport near the Chinese village of Lijiang was little more than one long dirt runway. There was no control tower, only a wooden two-story structure with a picture window on the second floor facing the runway. A Piper Malibu and a Cessna 1823 parked along the side of the structure. The area was almost bereft of any trees or people.

The only sign of life was a bulletproof Guangzhou-Honda four-door and its driver waiting for Siegal and Danielson as they deplaned. Goldberg stayed aboard the jet.

Two uniformed Chinese officers came out of the wooden structure and moved toward them. Speaking in Mandarin, the senior officer asked for identification. Danielson responded in like tongue and handed him some papers.

Impressive, thought Siegal.

"Good evening, Mr. Danielson and Dr. Siegal," continued the senior officer, speaking faulty English. "Our government has granted a travel permit for the two of you to view Lijiang University. You have been provided a driver." He pointed to the parked Guangzhou-Honda. "When you return, your plane will have been refueled and will be ready for takeoff."

Danielson thanked the officer and bowed. Siegal, in clumsy fashion, also bowed.

Turning to Siegal, Danielson said, "We're just a few miles from Lijiang University. On the way, I'll explain more of your involvement and offer you a firsthand feel of what we're up against."

The driver headed east. The early morning sun glared in their eyes, blotting out scant scenery along the way.

Siegal attempted to gain control of the conversation but knew he was in Danielson's arena. "You indicated on the plane you are concerned with some terrorist rats and that you want me to help smoke them out."

"That's a bit of an understatement. We want you to come up with information that will not just get rid of the terrorist we are currently concerned with, but all who will come up in the future. We need you to get into their heads—know what they're thinking before they think of it themselves. Each terrorist problem will be unique. But your job will be to find the common weakness in all of them. Many lives are at stake. And did I mention there can be no room for error?"

Feeling overwhelmed with the challenge, Siegal shook his head emphatically. "I'm definitely interested. But I'm not your man. In fact, I don't believe there is any person who can give what you want. I'm no mystic. I can't just point my finger at a person and say, 'You're a terrorist; I'm going to hang you.' I don't have that instinct. I'm just a psychologist who happens to know a bit about behavior. I work with probabilities, not one-on-one specifics. Besides, I don't even know what the hell a terrorist looks like."

Danielson gave a reassuring smile. "You're using a hell of a lot of "I's. Such honesty is refreshing. You just need to do the pointing. We'll do the hanging."

"I still think your trained super-profilers from the FBI or CIA can do the job much better than I ever could."

"I told you before. This problem is more complicated than their level of skill. Some of your lab research offers clues to identifying previously unknown instigators. For example, what happened to explain how your rats got out of their cages?"

Siegal felt his stomach clench. "How did you know about that? We never reported that to the Foundation. I can't believe you violated not only me, but those around me."

"I apologize for our investigation methods. We had to be sure you were the best person for the job. Our mission is that important. You can understand the mind of a rat, you can use the same logic to understanding human rats. A bit of a stretch, but in my mind, it makes sense."

"Can't say the problem doesn't intrigue me. Let's just say I accept your offer to be this super-sleuth. When would I start?"

Danielson pointed to the face on his watch. "How about right now?"

"You sure know how to romance a guy." Siegal held up his hands in surrender. "Is that it?"

"Not quite. In less than two weeks, there will be a meeting to introduce you to a secret group of world leaders, my bosses, so to speak. Until that moment, these participants have to remain nameless. That is the 'we' I have been referring to. At that time, you will have to withstand their rigorous questions. They have the final say whether you join our effort or not. Your only ally in the room will be me. After we visit the Lijiang site, you will have to say whether you are in or out. Neither I, nor anyone else, can make that decision for you. What I am telling you and what you are about to see is very sensitive and cannot be divulged to anyone."

The idea of testing his theories of rat behavior on humans enticed Siegal a great deal. "I still haven't said yes. In case I do, will I be a lone eagle or have a team?"

"You already have a damn good research team in Denver. Use them all you want. Just don't tell them what you're doing."

"I'll need expert human observation specialists who know how to work invisibly," said Siegal.

"Remember that pair of ill-fitted clothes, as you described them? There are actually four."

"And who is the hangman?"

"You've already met Sergeant Goldberg. He leads my quick-strike force."

"Okay, okay. You talked me into it. There's little chance I would refuse. My guess is you already knew that." Surprised how he suddenly felt more relaxed, he asked, "When do I really begin?"

"Remember last night there was a news broadcast about an airplane hijacking in Cairo? The White House indicated responsibility was an established group from Tunisia. Our sources tell us this may be the work of a previously unknown terrorist organization. After dinner, you watched film clips of the explosion at Lijiang University. Shortly, you will be able to conduct on-ground observation. It was raided about fifty-six hours ago. I think they're related and…"

"You want me to figure out why?" Siegal asked, still not sure of his role.

Danielson added, "I also want you to figure out who before they become a full-blown organization. Oh, and by the way, I guessed you would agree to join us, so I installed a green phone in your apartment in Denver. You will find it on your closet's top shelf. It's a direct line to my office. If I need you, I will call. To reach me, push the call button. I'm available twenty-four/seven."

"When did you have me figured?"

"I became hopeful when you bought your plane ticket to DC. I felt once we got together you would be drawn into the picture. But when you didn't show as planned, I became worried. I thought your damn independence would squash the whole plan."

THE DRIVER VEERED left between two small outcroppings of rocks. A matched pair of isolated cement block buildings came into view. Siegal recognized them from the satellite view on the video.

"I thought you said this was a university. I don't see any students or dormitories."

The Honda stopped next to a charred building.

"That's another part of the picture. Lijiang isn't a university at all," explained Danielson. "These two structures are only a small part of an ultra-secret research facility. Most of it is underground, safe from aerial viewing. Only a select few outside the Chinese government know of its existence. That anyone even knows of this place tells us how dangerous this terrorist is."

"I'm beginning to understand why you took me here. You needed me to see this place to get the full impact of the problem. This arson was no student reprisal. You must have students before you can have student unrest. Even I can figure that out. Knowledge of this secret facility has to have some serious roots."

"Exactly. Our terrorist is extremely resourceful, as well as intelligent. Now, Ross, where do you stand? You're the lynchpin."

"I understand how serious this is now. I want to help more than ever. I was mostly convinced before, but as they say in poker, I'm all in."

They toured the incinerated building and surrounding area. Smells of burned sulfur and charred bodies remained in the air. Within minutes they were headed back toward their return flight home.

A thought lingered in Siegal's mind that he kept to himself. *Why would the terrorist attack this godforsaken place?*

AS THE NEWEST member of the team stepped off the plane in Denver, Danielson shook his hand and said, "Good luck and good hunting."

Siegal's parting words as he deplaned were, "I hope I can convince the graduate team how boring his trip for ID was."

Siegal got into a taxi at the terminal curb. Thoughts ran rampant in his head. *What the hell have I gotten into? Danielson drew my curious mind like a magnet. As my WWII army papa said, 'In for the duration.' One big question. Am I Danielson's lynchpin or just a minor cog to fill some gap?*

"Tomorrow will be a very interesting day."

"What?" asked the cabdriver.

"Nothing."

TWENTY-TWO

MUCH HAD HAPPENED IN THE past twenty-four hours. A mentally and physically exhausted Ross Siegal dropped his bags inside the door of his apartment. He fought against collapsing with them.

He dragged himself to the closet, almost afraid to see if a green phone on the shelf existed. At the same time, he was also afraid this entire trip was an illusion…a nightmare. The phone was there. Picking up the receiver, the buzzing in his ear told him it was connected. *Ross, you aren't in Kansas anymore.* He flopped on his bed and collapsed into a deep sleep.

Morning came too fast. The nightstand alarm woke him with a start. He dialed a familiar number. "I'm coming in about an hour. Please tell Jerry I need to speak with him. It's about my trip."

Pause.

"He'll see you then," answered Ravid's private secretary.

SIEGAL BURST INTO Ravid's office. Not waiting for any of the preliminary salutations, he said, "I need to know. Is there anything about this so-called foundation you haven't told me? Are you part of it or not?"

Ravid got up from behind his desk. "Slow down. I promised, if you ever wanted to discuss whatever it is you're in, I'm here for you. You can believe me or not, but I know nothing about the Foundation or why they are interested in you."

"How can I know you're telling me the truth?"

"You can't. I can't prove what isn't tangible."

Siegal rubbed the thinning hair on top of his head. *I want, no, I need to trust Ravid. I have no one else. My best friends, Simi, BF, and Sally...all trustworthy, but no experience in matters this huge. And this is fucking huge.*

Siegal continued, not sure of what to reveal. "I'm just a college professor who likes to deal in animal behavior. I may be in over my head for what they require of me."

Ravid saw tears of frustration in Siegal's eyes. He buzzed his secretary for two hot teas.

Ravid was right. The hot tea relaxed him.

"Now tell me. What's going on?"

"You guessed right before. It's true, whoever they are, they want me, not ID. At least the CEO does. There's still a sifting-out process from a committee. They could change their minds at the last minute and I would be out in an instant. I'm used to rejection. And I usually don't mind a lot. In this instance, I don't want to be rejected."

"Then you have to let it play out. Most times, things work out for the best."

"At any rate, I will be putting in more travel time soon. How much, I don't know. I've had only this one meeting. No final details have been worked out."

"It sounds as if you already accepted their offer."

"I admit their offer sounds inviting. But you know me. I don't like change very much, especially when it's not on my terms. But I think…"

"I know, you're not going to quit because it's getting hard."

"For now."

SIEGAL SPENT THE rest of the day in his car driving around the city, hoping to clarify what he had seen and learned. In just forty-eight hours his whole life had turned upside down from the quiet research lab with his rats to the international world of counterterrorism.

It was after six when Siegal returned to his apartment. Simi used her own keys and was in the kitchen starting pasta alfredo. Seeing Simi in his apartment gave him a sense of normality. Rinsing out some dishes, she pretended not to notice him standing there. He snuggled up behind her. Feeling her warm body aroused him.

She ought to be a permanent fixture in my life. But not now. He deftly moved his hands beneath the long sweater she wore and discovered only warm skin, her nipples hard.

The two barely reached the bedroom. There wasn't time to throw back any covers. Foreplay, a nibble on the neck returned with finger kisses. The rest was pure animal lust. Unlike sex, you could turn off pasta alfredo, reheat it later, and still have a good meal.

"SO?" SHE ASKED as they ate.

"What?"

"You can't fool me. You didn't bother to call in at the lab today. What really went on in Washington?"

"I'll tell you soon, I promise." He knew this was another lie.

Kissing her on the ear, he said, "I love you."

The rest of the evening passed in quiet talk.

FOUR A.M., WAKENED by a phone ringing and half dazed, Siegal reached for the receiver on the nightstand. The line gave a dead signal. The ringing continued.

Wakened by the sound, Simi rolled over and punched Siegal. "Get the goddamn phone."

His head cleared. He looked across the room and realized the ringing came from inside his closet.

"Oh...the green phone." he blurted without thinking of Simi being there.

"The what?" she asked.

"The green phone in the closet," he repeated.

Still half asleep, he stumbled out of bed, stepped over the clothes strewn across the floor from their earlier madness, and reached up to the closet shelf. The phone light blinked in concert to the rings. Simi was there. Siegal knew any desire to keep his secret phone from her had vanished.

He closed the closet door from the inside, but it didn't keep the conversation private. "Hello?"

"Are you alone, or is your girlfriend there?"

"Yes, that's right," he stuttered.

"Get rid of her. I need to talk with you. I'll call back at nine sharp," said Danielson.

Siegal hung up and stepped back into the room. He could feel Simi's eyes tear through him.

"What the hell is going on?" she asked.

"It's my special communications line with the Foundation. Nothing to worry about." He leaned over and kissed her on the forehead.

She brushed it off. "I mean it, Ross. What's this bullshit you're dealing me?"

His face contorted, he stuttered a confession. "This foundation that's backing our research is really a front for the government to find a specific person for a particular mission. And that specific person they are looking for is me."

A surprised expression covered her face. "You hate anything that smells of government. You must be joking."

Siegal didn't smile.

"Are any of us at the lab involved?" she asked.

"It's no joke. I could never have been selected without any of you. So maybe the answer is yes. You all have a part. But there is also a secret aspect that only involves me. They're trying to find a certain type of research mind. One that can delineate a predictable set of behavioral patterns in certain humans."

"And they think you can do this?"

He nodded. "They think so. I just don't know. I don't know if anyone can. But…you know me. I like the challenge."

"Well, whatever it is, you can do it." Simi offered a warm kiss and reassuring squeeze. "You can do it."

There was no sense going back to sleep. They showered together, washing each other gently, and then made love under the undulating spray.

Lying in bed covered only by their towels, Simi finally spoke, "Who in the government? FBI? CIA?"

"Higher."

Her eyes widened. "You said Sally and I can help? What do you want us to do?"

"They think our rats escaping from their cages is important. Don't know why, but I need an answer. I hope you two will help me figure it out."

Simi sighed, hopping out of bed. "May as well get an early start. Drop me off at the lab, no library research today. We can grab a bagel and coffee along the way."

They dressed and left.

After dropping Simi at the lab, Siegal sped back to the apartment. Danielson was expected to call back at nine sharp.

TWENTY-THREE

SIEGAL LOOKED AT HIS WATCH. 9:02. First it's the damn traffic lights all turning red against me. And then those fucking cone patrol people doing street maintenance. I've never seen so many mid-morning retiree crawlers driving slower than the speed limit and changing lanes without signaling.

He could hear the phone ringing as he approached his door. His nervous hands dropped the door keys to the ground, wasting more valuable seconds.

"Shit."

The indefatigable ringing continued. "Finally!" He threw the door open, banging it against the wall, and rushed to his closet. One look at the nightstand clock told the bad news. It was nine-eleven. He picked up the receiver.

"I said nine sharp, not nine-ish. You're late," spat Danielson. "We're not on professor time."

"It won't happen again. I promise you."

The anger he heard in Danielson's tone was different. He had judged him to be businesslike, but this response was sarcastic; totally different.

"It's not promises that will win this war. Its action. What answers have you come up with about Flight 234 and the Lijiang Laboratory raid?"

"I really didn't have time to…"

"You had plenty of time. You've had all day but instead wasted it driving aimlessly around town."

"You had me followed?"

"I will repeat it. One more time. This is not a college exercise."

"Screw this. If you don't think I can do the job, say so and I'm gone. I never asked to be involved," spit Siegal. He surprised himself. "I've had it up to here with your cloak-and-dagger routine. I've lied to my friends and made my relationship with Interaction Dynamics iffy."

Danielson shot back. "I'm not your psychiatrist. I don't want to hear all your problems. There is more pressing business. I need you for this job. So get your head on straight."

Siegal took a deep breath to calm down. "Okay, I'm back. I take it you wanted to tell me something. Surely you didn't call just to chew me out."

"You'll be meeting with my committee on the twentieth, nine days from now. It's all the time I can manage for you to prepare. If you pass scrutiny you're a permanent player."

"I don't know why I keep agreeing to stay involved."

"I knew you would. That's reason enough."

"Are you God or do you just think you are?"

Danielson laughed. "Nothing so supernatural. I just know what motivates you. What turns your wheels, so to speak. I'll tell you about it later."

"What else can you tell me to help my cause a little more before I meet your committee?"

"I've named this group The Summit of Six, codenamed SOS. I don't know what else to add. Just remember, it's your brains they want, not your material."

"You seem so sure I will be accepted."

"I'm betting my life on it."

"Mine too, I'm sure. I'm guessing we will be talking about the hijacking and the raid. The two events don't seem to be related, but both not claimed by any group makes me believe they may have been initiated by the same organization. And just like you, I also think the organization that did them is new or you would already know who it is."

"That kind of thinking is why I want you on deck. And don't be afraid to call them terrorists. That's what they are."

Calm and back in his analyzing element, Siegal added, "To make better guesses, I need more information. Details, reports, and whatever else you have."

"You'll get them by special courier tomorrow. The more conclusions you bring to the Summit, the better. Remember, nine days."

"Working with only two observations isn't very much on which to base conclusions, especially for a researcher like myself. I'll do what I can."

Siegal studied the calendar on his watch. "The twentieth is on a Thursday. That's BF's birthday. If I'm not there, he'll be very disappointed. I need an excuse to be out of town. Can you do me a small favor?"

"Name it."

"Send a letter from the Foundation insisting on my being in Washington."

Danielson laughed again. "Doing the spin is child's play. I'll overnight the request. You'll have it first thing tomorrow. Remember, you must be very sharp for your meeting with the SOS. I suggest you not party too hard the night before and not have your fave stay over."

Siegal knew it wasn't a suggestion. *Not sure it's any of your damn business,* he thought to himself.

"You will be picked up at your apartment. Ten-thirty a.m. on the twentieth. Pack some warm clothes. Sometimes it gets chilly this time of year."

The phone line went dead before he could ask more questions.

Siegal felt a surprising nervous rush. It was something he hadn't felt since the first time he made love to Simi. He vowed that someday he would research the relationship between danger of the unknown and sexual urges in humans. Maybe a one-person case study.

The challenge by Danielson to expand the cutting edge of knowledge was almost too much for his system. He wanted answers. All he got were questions.

Who is this terrorist? How can I learn about him? Why did the terrorist select these two actions? I can make some sense of the hijacking, but attacking a remote research facility in northern China makes no sense at all. Tom Danielson is some bigwig in Washington, but who is he really?

Siegal's fingers toyed with the calculator he kept handy on his dresser. Speaking out loud, knowing there was no one to listen, he said, "Nine days. Two hundred and sixteen hours. Twelve thousand, nine-hundred, sixty minutes. Seven hundred seventy-seven thousand, six hundred seconds. Not much time."

SIMI, ARRIVING EARLY at the lab to feed and weigh the rats, hoped to spend her day at the library working on her dissertation.

She opened the storeroom door.

"Holy shit. Those little bastards got out again. We even added wire twisties."

Sally walked in. "What's happening, girlfriend?"

Without looking up, Simi said, "Look. Those extra twisties keeping the cage doors closed are all untwisted."

Sally looked at the cages. "One cage had its twisty gnawed. The others had almost no apparent gnawing."

"Lots of copycat behavior," said Simi.

"Are you thinking the first group taught the others how to escape?" suggested Sally.

"They watched us open the cage hundreds of times. We inadvertently taught them. Once the first rats escaped, the others copied their success," said Simi.

"Smart bastards," said Sally. "We're going to need padlocks from now on."

Siegal walked in, hearing only the last part of the conversation. "I agree. Gather around, ladies. We have some serious work to do. I have to meet with the Foundation soon. I'm not sure when. I need answers for them. I think the rats' escaping is important. And helping each other showed unique teamwork. Social behavior like that, we attribute more to humans. They may be using vocal communication."

"What data do you need? With our new computers, it should be a snap," said Sally, gathering the last of the escapees.

"It's not measurable data they want. I need to know what the rats tell us that we don't measure by computer. How did they cooperate with each other, and why?"

"Answers from the outer limits," said Sally. "Fearless leader, when do we start?"

"Yesterday," he said.

Simi printed out new data sorts showing the rats' nighttime activity; Sally cleaned off the worktable and placed them in several piles as Simi gave them to her. Siegal, resorting to old habits honed before computers, taped sheets of flip-chart paper on the walls and drew trends. They reviewed every document to date, beginning with mating—who chose whom and which rat did the deciding.

It was long after dark when they broke their concentration. No extracurricular socializing tonight. This was not the time to waste energy.

EARLY THE NEXT morning, the team was back at it. Simi brought in fresh doughnuts and started the coffee before Siegal and Sally arrived. Alongside the donuts, she placed a letter she had found taped to the lab doorway.

Siegal opened the letter, pretending not to know its contents, and handed it to Simi to read out loud.

"It is from the Foundation," she said.

Dear Dr. Siegal,
We felt your meeting with us was very productive. However, at our last board meeting, it seemed there were a few unanswered questions we had regarding your results. In order to explore these further, we need you here in Washington to meet with us on the twentieth. Bring any results you have not yet sent us.
Sincerely,
Director

Ear-numbing silence filled the room. The hard copy date reiterated the meeting's significance.

"Well, now we know when 'soon' means," said Simi.

Sally went to the whiteboard and wrote numbers zero through nine. Then she crossed out numbers eight and nine. "Let's see. That means we have seven days left to get your answers. Really only six days if you count one day for travel. And we don't even know what to look for."

"Sally, what have we found out in our initial search?" he asked.

"That's simple. Offspring of maze-trained rats learn faster than those of untrained rats. Heredity, I'm thinking."

"Good as far as that goes. But exactly what do they learn faster? What is the cognitive process? And, are they talking to each other?"

Sally answered, "Our studies only explored learning rates on similar mazes."

"Then we're missing some vital information," declared Siegal.

"Do you want all this fucking information before or after lunch?" asked Sally.

Siegal continued without acknowledging Sally's sarcasm. "Tomorrow will be fine. Find out what we're missing." He turned to Simi. "What are your findings?"

"Maybe we're leaving out some important social interactions. After the first time our rats escaped from their cages, I started twenty-four-hour surveillance. We never did any social charting before, but we can do so now with our new video cameras, courtesy of the foundation."

"I'm very interested in any gut-level feelings you have. Don't leave anything out. I'll decide if it's unimportant. Or, at least, the Foundation will. Any insights, chart them on the wall. Mistakes are better than holding anything back." Siegal tried to appear casual, but there was tension in his voice. "I have to check in at ID and see what is happening there."

SIEGAL SAT IN his office at ID, checking his emails and making notes. He didn't notice Ravid standing in the doorway. Closing the door behind him, Ravid pulled up a chair.

"I think I know you pretty well. You're getting very involved with the Foundation and you aren't comfortable."

Siegal's silence said yes.

Ravid asked, "Care to talk about it?"

"I can't tell you any more than before. You're right about one thing. I wish I'd never heard of the Foundation. Better yet, I wish they'd never heard of me." He rubbed his head. "I got a letter today. Fact: they expect to meet with me in little over a week. Fact: they need some data we don't have. Fact: they could pull the grant if I don't come up with what they want."

Lie.

Siegal paused a moment, then continued. "We'll be busy at the lab right up to the time I leave. I need time out of the office."

"How many days are you talking about?"

"Nine, maybe ten days."

"Do I have a choice?"

"It's that I have no choice," Siegal said.

"I don't like it. We're heading into our busy season. I'll find some-one to cover, but do this to the firm again on such short notice and you'll have to be released. I don't like saying that, but I'm running a business and have to have dependable people around me."

"Do whatever. This foundation draws me in like a magnet."

"Tell my secretary to do the paperwork." Ravid left without an-other word.

TWENTY-FOUR

FIVE DAYS AND COUNTING TO have answers for the SOS's questions. The graduate assistants were in a frenzy determining how the rats twice escaped their cages. They sought answers, but none came.

Simi took up residence in the storage area where the experimental rats were housed and continued to look at videotape activity. She called out to Sally. "Everything looks normal during the early evening hours. The rats just milled about in their cages. And, holy shit, abrupt activity began in one cage. Then, by some means, transferred from one cage to the next ending in a coordinated untying of every twisty." Sally asked, "How were they suddenly able to transfer the knowledge to each other?

Between Simi's storeroom and Sally's battleground, the worktable in the main room, there were no answers to be discovered. Certainly not on this day.

Siegal looked up from his desk to offer encouragement. "You

ladies are the brightest graduates on campus. If anyone can make sense of what happened with our rats, it will be you."

He turned on his computer, not to calculate complicated formulas but to create Word documents, one of the few skills this technophobe mastered. He typed his thoughts to help him visualize what he needed to focus on.

STEP I: DO FURTHER ANALYSIS OF THE CURRENT DATA
STEP II: DETERMINE WHO IS RESPONSIBLE FOR THE HIJACKING OF FLIGHT 234 AND THE FIRE AT LIJIANG AND WHY?
STEP III: MAKE PARALLELS OF RAT ACTIVITY WITH HUMAN BEHAVIOR.

He imagined rats walking on two legs and doing human things; these images began to blend in to the shadows of the afternoon sun as it beamed through the single lab window and danced on the opposite wall. He shook himself and returned to the computer.

STEP IV: MAKE INFERENCES WHY THESE TWO INTERNATIONAL EVENTS TOOK PLACE? AND WHY NO ONE TOOK RESPONSIBILITY?

What do I know that can tie these two events together? Nothing. Nothing at all. Damn it.

His hand slammed the desk in frustration. The wall shadows transformed into images of the hijacking. He saw all flight passengers freed without injury.

It doesn't make any sense. Even some wannabe terrorists would try to claim responsibility for action. And for what purpose was either executed? I have no facts that tell me they were done by the same group. Only my instinct tells me they are. My only clue is they took complex surgical planning. Danielson, I need that package you promised.

He doodled a devil on a paper pad. Over the horned head, he printed DANIELSON.

In what seemed like only minutes, the team broke for an early dinner. "Armies don't do well on empty stomachs," announced Sally as she ordered pizza and Pepsi from Domino's.

They discussed their progress and non-progress while eating.

Sally started, pointing to her loads of disorganized data. "As you see, I have a good case of the piles. By the end of today, I'll have those rats organized in marching order. Tomorrow I'll start putting the little bastards through their paces."

Simi volunteered next. "I was amazed at how organized they were. It was like a leader in the first cage told the others what to do. Can you guess who lives in that first cage?"

"I'll bet it was Tigger," guessed Sally.

"We haven't taped their squeaking. We should buy some sound equipment to do this."

"But in the meantime," said Siegal, "we can only assume they have a sophisticated communicating system far beyond what we ever imagined. There isn't time before I have to meet with the Foundation. It will be part of our future studies.

"As I recall, we kept them together in family groups," continued their mentor. "This was for nurturing purposes and it just seemed to be a simpler way of keeping track of them. Why don't you mix them up? Combine naturally timid and aggressive rats in the same cages. See how opposites react to each other."

"We're on it," saluted Simi. "Sally and I will design some experiments this afternoon and start observations in the morning."

The only sounds for the rest of the day were the noises of three individuals doing their own thing. That meant Sally doing her periodic swearing, Simi yelling every time she was bitten by over-hungry experimental rats, and Siegal cheering every time he made a basket with the crumpled papers of half-started printouts from his computer.

THE SEVENTEENTH. THREE days before the meeting.

Simi painted T's and A's on the rats' backs. She made one cage of only A—aggressive—rats, one of T—timid—rats, then randomly mixed the other T's and A's in the three remaining cages. BF volunteered to help build research mazes.

"Group older rats and naïve rats in the same research mazes. Look for any form of communication among them," said Siegal.

On the morning of the eighteenth, Simi came out of the store-room. She had tears in her eyes. "One of the timid rats was killed last night in one of the randomly mixed cages."

"Oh, no," Sally murmured.

"Very interesting," Siegal said.

TWENTY-FIVE

MIDMORNING ON THE EIGHTEENTH, THERE was a knock at the lab door. Siegal answered. An express courier handed him a certified envelope. The return address read "THE FOUNDATION." The lab team was so busy with their own work, they didn't notice its arrival.

Finally, the reports from Danielson. Or a *booby trap? I'm getting paranoid? Danielson and I are on the same side…I hope.*

He tore open the flap and let two discs slide out onto his desk. The first was labeled *Lijiang Raid.* Having just experienced the raid in China, he picked up the second, *Hijacking of Flight 234,* and slipped it into his player on the computer. He plugged in his ear-phones so Sally and Simi could not hear.

In a few moments, he heard Danielson's voice introducing the event. "This report is a compilation of photographic observations, voice recordings, and computer-generated actions as they must have taken place. It all started at the airport in Alice Springs, Australia."

Airport security cameras showed a bearded man getting off an arriving plane and proceeding on the open tarmac toward the passenger building. He was carrying a didgeridoo, an aboriginal five-foot flute. He tripped. A bundle of sharp pointed sticks, similar to the ones used to make deadly spears and arrows, slipped out of the flute's open end onto the tarmac. The bearded man got up, leaving the sticks on the ground, and continued into the terminal.

Danielson's voice explained, "Security later found a false beard and the didgeridoo hidden in the men's room stall."

The computer images continued. On the continuing flight to Melbourne, five individuals in their late teens or early twenties exited the terminal along with other passengers and boarded the plane. One of the five knelt where the sticks fell and picked something up.

Danielson's voice said, "This all happened outside the security gates."

Clever, so casual. Extremely well-planned and professional. Just like the raid at Lijiang.

Generated images showed the five taking aisle seats. It showed one of the hijackers taking what appeared to be a fishing line with small wood knobs at each end from his pocket. He walked up behind a cabin attendant and looped it round her neck. Three others, now in possession of the wooden weapons, poked them at the hearts of their seat mates.

"At that time," said Danielson, "what we determined later, the oldest hijacker, estimated to be at least thirty, stood and demanded to speak with the pilot. The second attendant led him to the plane's intercom.

"Interesting. Not one individual or group has come forward to claim responsibility. Why? As a behaviorist, I believe people, like rats, are motivated by rewards. The rule is consistent. What are the rewards for this event?"

"Did you say something, boss?" asked Sally, pausing at her sorting and piling.

Siegal pressed pause. "I didn't realize I was speaking aloud. Ah, no. Just go back to what you are doing." He pushed the play arrow and the disc continued.

"The man, speaking in a reported Eastern European accent, told the captain he had just commandeered the plane. He said his people had weapons pointed at the hearts of three passengers and another had a fishing line pulled tightly around the neck of an attendant. And as long as his directions were followed, no one would be hurt."

The pilot turned on the plane's tape recorder and asked, "Why would you want this plane? We don't carry enough fuel to travel much beyond Melbourne."

"Don't think I am stupid, Captain. I want to speak with airport security in Melbourne. Put me in contact with them…now."

After a short time, a new voice came over the intercom: "This is Colonel Christopher of the Melbourne airport security. Who am I speaking to?"

"It matters not who I am. Just obey my instructions and I promise you no passenger or crew member will be harmed at this time. Do you understand?"

"Yes, what are you asking for?"

"When we land, I demand you fill this plane's fuel tanks for a minimum ten-hour flight.

"Go on." Then speaking away from the phone, Colonel Christopher ordered snipers in the terminal aimed at where the Alice Springs plane would park. Turning to his staff, he asked, "Can anyone tell where the hell these guys come from?"

"Sorry, sir. No."

"Shit," came Colonel Christopher's off-microphone comment.

"Now listen carefully," barked the hijacker. "Do not attempt to use snipers. We have a spotter in your terminal who will phone me to assure this takes place. Do you understand?"

"Why are you doing this?"

The question went unanswered.

"Once we land unhindered, all passengers and crew of this flight except several hostages will be released."

"Qantas flight from Alice Springs on its final approach," announced the control tower. "Any special instructions, Colonel?"

"No. Just have the sharpshooters stay hidden but ready for any opening. And wait for my orders."

Siegal, almost forgetting to breathe, continued to listen.

"The plane landed and taxied to an outer runway," explained Danielson.

"Hurry with the refueling trucks. I have little patience," demanded the hijacker.

"Yes, yes," responded the very nervous security colonel.

"Good. As soon as we are refueled, we will release all international passengers and several Australian nationals along with most of the flight crew. Soon after that we will leave your airspace."

Tanks filled, Qantas 234 taxied into position and took off. Global tracking followed their path. Interceptors followed but did not engage.

"CAIRO, EGYPT, THIS is Qantas 234 requesting permission to land."

A third tape was added to Siegal's DVD. "This is Cairo air traffic control. We have been in contact with Melbourne airport. They have informed us you have been commandeered and there are several hostages on board. What are your instructions?"

The Qantas pilot responded. "I have been ordered to land. Complete compliance assures the hostages on board will not be harmed. They have already released all but twelve passengers. I tend to believe them."

"Thank you, Qantas 234. You are cleared to land. Use runway E-27. Good luck."

The pilot added, "I have just been handed more instructions. They demand an armored vehicle, large enough for twenty people, to meet the plane. Also I am to park on an outer landing area."

"Roger that, Qantas 234."

Minutes later, the plane touched down and taxied to a stop out of range from any sharpshooters stationed about the terminal. Computer images showed the side door opening. The pilot and co-pilot were pushed out. Each hijacker, with hostages around them as body shields, transferred to the armored vehicle and drove toward an emergency exit.

"We pieced together the next bit of information," said Danielson's voice. "Outside the airport, the armored car drove to three wait-ing SUVs. The hijackers divided their hostages into the SUVs and drove in different directions toward the bustling streets of Cairo. Then each, using different escape routes, disappeared into the endless Sahara Desert. Within an hour, all hostages were freed. Egyptian authorities found two bodies in the desert where the group traveled. Both were shot in the head execution style. They were not the bodies of any hostage. Either they found new victims, or they were part of the initial hijackers. We think the latter at this time."

The detailed planning, from the boarding of the Qantas jet to the carefully executed escape in Egypt, reinforced Siegal's thinking that he was not dealing with just any terrorist group. Their head terrorist was like their lab rat, Tigger. Smarter. Much smarter than the rest.

A troubled Siegal turned off the DVD. *Why would they go to all that trouble and gain nothing? Is it because they could? There had to be more.*

THE LEAD HIJACKER ordered his SUV to stop by a roadside oasis. He sipped a hot tea as he dialed a number on his cell phone. "It was clean, sir. Everything went as planned."

"And the other matter?"

"That was taken care of as well."

The two men laughed.

TWENTY-SIX

"HEY, ROSS, HOW'S IT GOING?"

Siegal whispered into the phone, hoping his graduate assistants would not hear. "You? Calling in the middle of the day at the lab? I figured you only call in the middle of the night when I'm asleep."

"I couldn't wait. I'm guessing you already had a chance to view the reports. You only have a couple more days before meeting with the SOS. Tell me your thoughts."

Siegal held the discs in his hand. "Both events were planned out in great detail. Very professional. Yet according to you, no individual or group claimed responsibility. I keep asking why."

"And?"

"I think this terrorist is checking out his skills. Sort of sowing his oats to see what grows. Maybe even to see what kinds of reaction he gets from our side."

"It sounds too simple," said Danielson.

"Simple can be good. Another idea also crossed my mind. The

actions may have been training exercises, especially the airline hijacking. In both cases nothing was gained, at least not from what your reports suggest. I still haven't figured out their motivation."

"Anything you want to ask me?"

Siegal thought for a moment. "I wonder about the bearded man who got off at Alice Springs. This organization is too small to leave him out there hanging. Could he be the king rat?"

"Good question. The action at Alice Springs was so casual; the airport cameras caught the action but nobody picked up on it until later. You may be right."

"That would confirm that the organization is still embryonic. One leader, probably one main hatchet man or whatever you in the business call him, and a few insiders."

"Good thinking, Ross. Keep it up. You'll be great at the meeting."

THE WHITEBOARD SHOWED Siegal had one day left to come up with something important to impress the mysterious Summit of Six. As of this moment, he felt he had no answers at all.

Remember, Danielson said it wasn't what I know, but how I think through problems. I hope he's right.

At noon, Siegal volunteered to order lunch. A steady diet of olive oil and greasy pepperoni was getting to his digestive system. He needed some real food.

"Clean off a corner of the worktable, guys. I'll be back in twenty minutes with lunch. I'm getting Chinese."

When Sally reached over to take the last piece of sesame chicken, her cleavage under a summer tee was impossible to overlook. Neither Ross and Simi nor the love pair of BF and Sally had been together for the past week. Too busy.

Sally saw everyone's eyes focus on her. "Cool down boys. We have a job to do here." She attempted to change the group's mindset. "Let me tell you what I've found so far. I grouped all the little bastards into test pairs. My design combines all three activity categories: mazes, lever pressing, and shock avoidance."

BF said, "It looks like we're conducting plans for the reenactment of the Bataan Death March. Will your experiments get significant results in time for the boss?"

Without being aware, BF was gently touching Sally's thigh as he talked. First it was Sally displaying cleavage, and then it was BF's touch.

Siegal sensed the sexual urge swelling in all of them, including himself. "As leader of this band of thieves, I say we all need some privately paired study of our own. I order us to shut down for the afternoon and meet back here for the last day tomorrow morning. Whatever we have has to be enough."

Before leaving, Simi crossed off one more day. Siegal watched as she did and doubted there would be enough to satisfy the Summit.

THE HALF DAY and evening off did wonders for the team's energy level. They met back at the lab before eight, ready to continue their projects. At noon they gathered for lunch and to share results.

Simi started. She turned on the television monitor and put in a disc. "I've charted something very interesting. I taped heightened aggressive behaviors in a couple of our cages each time leading to a timid rat being killed. It was like an organized gang attack. I don't believe it was random. According to our boss, all behavior has a purpose. The slain rat was killed on purpose. I'm guessing he didn't fit the mold of the rest."

BF asked, "What else do your tapes show?"

"I followed who I thought were two more rats active in the great escape." She put in another disc. "When we placed them together during our earlier experiments where they were caged with their paternal families, they acted friendly. Second observation. In every situation where these rats were placed with nonfamily members, the more passive rats were denied food pellets by their cage mates. Now watch this." She used a split screen to show aggressive behaviors in two cages at the same time. "Just prior to any bully behaviors, the activities in both cages were identical. Now it gets really interesting. Just prior to the killings, the lead rats retreated to the far part of the cage and privately groomed themselves. The other rats did the dirty work. In this last disc I want to show you, one rat groupie stalled and hesitated in the massacre. It was also bullied and slain."

Sally asked what happened when two or more identified aggressive rats were in the same cage.

"Interesting that you should ask. I never observed a battle for leadership. In any cage, one boss, one gang. No problems. I'm guessing that when there was any dispute, the rats would side with one and ultimately slay any other. I didn't have time to observe this development in the time Ross gave us."

Siegal concluded, "Our rats could be models for human behavior, especially describing gang behaviors. Then, thinking to himself, *Simi unknowingly discovered a parallel—why terrorists in both the Lijiang raid and the hijacking were killed. They were misfits, whether they were American agents or not. They were handled with equal, and deadly, disapproval.*

"Good going, sweetheart. You're getting the results I need," said Siegal. *At least I hope.*

It was Sally's turn. "I ran an experiment four different times using different combinations of fast learners versus normal learners."

"And?" Siegal asked.

"As I expected, groups with a history of fast learning continued to demonstrate superior learning rates. Rat groups lacking in at least one of the skills always did the poorest. One perplexing problem showed up after the task was learned. The smart maze-learning rats, when teamed with lower-functioning rats, distanced themselves from the others and tried to climb out of the maze. The walls were too high for them to get out by themselves. But catch this: one smart rat herded its naïve maze mates near the wall and climbed over the top of them, thus enabling an escape. The remaining rats just watched and wandered around seemingly perplexed." She smiled, then added, "I guess that's about all I have to report."

"Hell", said BF. "This unexpected creative behavior has never been witnessed before. Right, boss?"

Siegal nodded. "The rats were creating coordinated strategies. They were thinking in unique ways. This is what I need for the Foundation. The rest is up to me. I'm going to bury myself in my apartment until I have to leave tomorrow. Please, no calls unless personally reporting your own deaths. I need to get a handle on all of your information. You're on your own for a while. BF, I apologize in advance for having to be away on your birthday. Have another one next year. I'll be there. Oh, will you cover my classes till I get back?"

The team walked Siegal to the parking lot, carrying their research and loading it into the trunk of his car.

"I think I have the answers I need. I could never have gotten this far without all your help. You guys are fantastic friends—one of a kind."

IT WAS ALMOST nine o'clock. His mystery ride would arrive soon. He double-checked his luggage, making sure it included a heavy sweater. *Where is this meeting? Who are The Summit members? What is really expected of me? Soon enough—I'll know soon enough.*

TWENTY-SEVEN

A BLACK LIMOUSINE DROVE UP and parked in front of Siegal's apartment building. He was waiting outside when it arrived. Ben Goldberg stepped out of the driver's side, took Siegal's overnighter and briefcase crammed with his research notes, and placed them in the trunk. With only a nod of recognition, they were off.

Goldberg headed directly to Denver International Airport. This ride reminded Siegal of mystery, fantasy trips he'd read about in magazines while waiting in his dentist's office. His only hint that the end destination was not Washington, D.C., came from Danielson suggesting he pack some warm clothes.

Siegal attempted to learn their destination. "Where are we going? The mountains of Virginia?"

Goldberg said nothing and steered toward the outgoing passenger level and slowed. Siegal prepared to get out of the car. To his surprise, Goldberg did not stop at the arrival doors, but maneuvered the limousine through a series of security-patrolled gates to a small side door near the back of the terminal and honked twice.

The gate opened. Danielson appeared behind it. He looked around for any prying eyes, then waved to a person standing in the shadows. A gray-haired man, in casual attire, stepped into the open, followed by a pair of suited individuals. One of the suits took the gray-haired man's luggage and stowed it in the limo's trunk.

The door to the limo opened. Danielson nodded a silent hello as he and the stranger entered and took seats facing a stunned Ross Siegal.

The mystery man's face was familiar. Even Siegal, who almost never watched television nor read political sections of a newspaper, recognized the stranger sitting across from him.

He swallowed impulsively. "Are you…the President…or a looka-like? Just another joke Danielson devised to keep me interested?"

"Some people in the other party call me a joke. But I'm the real thing."

The gray-haired man recognized Siegal's nervousness. He tried to offer some comforting words. "I know how you must feel, Ross. And you have every right. Believe me. I've been there many times in this business. But if I know Tom, he had good reason to select you for this job. Fortunately, his intuition has never failed me." He gave a reassuring pat on Siegal's knee. "Yes, I know you'll do just fine. In our haste to get on our way, Tom forgot to formally introduce us. I'm Elwin Russell." He reached across the seats and extended his hand in friendship.

"You mean President Russell?"

The president gave his political smile, one that earned him many votes in the past.

A muffled slam of the trunk indicated the luggage was deposited. A tap on the top of the car by one of the suits and Goldberg eased the limo out of the airport. The two suits got into an SUV with four others and followed closely behind.

Once on their way, the three men in the back seat exchanged pleasantries and talked a bit about the weather. Not one word was uttered about the meeting to come.

Siegal's previous feelings of mistrust for Danielson returned. His willingness to be involved became more tenuous. He avoided his traveling companions' eyes by pretending to be interested in the scenes outside the window. They were still in Denver and Siegal contemplated jumping out of the car at a stop sign, which right now seemed like an excellent alternative to escape this secretive behavior.

The limousine gained speed as they exited the city heading west. Jumping was no longer an option. Here he sat next to the President of the United States trying with all his willpower to trust the ranking political leader of the nation, when in fact, he had little regard for the integrity of any politician.

The limo continued, first on I-70, then onto US 6, taking the new highway toward Central City and Blackhawk.

Siegal tried to move the conversation toward the meeting.

"I'm sorry for sounding rude. I do appreciate your confidence, Mr. President," Siegal continued. "I'm sitting here with a boatload of documents, most of which I have not yet fully digested and I'm getting ready to report to the board of directors, this Summit of Six, whom I have never met. Can you at least tell me what I could have done to be better prepared?"

The president spoke. "I repeat, I'm sure you'll do well. I will say this. It's not what you have to report. They want to hear how you feel about the material you have and how you would use it. Like I said, you'll do just fine."

Another pat on the knee followed. Siegal flinched in an attempt to avoid the contact.

"We're still in Colorado. You mean this meeting is almost in my backyard?"

Danielson didn't reveal any more of the mystery. "When we get to the chalet, you and I will discuss things. I'll try and prepare you for tomorrow's meeting. But for now, relax." Then, looking out the window, Danielson said, "I always enjoy riding through these canyons. God and nature are amazing architects. The scenery is so much more beautiful than the sterile white marble canyons of Washington."

Siegal remained nervous. Staying in Colorado gave him some security. He first felt they were meeting at some resort hotel with fancy rooms and catered dinners. When Danielson talked of a chalet, it made the meeting seem more intimate, more mysterious. "I suppose I'll learn soon enough, won't I?"

Siegal's last question was answered with one word.

"Tomorrow," said Danielson.

President Russell looked at both, then returned his attention to some papers he had on his lap.

Goldberg maneuvered the cumbersome limo through the narrow streets of Central City, once the gold-mining capitol of Colorado and for a short while, the entire Gold Rush. Just past the downtown area, he turned onto a little-traveled private mining road and came to a stop in front of a secluded log residence. The chalet, as Danielson named it, was surrounded by pristine pines and aspen. It was easy to imagine the area looking much the same to fur trappers and miners of the 1800s.

The Secret Service SUV behind them stopped at the base of the road. Siegal watched the six agents exit the car and spread out into the woods.

GOLDBERG'S LONG ARMS handled all the luggage at one time. A seventh agent met them at the front door and escorted each to their individual rooms.

Siegal looked to Danielson. "Does the president always have this much security around him?"

"It's the way it is with presidents," said Danielson. "He often has more for special occasions. I'll meet you in your room, say fifteen minutes?" Danielson turned away, and then almost immediately turned back. "It's almost lunchtime so I'll have some sandwiches sent up. I want you to stay there for today, and that includes dinner. There will be plenty of time tomorrow for you to meet the SOS."

"All this secrecy," Siegal exclaimed. He could sense his anger igniting. "I feel I'm getting initiated into a fraternity. I'm not enjoying this game-playing one damn bit."

Danielson said, "Believe me. This is not a game. It's my judgment call. This is the best way to handle your introduction. Everything will become clear in the morning. I'll see you in fifteen."

Once in his room, Siegal felt his face redden. Not only was he angry at the way he was being manipulated, but his mistrust in Danielson remained high. He wondered again if there was any possibility of escape. He looked out his window and saw rocks at the bottom. He estimated it was twenty feet to the ground. Too dangerous for a man of Siegal's age. Sneaking out the front door when everyone is asleep was another alternative. He shook his head. Too many Secret Service agents out there in the dark.

Siegal normally enjoyed solving mysteries, especially psychological ones. And now he was not only watching the mystery unfold, he was in the very middle of it. His mind spun, imagining all kinds of international horror scenarios.

A knock at the door put the brakes on his thoughts. Siegal hesitated opening it. *If I chose not to open it, would everything disappear? Would I suddenly wake up discovering everything is just a dream?*

A second knock. This time louder. Siegal stood frozen in the middle of his room. The door opened as if it had a life of its own.

Goldberg stepped in, bowing slightly so as not to bump his head on the wood frame. He held a tray with a half-dozen tuna salad sandwiches, some potato salad and a six-pack of cold ODL. Old Dog's Leg was like a warm letter from home. For the moment, it made Siegal feel calmer.

Danielson followed, wearing a blue sweat suit. Seeing Siegal looking out the window, said, "It's a long drop."

Siegal continued looking but didn't focus on anything in particular. He almost never took time off to sightsee the Rockies. His life was totally encompassed by his rat lab, work at ID, and of course, Simi Block. "Just enjoying the scenery. I appreciate the nice room, food, and scenery. Is this more of a set up than a friendly gesture?"

"A little of both. You'll have to make up your own mind. As of this moment I'm only the messenger."

"You bother the hell out of me. You treat me like either a friend or a celebrity. Believe me, I don't feel like either."

"Sorry about that. I don't mean any harm by it. It's my way of taking charge of things."

The apology surprised Siegal. It was the first time he'd ever heard Danielson apologize for anything. It gave him newfound power.

"I also apologize some for the secrecy. My style is to work with people on a need-to-know basis. Trust me on this. Once you are accepted by the SOS, there will no longer be any secrets from you. Any questions you ask will be answered with complete honesty."

"Then why do I sometimes feel I'm the pawn in this chess match?"

"I need you. Russell and I have gone out on a limb with that assumption. Your integrity and loyalty to an ideal make you a person above reproach. You can't be bought. I can't say that for a dozen people I've known. You, my very good friend, are one of a kind.

Even the promise of an open-ended grant couldn't persuade you to give up on your ethics."

"You're right about that. I didn't want your grant. I only accepted it for my grad assistants."

A knock on the door stopped the discussion. "You guys were talking so loud," said Russell, who was dressed in sweats matching Danielson's except that his bore the presidential crest on the left breast pocket. "Thought I had to come in before it got physical." Changing the subject, he said, "Anything new?"

"Ross is feeling left out a little. It's not about what we're asking of him. It's the closed-door secrecy this mission requires at this moment. Scholars aren't used to it like we are."

Russell responded. "Even us politicos have felt that way at times." He turned and looked directly into Siegal's eyes. "Tell me, Ross, are you a quitter?"

Siegal felt the man's full power. "I don't think so, sir. No, I'm not a quitter. But I have free will and can pick and choose my actions."

Danielson cocked his head. "If your action is to quit, then you will have to go through what we call a deep brainwashing. Not pleasant, believe me."

Siegal thought for a moment. "So I'm already here. As you once suggested, I may as well see the rest of the movie."

Danielson smiled. "I've studied you more than you will ever know. There is one part of your psychological drive that makes you want to see this through."

"And that is?"

"You are being given the once-in-a-lifetime chance to do something every behavioral psychologist seeks. We believe you, and only you, can take simple rat experiments and translate them into human behavior beyond what anyone else has ever done. And in doing so, you may just save the world from another terrorist."

Siegal paused. The motivation for new knowledge was more powerful than any other argument Danielson could offer.

"Suppose I meet with your Summit group and fail to meet their expectations. What happens then?"

Danielson sat back in his chair. "You will go back to your lab. No one outside of the SOS will ever know where or what you've been through. Funding for your research will continue. This may not be important to you, but it guarantees that your graduate students will receive the best learning experiences. Tomorrow will be your dog-and-pony show. I can guide the direction a little, but that's about it. We'll see you in the morning. Be ready at nine-thirty sharp."

The two offered smiles of encouragement as they left.

TWENTY-EIGHT

SIEGAL SLEPT SOUNDLY FOR THE first time in many days. He, not Tom Danielson, controlled his future. He was his own behavioral experiment.

After several knocks, each louder than the previous, Siegal woke.

"Excuse me, sir." It was the deep voice of Goldberg. "It's almost eight thirty. I brought you breakfast. I will leave your tray on the table by the door. See you in one hour."

One hour. One hour to discover my future.

"ITS NINE-TWENTY-FIVE," BOOMED Goldberg's voice outside Siegal's door.

Siegal took the last sip of coffee and was escorted downstairs to the dining room to meet Danielson's secret Summit of Six.

Siegal surveyed the dining room landscape. A long buffet of

black African oak hid most of one wall, a matching credenza reaching almost to the ten-foot-high rafters covered another, and in the center stood a large banquet table and chairs. President Russell and Tom Danielson sat at the table waiting for him.

"I thought I was to meet with a group of six members. I only count coffee service for three. Where are the rest?"

"They are here—only electronically. It would be difficult for these individuals to be here anytime we need to talk." Danielson pointed toward the buffet.

Siegal focused on a complicated set of wires and electronic equipment attached to a large plasma television screen. "What's this stuff for?"

"You'll see in a moment, Ross," said Danielson.

The absence of others in the room made Siegal's anger from last night return.

"Another one of your Washington insider jokes?"

Siegal attempted to leave but was stopped in his tracks by Danielson's strong arms, developed from his Navy SEALS days.

"Hold on. Do you recognize what this electronic setup is?"

"Of course. We used this at ID to communicate with our out-of-town clients. I never liked these gadgets. My choice is to meet my jury face-to-face.

"Members of the SOS are too important to be traipsing about for every meeting they attend," said President Russell. "Each of them has similar setups so they can communicate without leaving their home office. I have one in my basement. I believe being here in person with you is more important."

Danielson flicked the power switch. "Sit down and meet the Summit of Six."

The flat screen flashed to life and cordoned itself into four quadrants.

SIEGAL STARED AT the screen. He recognized them as leaders of their own countries. "That tells me there are four. I'm guessing you, President Russell, are number five. Who's missing?"

"Five is correct. But what you didn't know is that I'm the group's chairman," said Danielson. "Making six. Secrecy demands that we meet this way without leaking our get-togethers. Each can be in their own situation room without raising the antenna of their own media."

The president added, "This is your private situation room, Dr. Siegal."

Each person, in turn, nodded in Siegal's direction as he was introduced to them.

Siegal felt his heart race. *This is no fucking fluke.* He took a drink of coffee before speaking.

"Gentlemen, how can I be of service to you?" His question came out as a total surprise. It was not the succinct front he planned.

"Dr. Siegal," started King Ishmere, "did anyone explain exactly why you are here?"

It was not a question Siegal expected, especially as the first inquiry. "A little. I met with Mr. Danielson several times. We discussed my rat behavior experiments. Then we moved to topics more in the realm of human behavior. He indicated you were looking to uncover a new brand of terrorist and felt I would be an important asset to your team. Then he asked my views of Flight 234 and the Lijiang raid. I told him neither instance was in my field of expertise. And then he said, 'I'm guessing it will be soon.'"

King Ishmere smiled, "I trust your field of expertise, as you say, is broader than you imagine."

President Cho-Se interrupted. "King Ishmere, I think we are pushing the gentleman a little too fast. Even I was impressed to think that all of us would care to gather in secret with a singleness of purpose. Please, Dr. Siegal, go on. I want to hear about your rats. Tell us what you found that relates to our terrorist problem."

Siegal cleared his throat. "Along with my two graduate assistants, I have been working on a unique approach to behavior testing. By intermixing rats from previous studies with new rats, we were able to study behaviors between generations, investigating hereditary trends that before were only guesses. One morning, we came into our rat lab to discover our rats running loose. We felt their escape was not just an accident since the escape occurred twice, even though we had taken certain precautions. Some unique problem-solving, tied with sophisticated communication, had taken place."

"And what does your interest in laboratory rats have to do with understanding our terrorist problem?" asked Sokoloven.

"A good question, sir. It caused us to look at different social interactions between them. Groupings developed around dominant rats who seemed to bully others into doing their bidding. This had never been observed before in classical behavior research studies. My graduate students are looking carefully at those social groupings as we speak."

Siegal stopped, hoping for more questions. None came. He felt sure his chance to impress the SOS was blown. Bowing his head as a sign of submission, he said, "Thank you for your time."

After moments of silence, President Galdet said, "I think it is time for you, Dr. Siegal, to take a short break. You may have something to do in your room."

Danielson turned to Siegal. "We will need you back later."

Siegal excused himself. He thought about packing and thinking what he would say to his team at the lab. Before he had time to do anything, his oversized alarm clock knocked on the door, reminding him it was time to return. When he re-entered the dining room, there were no smiles, nothing to give any clues where he stood with the Summit members.

"Well, Dr. Siegal, we are ready to proceed." The assured voice of Chairman Danielson overwhelmed Siegal. Not what he expected.

King Ishmere continued his jabbing. "You are Jewish, are you not? I hear many of your America's most prominent psychologists are Jewish. Do you think this is why you were chosen to be here?"

"As I believe many of your people are experts in oil geology and technical engineering."

King Ishmere responded. "A very good retort. A quick wit and subtle sense of humor. I commend you for speaking so well on your feet. I was expecting a much less intelligent response."

"Do you have any more to add about your rat studies before we go on?" asked Danielson.

"Not much. Like I said before, we discovered the rats were communicating with each other. Not just by pointing or squeaking, but were sharing complicated information." He explained how the dominant rats used others as tools for selfish purposes.

Each quadrant displayed smiles. He piqued their interest for sure. Only he was not sure whether they were just curious about the rats or learning more about him.

President Sokoloven asked, "Doctor, why do you think knowing about your rats will help us subdue our new terrorist?"

Siegal paused, trying to remember his notes. "We started looking at how the rats developed social relationships. Some rats readily grouped together. Others were excluded. Three times, dead rats were found in three different cages. I felt that if it happened only once, it would have been a unique event. Recorded observations following the rats' behaviors at night showed the movements within these cages were similar."

"And what was that?" asked Sokoloven.

"A dominant rat would emerge. At first, all the rats would group around the dominant rat. For some unknown reason, one rat would be nudged away. From then on, the dominant rat would ignore the shunned rat. The same ritual was always followed by the rest of the pack—picking on that shunned rat until it was killed. If two dominant rats were placed in a cage with a neutral group of rats, one would always emerge as dominant and the other would be shunned, and ultimately slain, by the pack. Some rat groups never developed a dominant leader. I believe this last point is important because it shows there is something in their genetic makeup that leads some rats to be dominant leaders, some to remain followers, and others to be outsiders. I believe there is a direct relationship with my rats and a terrorist group. Each successful group has one leader, controllers, followers and outsiders, an almost impregnable paradigm."

"I'm intrigued. Go on, Dr. Siegal," said President Galdet.

"If what I discovered in the rats holds true with the terrorists, stopping members of the pack has no impact. It is imperative to find the leader and chop off his head. The rest of the pack becomes directionless and can be taken."

"And, Doctor, how were those human victims in the terrorist groups chosen?" asked Sokoloven.

"I don't know."

"Oh, you may not know now. I think soon you definitely will. I urge, and I speak for all of us here, that your clarification is not delayed too far into the future. Tell me, do you believe your rats are acting similar to our terrorist?"

"I am sure of it. The people slain at Lijiang and Flight 234 didn't fit the accepted mold of their group."

"And the head terrorist saw fit to eliminate them?" asked Russell.

"It is logical," responded Siegal.

"Dr. Siegal," explained Danielson, "there is something we haven't told you. One of the two killed in each event was an agent of ours. Do you think the terrorist leader knew about them and that's why they were killed?"

"Being spies for you had nothing to do with it. I think both were identified as misfits. Maybe they were too inquisitive or just wore the wrong clothing," answered Siegal.

President Galdet spoke next. "Monsieur Doctor Siegal, you said your research team was looking at heredity, attempting to tie in special traits to families. Is this like the acorn not falling far from the tree?"

"I have spent most of the past week trying to understand. I know it's important but, again, I only have questions."

"Dr. Siegal, tell us what you think. We can decide if it is important."

Siegal continued, "We were beginning to discover that leadership and followership runs in families. But this tendency did not always follow from parent to child. Sometimes it skipped generations for no logical reason."

"And you think this is important?" President Galdet asked.

"I do know the greater our predictive factor, the better we can understand your terrorist. So far, we can statistically predict certain behaviors with an eighty percent degree of accuracy. The final twenty percent is still a guess."

Questions stopped. Siegal, once again, was about to apologize. After tense silence, Cho-Se bowed his head and smiled. The rest nodded their heads in approval. Siegal was in.

"Our time is up for today," said Danielson. "We will convene tomorrow at the same time, as agreed." He turned to Siegal. "The hard questions will come then."

TWENTY-NINE

THAT NIGHT, SIEGAL'S MIND CHURNED, thinking about the past several weeks after becoming aware of Danielson's involvement with the SOS.

If I'm so fucking important. There are so many parts of the puzzle which need filling in before I can become useful. Why is this terrorist so dangerous that five world leaders put aside their political differences to combat this evil force? And what about the hijacking? Maybe it was a training exercise. But setting fire to the remote Lijiang facility makes no sense at all. I want straight answers. And I want them now. My life is too important to be made a toy by these politicians.

DAY TWO, SIEGAL did not wait for his personal alarm clock to let him know when to go downstairs. His troubled night made him hungry. While eating some eggs and a bagel from the buffet, Danielson, followed by President Russell, came in and sat beside him at the large table.

"You made me look pretty good yesterday," said Danielson.

"You know," Siegal said, "you could have keyed me in on the SOS membership."

"Would you have said anything in a different way? I think not," said Danielson as he powered up the giant screen.

"Good morning, gentlemen," said Danielson. "Are there any left-over questions from yesterday?"

"Tell me, Dr. Siegal," asked King Ishmere, "what do you think about a certain airplane crisis that started in Australia and the raid on a chemical lab in China?"

"They may be related, King Ishmere. But I have no specifics. This very clever person knew exactly what he was doing...even both events resulting in casualties of their own members. In my mind, there can only be two logical explanations. Either an under-financed group is attempting to make a name, or these events are part of something bigger. I personally believe the latter. Our terrorist has a personal agenda."

King Ishmere continued. "Suppose we add a little to the equation. You see, there were some details left out of both stories."

"I beg your pardon?" Siegal felt his neck muscles tighten. "And what details are these, sir?"

"There was some information left out of the news reports in order to keep the depth of consequences to a minimum. We learned the terrorist used local individuals to carry out each incursion."

"This new information could be important," said Siegal.

President Galdet asked, "Why is that?"

Siegal sipped his coffee, helping him clear his mind for the question. "First of all, it tells me that his pitch to win new converts is a slam dunk. And secondly, he probably intends to use most of them only once. Cut groups, I think they're called."

"And this," asked Galdet, "makes our job of tracing the leadership more difficult?"

"Exactly," responded Siegal.

"Please go on, Dr. Siegal," said King Ishmere. "And tell us why this terrorist kills his own kind?"

"Your second question is easy. He used the killings to keep the rest of his troops in line through fear. The same I found in my rat studies."

King Ishmere continued his questioning. "Why not kill some of the passengers of the airplane? I think this would have shown the same effect."

"Not necessarily. They were of no consequence to his goal. These victims were weak links, not trusted, and had to be eliminated."

Still feeling angry from being left out of the information loop, Siegal decided to confront the delegation. "Gentlemen, I think everything I've said this morning is not really news to you. I believe you had come to the same conclusions through your combined intelligence forces."

Siegal took their silence as a yes.

"Is anyone going to tell me more? If not, then I don't believe you need me."

Russell broke the stalemate. "You are right. The truth is, we have tried and failed to infiltrate terrorist cells in the past. We didn't tell you specifically about two of the slain victims. Both were attempts by our CIA at embedding informants within the organization. We need your behavioral expertise to keep our agents on the inside from getting killed."

"What makes this terrorist so different from the ones already out there?" asked Siegal. "It seems to me that this group commands most of the world's intelligence as well as military might."

Danielson explained, "This terrorist is willing to take on all of us with no doubt about his success. And when he succeeds, our fear is others will follow his model."

"And how do you suggest I identify these caped marvel agents? I have no network to work with."

President Russell said, "How you do it is your decision. Chairman Danielson has as much information as we have. He is instructed to be of complete assistance to you and have all his resources at your disposal. Anything else you wish to ask?"

"Actually several questions have crossed my mind. The first one is, when do you need my conclusions?"

Chairman Danielson answered, "We don't have a definite deadline but we feel he must be already planning some new attacks."

Siegal's mind was whirling. He was starting to formulate a plan.

"Well then, I think my first inclination is to determine the character dimensions of the terrorist organization, which I think is similar to my new rat social model. A leader, top advisers, and feet-on-the-ground types to do the dirty work."

Danielson stood up. "Are there any further questions for Dr. Siegal?" There were none. "And, Dr. Siegal, is there anything else you wish to ask us?"

"One more, Mr. Chairman. Why attack the obscure, ultra-secret laboratory at Lijiang?"

Siegal asked the question no one wanted to hear. He could tell from the silence: they all knew the answer.

Danielson said, "I promised Dr. Siegal he would get every one of his questions answered. President Cho-Se, please explain."

President Cho-Se began. "Initially we reported the fire at the laboratory as a student accident. This, as you well know, was false."

If Siegal had felt the weight of silence when he asked the question, it was even heavier now.

President Cho-Se continued, "We were experimenting with some unique chemicals at Lijiang. It was important to keep the experiments very secret. If any hint of what we were doing leaked out, the world, including all of you here, would have forced us to halt our activity. Somehow this terrorist discovered what we were doing."

Siegal saw a look of humility.

"We were developing a toxic drug, deadlier than Sarin gas. But our goal was not to develop a weapon to kill people. Dr. Siegal, you saw the carnage at the laboratory. We first thought there was an accidental fire. Every trace of our work was thought to have been destroyed in the blaze. Our investigators discovered that four containers holding our toxin were missing. We have now concluded that the chemicals inside these containers were taken intact before the fire and exported somewhere outside China."

"Tell me more about the missing toxin, President Cho-Se," asked Siegal.

"We call it V-32. It is a virus developed from a series of complicated distillations. It is extremely virulent and attacks through the air. Once a person or animal comes in contact with the virus, death comes within hours. As you all know, we have many cities that have become inundated with germ-carrying vermin spreading disease. We planned to use the virus to clear these areas, making them more habitable for our population. The advantage of V-32 is that within a few hours, the deadly effect mutates and the contaminated area is again safe for life. We were beginning work on how to dispense it, since it can penetrate most biohazard-protective gear."

"How much was taken and what destructive power would that amount have?"

"We only developed 200 cc's. We estimate this would effectively endanger an area as large as one hundred square miles."

"Two hundred cc's. Sounds limiting."

"Not so, Dr. Siegal. The virus works as a culture. It is stable at zero degrees centigrade, but at room temperature it can double in volume every three to four weeks."

Siegal said, "If it's a liquid, than something as simple as a fly sprayer could be used. But that would not only kill the cut users, who the terrorist could care little for, but his midlevel people as well. He seems to lack a delivery system he can safely use. Which is why he hasn't used it to date. But it doesn't mean he won't do something evil."

A sober President Russell spoke. "Gentlemen, I believe the clock to combat this terrorist started right after the Lijiang raid. It is only a matter of time until our terrorist finds a way to use this virus as a weapon of mass destruction. We have to be ready."

PART THREE

ONCE UPON A TIME, THERE was an ant who kept bragging how strong he was. All the other insects became tired of his bragging and challenged him to prove his strength. The ant proclaimed he could move a whole mountain. They all laughed at him until he actually did it…one grain of soil at a time.

Ram Das, *Grist From The Mill*

THIRTY

MEETING CONCLUDED, RUSSELL AND DANIELSON returned to Washington for business as usual. Siegal returned to Denver for the comfort of his own bed.

Ten o'clock the next morning, Siegal arrived to an empty rat lab. The team, even BF, were elsewhere. His only clue to them knowing he existed was a sticky note on his computer:

WE HAVE YOUR CLASSES COVERED.

Thank goodness for the guys. Covered my butt. But who covers my butt if I fail with SOS?

Siegal called Jerry Ravid at ID, asking for an appointment. Ravid's secretary asked the purpose.

"It's to discuss the Foundation."

She offered a three o'clock opening. He gave a quiet thank you, scribbled a reply on a sticky note that he would be gone for the rest of the day, and attached it to the lab door. Siegal got in his car and drove around town, ending up in ID's parking lot just before three.

RAVID'S SECRETARY MOTIONED him to go right in. Ravid had set two chairs around a small coffee table in preparation for the meeting.

"Sit down. Coffee?" Ravid signed coffee to his secretary.

The atmosphere in the room felt different to Siegal. It wasn't that he was ever unwelcome. Always before it was on Ravid's invitation. Today was different.

Ravid started the conversation. "My secretary said you wanted to discuss something about the Foundation grant you're on."

"It is and it isn't."

"Okay. Let's start over. Your name is Ross and mine is Jerry. This isn't a meeting, just a conversation between friends. My guess is you came here to bounce off some ideas. However, you seem to be acting more like you're an unmarried pregnant girl deciding to tell her mother of her predicament. Am I close?"

Siegal nodded at the metaphor. "I'm just not sure how to proceed. There's a lot to talk about, but not much I can actually divulge. If I skirt around the specifics, please bear with me. I'm limited to what I can say."

Ravid leaned back in his chair, giving Siegal more space. "Say what you want. I'll just listen."

Siegal sipped some coffee. "I met with the Foundation. Only it's not a grant-funding source as I was made to believe. It's actually a secret organization who thinks they need my special psychology skills. Do you know anything about whom I'm involved with?"

"I'm not in the loop. But about these skills. Can you talk about them?"

"They think I can give some very sensitive input. I agreed to work with them because…"

"Because?"

"Because what they want to do is of extreme importance."

Ravid leaned forward in his chair. "I take it this is more to do than ordinary Foundation activity and research in your rat lab."

"A whole lot more." In a halting voice, Siegal added, "This enigma has me in over my head. Everything in Denver is crowding my thinking. I need space to think. One part is to distance myself from ID."

Ravid suggested, "I don't control you and I don't want to lose you as a staff member. If what you're doing is so important, I won't hold you back. I'm offering you a leave of absence from here if that will help your dilemma. You can come back when your world changes."

Both men knew it was just words and the leave would be long-term at best. Ravid patted Siegal on the knee similar to what President Russell did in the limo a few days ago. This time Siegal did not back away. It felt sincere.

Ravid stood. "I'll have my secretary pack up your office and send any personal belongings to your apartment tomorrow. There will be no letters of resignation or any other papers relating to this move in your personal file."

They traded final handshakes.

Siegal left, unsure whether he was relieved or not. In his heart, he knew this was the last time the two would ever speak as co-professionals at ID. He had broken one of the three ties that held him to his current life. The second tie would be harder.

IT WAS AFTER eight when Siegal entered Quandary's for what he thought would be a late dinner with his friends. They had already gone. Feeling relieved at not having to talk to them there, he ordered a takeout sandwich and went home to contemplate his next move.

The first thing he did once inside his apartment was to glance toward the closet and the green phone. There was no blinking light. Next he checked his answering machine. It, too, indicated no one had called. It was as if the team, and especially Simi, were waiting for him to initiate any communication. Siegal knew it was his secretive behavior in the past couple of weeks that isolated all things familiar and warm.

He had to make the first move.

"Hello, this is Bill Feinberg. I'm sorry I can't come to the phone right now. If you know me well, then you probably know where I am. If not, then just leave a message. I will respond when I have time."

"If you can take a break from your romantic activity for a minute and gather your messages, then meet me in the lab at nine tomorrow. Ask Sally to be there as well."

He next called Simi. The conversation was businesslike, not one between lovers.

"Ross, where have you been? Are you all right?"

"Yes, I'm fine…I guess."

"I was just warming up some leftover fettuccine and garlic bread. There's enough for both of us if you want to come over."

Choosing between a cold, greasy sandwich from Quandary's and being with Simi offered no contest. He dropped the sandwich in the disposal. "I'll see you in a few minutes."

THEY SAT QUIETLY at her kitchen table sharing warmed-over fettuccini, cheap wine, and garlic bread. It felt good to see her. He had only spent two days in the mountains, but it seemed an eternity since they had been alone without the pressure of deadlines.

Siegal's responsibility to SOS consumed his psyche and promised to suck every ounce of his energy before it was over. SOS, not Simi, had become his emotional partner.

The dinner candles, measuring time, burned down and flickered out. There were no words, only sounds of the wine bottle clicking against their goblets as the two gazed at each other. Simi stood, walked behind her lover, and with gentle fingers massaged his stressed neck muscles. They turned to each other and their lips met.

Hand-in-hand, they walked to her bedroom. Slowly they undressed each other. Ross picked her up and moved to the bed. Naked, they came together.

Simi's body felt wonderful as she moved in perfect rhythm to his. She was the therapist and he the patient. Totally spent, they fell asleep in each other's grasp. There they remained entwined until the first rays of daylight.

Facing each other in bed, Simi whispered, "Are you okay, Ross?" It was her first question regarding his meeting.

"If you mean with the Foundation, it went very well. The data you all helped collect kept me in good stead. Everyone was happy." He mouthed the words, but wondered if he was convincing.

He needed to change the subject and hoped Simi would go along. She did.

"Before I forget, thank you and the team for covering my classes. The extra day with the Foundation caught me by surprise."

"I take it that you don't want to talk any more about your meeting, or should I say, your green closet phone co-conspirator?"

"I'll tell you about it later." The last statement was a lie, something he hated to do. But come to think of it, the whole ruse of there being a Foundation was just one big lie after another.

"I called BF last night and asked that we meet this morning at the lab," Siegal continued. "There are a lot of things to clear up and it's best if we do it together."

Simi curled back up into Ross' arms and was already back to sleep before the last words were said. Siegal fell back to sleep as well. The last thing he thought before dozing was how natural and good it felt to be with her.

SIMI AND SIEGAL arrived promptly at nine. BF and Sally were late. They brought fresh donuts as a peace gesture. Simi had made the coffee while waiting.

Following their regular routine, the team first had their coffee and doughnuts before business. No words were exchanged except for the usual hellos and other minor gossip. Then the rats were attended to. Finally, they sat down around the table with a second cup and the real meeting began.

BF broke the silence. "Enough of this bullshit, Ross. Things seem the same but they damn well are not."

"Well," started Siegal, "for the past several days I've kept you consumed with our rat studies for the Foundation. I believe I have been selfish in this regard because you all had other responsibilities. You all have academic lives. The term is almost over and it creeps up if you let it. BF, you have classes to teach; Simi, your dissertation is due in the next couple of months; Sally, there's finals to get ready for. I think these are the highest-priority issues to resolve. So for now, the lab, our current research, and yes, even the Foundation grant money has to take second chair to your personal needs."

Sally spoke up. "I don't get it. I guess I can understand you giving up the Foundation grant money. You have always been stubborn when your back was up against the wall. But giving up the lab and your research is something I don't get. The stuff we discovered will open the behavioral science world and kick all those grey beards in the ass. Why would you even suggest giving that all up?"

"The Foundation has thrown me a curve. I don't mean to give up all the lab experiments. They're doing well and only year-end publications are necessary. BF, while I'm gone I am hoping you will take charge to lend a Ph.D. title to these publications. I can't tell you how long I will be tied up off-campus. Hopefully shorter than longer. If what we discovered is really important, then others will pick up the results and begin duplicating our studies to verify our results. Questions?"

Siegal saw the wind being let out of their sails. For the past several days, they'd been going full bore. And now they were told to shut it down to a maintenance level, just like that, and for no reason they could accept.

"You all finished with what I needed. Now I have to carry on alone."

Sally was not about to shut down. "Are you playing with us? The lab has just been fun and games for you? I just don't buy it."

"Sally, I am not playing. The rat lab is a very important part of your learning and my life as well. I tried to give you a chance to experience a very different way of studying animal behavior. You and Simi are the best students any professor could have working with him. But you would have been just as spectacular under a different philosophical approach. And, BF, you're on the road to becoming a great full professor. I only hope all this is temporary and I'll be back."

"So, Ross. Oops. I mean Dr. Siegal. This sounds like umbilical cord-cutting time." Simi's show of sarcasm could not have been better timed. "What could the Foundation offer you to make such a sudden shift?"

Siegal paused for a moment. He was cutting them off—and out of his life. There was danger if they discovered too much about the terrorist and the Summit of Six. "As much as I want to say more, I can't. As you complete each research project, initiate plans to farm the little critters out to science classes in the different area public schools where they can be assured of a pleasant retirement. Or, keep one or two for personal pets."

Simi asked, "Are you sure we're ready to be let out without you, our safety net?"

"A story once imparted to me by a practicing yoga teacher, Ram Das, tells of the time when he was a young student in India. Each time he asked his teacher if he was ready to go out into the world, his teacher's response was always, 'Not yet.' This went on for some time until one day he approached his teacher and rather than asking, he simply said he was ready. The teacher answered, 'Yes, my son, you are.' And indeed, he knew he was. Ram Das left India and became a great teacher in his own right. And now I say, 'Yes you are.'"

"Sorry, Ross," BF said, getting into the conversation, "but I don't recall any of us asking to leave your circle."

"Possibly not, but maybe you need a little nudge from the nest. You told me without asking."

Simi stood up and saluted. "Aye aye, sir. Your orders will be met without question." She paused as tears formed. "And what exactly are your plans? Do any of them include me?"

"Right now I feel worse than all of you. The three of you are my entire world. That is, until now. We've always been open with each other and I intend to be as frank with you as I can. There are just some things I cannot say. I have been sworn to secrecy. There is more. I will also need to leave the university. My relationship with the Foundation was cemented in these past couple of days and now it becomes a full-time responsibility. I will be moving into their western office very soon. In the meantime, I will keep my apartment in Denver."

Turning directly to BF and Sally, he said, "I think it's clear that your relationship will culminate in something more permanent. And, I hope that means marriage. I am going to recommend that the university hire Simi, by then Dr. Simi Block, to take my place on staff in the psychology department. If not, I'm sure you'll find a good opportunity elsewhere. I think the Foundation has enough strings to help all three of you if you need it. As a tradeoff for me working with them, they promised they would help."

Siegal looked at Simi. "I cannot think of a life totally without you. If we can be together at times, I would like that. However, you have to be free to make other choices."

"That's not exactly a kiss off," said Simi, "but it sure comes close." She remembered her first marriage, which ended when her husband walked out on her without a goodbye. Until now, she protected herself by staying out of other close relationships. Falling in love with Ross Siegal was never intended. Simi was angry. She wiped her tears and tried to act brave. "Okay, guys. We have lots of work to do. There are rats to attend to, research studies to finish, theses to write, and courses to finish. Fuck this whole damn scene. Just fuck it all."

They finished their work in the lab and left.

THIRTY-ONE

ALONE, SIEGAL TYPED T-E-R-R-O-R-I-S-T IN Wikipedia for synonyms. One synonym caught his eye.

Zealot: n. An immoderate, fanatical, or extremely zealous to   a cause. Synonyms: extremist, crank, bigot, fanatic.

He Googled "zealot". Over a hundred links popped up. He read them all and printed those most promising. Those were Knights of the Crusades, Middle Eastern priests, Spanish Inquisition leaders, the Ku Klux Klan, Nazis, freedom fighters with subheadings of skinheads and white supremacists, and colonial Tea Partiers.

Educational, but nothing to help me organize this terrorist in my own terms.

Turning his head toward the storage closet, he shouted, "Hey, rats, you acted more like my unknown organization. Why didn't Google list you?"

Siegal's frustration soon had him rubbing his overworked eyes and scratching his thinning hair. Then a smile formed on his lips.

What makes them alike is one common thread. Their victims are looked upon as inferiors and need extermination. But does my rat terrorist group fit within this definition? At least I don't think so. Would any of them set fire to the lab or hijack an airplane? A mass killing would be more likely. There must be other kinds of terrorist groups.

"Hey, rats. How about this? Why can't a terrorism group develop differently, not out of a sense of mission but out of boredom or misdirected sport? Let's call them Ennuis, weary with their current state and seeking action to upset the status quo. Ennuis, as they mature, can develop some common purpose. In contrast with zealots, leadership is not easily identified in the beginning."

Nothing hits me yet. There must be some other group or groups. How would I define it?

Siegal jotted some notes on a legal pad, his way to focus using his rats' behaviors as a model. "Directives by the leader are handled by the lieutenants. Often heartless, cruel, and bloody."

"It can be like a king and an evil prime minister, as in the story of Queen Esther and Purim in the Bible. King Tigger, I'm talking about you and your underlings."

Siegal added more notes. "This third category's purpose is to develop power over a person or group."

"Aha. Gotcha pegged."

Now all I have to do is figure out who or what they're trying to take power over. And then how they are attempting to actuate their heinous takeover.

SIEGAL REMAINED AT his lab desk for the next day, separating himself from his researchers. He even swore at Simi when she accidently brushed her breasts on his shoulder on the way to the pencil sharpener. From then on, Simi, Sally and BF avoided talking to him. He became their invisible man.

The stress of keeping notes and printouts hidden from everyone made concentration so difficult, Siegal decided to set up office in his apartment kitchen. Except for the formal request to leave City University, the break from his old life was almost complete.

THE GREEN PHONE'S ring startled Siegal.

"Ross, how's it going?" The salutation was friendly enough, but Siegal knew the question was all business.

"I don't know. I've theorized there are three categories of terror- ist groups. I think I'm beginning to understand our target. But now I'm stumped on where to go from there."

"Want someone to bounce any of your ideas off? It's my job to be available whenever you wish."

"I do my best thinking alone. Give me the weekend." He hoped he had another day, given that the terrorist had control of the dead- ly V-32 virus and would use it at any time. "Then we should get together."

"Okay, pal. Just look in the mirror every so often. The person you see there is very bright and I know he'll discover the solution."

Siegal, inhaling his sense of frustration, hung up the phone without a goodbye.

Was Danielson's calling a subtle way of pushing me? Maybe he thinks I'm going too slowly. I'd rather bounce my ideas off the research team, or better yet, Ravid. Both choices, of course, no longer possible. Danielson is my only choice.

He opened an icy ODL and settled back to his notes. It was impossible to find a clear space on the kitchen table. Siegal's style was to throw nothing away. Even the floor was mostly hidden by books, articles, and computer printouts. He became the insect in *The Metamorphosis*. Dr. Ross Siegal was morphing from a behavioral specialist into an expert on terrorism.

He turned to his laptop and typed:

Category I: RELIGIOUS ZEALOTS
1. Get others to think their way
2. Destroy those who do not think their way
3. Make the fear in others the motivating payoff
4. Has an identifiable leader but subordinates carry out the program of terror
5. Could use different events as tryout activities and to 6
6. Keep every member on a readiness program

Category II: TERRORISM FOR SPORT—ENNUIS
1. One or a few people start trouble
2. Initial motivation to move against someone or some idea
3. Other groups and subgroups piggyback the activity and claim their own purpose for existence
4. Hard or even impossible to trace subgroups back to the primary group
5. Leaders may be extinguished but the lieutenants and subgroups carry on with just as much vigor
6. Motivational payoff is kinship within their subgroups and sometimes with the primary group
7. Thrill-killers and other sadistic attacks on others

Category III: PURPOSE IS TO OVERTHROW— REVOLUTIONARIES
1. Probably political
2. Guerilla groups set up to overthrow a government or regime

3. Ruin an election
4. Play on internal weaknesses within a specific population or ideal
5. Life and welfare of subordinates are incidental
6. Motivation is geared to complete success of the plan
7. There is a singleness of purpose although not every mid or lower level individual in the group may know what it is
8. Control from top to bottom is very tight
9. There is only one leader

Not waiting for Monday, Siegal went to the closet and activated the green phone. "Mr. Danielson is not in his office. I will relay that you called."

It seemed like hours but was only a few minutes when the green phone rang. "What's up?"

"I'm in a deep pit and need a rope."

There was a short pause at the other end of the line. "I'll meet you at the chalet on Monday afternoon. Go up Sunday and have a steak in Blackhawk. Oh, and take some extra clothes in case you decide to stay a few days."

The offer was a good one. Siegal realized as of late, his most exciting meals were peanut-butter-and-jelly sandwiches followed by too many ODLs.

ON MONDAY AT the chalet, Siegal took an early morning walk to clear his head before Danielson's expected arrival. By the time he returned there was a car parked in front. It was not the typical black van used for government business, but a sleek yellow convertible.

Siegal's favorite bodyguard opened the car door and greeted Danielson with a salute.

"Good day, Ben. I trust my room is ready," said Danielson. Then meeting Siegal at the chalet's front door, said, "I hope you have a fresh pot of coffee brewing in the kitchen. We can sip a fresh mug and breathe a few moments of fresh mountain air out on the patio before getting down to business. That would give me a chance to un-wind after my red-eye flight from Washington and the drive up here."

A FEW MINUTES later they were sitting at the large dining room table. Siegal spread out his notes.

"Bring me up to speed."

Siegal shuffled papers, pointing out specific parts. "My first step in understanding our rat was to learn what terrorism is. I broke it down into three basic categories. What really complicates the para-digm is that within any single category, the other two categories also exist. I determined our terrorist is most like my category-three type. Do you agree the breakout seems logical so far?"

Danielson nodded. "I've never seen these breakouts in quite this way before. For example, your category 'Terrorism for sport' is entirely new to me. But it makes sense. I always thought that acts like school shootings or bombs in public buildings were some-thing on the edge of being straight criminal behavior, or at least being done by kooks. But now I can see them as part of this whole scheme. Where are you taking this?"

"We need to be looking at a form of terrorism that seeks to over-throw something."

"How so?"

"My first two categories require a certain amount of notoriety. Zealots and sports groups need the public media. They want their names known. Our terrorist is neither asking nor seeking any spe-cial publicity. Are you still with me?"

"I am so far."

"Okay. Look at my category three. This form of terrorism leads to an overthrowing of something, someone, an ideal, or some political entity. I'm convinced we are looking for a group that is setting up to overthrow whoever it is they want to overthrow. I just don't have enough data yet."

Danielson asked, "What else do you need?"

"Tell me, are there any of your infiltrators still in this terrorist organization?"

"No. The two you know about were our last successful embeds. Or, perhaps I should have said partially successful embeds. We're not clear why they were singled out and killed. It may help if you figure that out."

"Two. Hmm. One in Egypt and one at Lijiang. Both killed in a similar manner. No wonder you felt so sure the two incursions were related. I based my judgment on both being so well-designed. The operatives who were killed somehow didn't fit the exacting profile of our category-three terrorist organization. Remember, I theorized there was a strict line of command-and-obey. These two didn't fit in. Can you get me complete files on your two agents? I need to know what those agents were doing to get the terrorist's attention. And, if possible, I would also like to have complete workups on any you attempted to place but were unsuccessful. Understanding failures is just as important as successes."

"I think it was more dumb luck that they were accepted, but we never found out how they were singled out as being undesirable. Everything happened so fast, they weren't able to contact us before being killed."

"They were accepted for a reason. They were also killed for a reason. And both of them are different. Very different. I need time to think it out. Can I stay on here for a few extra days? I need my privacy away from my friends."

"I'll have those reports emailed as soon as I get back to my desk. My intuition tells me that things are moving. You may not have much time."

Danielson turned to the buffet behind him. He opened one of the storage doors, which usually held the wine and other beverages, to expose a green telephone with a little red light, a twin to the one in Siegal's bedroom closet.

"You don't miss a trick, do you?" quipped Siegal.

"There's also a case of ODL in the fridge. Stay here as long as you like. As far as I'm concerned, the longer you stay here, the better. A good place to work, undisturbed. The pantry and refrigerator are stocked, and there are plenty of fresh bagels. My men will check on you every day and refill anything that runs out. If there are any special requests, leave a note on the patio window. Food and other necessities will be left out there so no one will see your work. Only be sure you put everything away every Friday afternoon. A crew will come in on Saturdays to change sheets, towels, and generally clean up after you. Mi casa. Su casa. Consider this chalet your private refuge."

Danielson changed the subject. "How's your other life? You know, the one you had for most of your time on earth?"

"The toughest break is Simi. I miss her when we're apart. I let her know we couldn't remain close but would try to see each other on a limited basis as long as she wished. As you know, I've broken all ties with my friends. I need to break one more, my position at the university," he said, rubbing week-old stubble.

"On one hand, you're maybe in control of the world. On the other hand, you're completely without control of your own life." Danielson gave Siegal a pat on the back. "I have to go now. I'm as close as your green phone. Good luck. Better yet, good hunting."

THIRTY-TWO

NOTHING IS WORKING. I NEED to focus. Why am I at a loss? Where are my rats I can talk with? I asked to be left alone so I have freedom to think. Instead this dead silence locks me in, making me a prisoner.

Siegal tore a sheet from a flipchart pad garnered from the rat lab and with a black felt marker he drew a likeness of their pet rat, Tigger, with a black stripe down his back. He taped it to the wall. Then he took a red felt pen and painted a nose.

He went to the refrigerator in the kitchen and retrieved an ODL. "Now, my rat friend, where are we? Oh yes, we need to dissect this category three terrorist group."

Siegal searched through his pile of printouts. Finding the one he wanted, he addressed his cartoon rat, "Item one: purpose is to overthrow. But to overthrow what, how, and why? Tigger, there are two dichotomies. Violent types are after political control. Nonviolent types are interested in overturning ideological dogmas. I believe the character of our group is politically motivated but has no compunction against killing to enforce its goal."

Siegal finished his beer and collected another from the kitchen.

"Tigger, I know Danielson is in a rush, but don't you push me. Let's think this through. Two embedded American agents were killed at the hands of their own and while they were involved in destructive incursions. They could have been killed at any time the leader chose. I believe this head terrorist showed violence not as a cruel action but as a well-thought-out demonstration of his power over the others." Satisfied with his thinking, Siegal banged his fist on the table in victory. "Done."

He taped another sheet next to his Tigger drawing. "This feels more like home, having sheets of paper lining the lab for brainstorming."

He scrawled:

Category III leader comes into power by:
1) Election   2) Overthrowing a previous leader
3) Ascension   4) No one else wants the job
5) Controls finances   6) Has more knowledge
7) Has an idea others would like to make happen

"Okay, Tigger, which ones fit our leader?"

Siegal underlined the last three. "Tigger, the combination of finances, knowledge, and ideas makes our top rat a very powerful individual with considerable attraction. Any pretenders could easily be eliminated. Chopping off any lower members will not weaken the pack. The only way to neutralize the organization is to eliminate the head rat."

Siegal's mind burned with ideas. "We need to infiltrate the organization somehow. I must know about the two agent moles. Initially, they fit the mold and were invited in at the lowest level far removed from the leader. Whatever they did in the process identified them as outsiders. Why? What did they do wrong? I know their job was to learn about the organization and who was their leader. But the level-three culture of the terrorist group made this impossible. I think too much was expected of the agents."

"Where do we start, Tigger? Question: does this leader consider himself evil?"

Siegal thought he saw his cartoon rat shake his head no.

"I agree. It would be difficult to recruit cut group people if the joiners did not believe the purpose was more important than the process. The now dead moles entered the organization believing the leader was evil, and this may be one reason they were singled out. But, how would the leader know that? I'll come back to this."

Siegal stared at the chart. "Control the purse strings and you control the organization."

"Makes sense, Tigger. No more discussion." The next item was "Knowledge."

"People with knowledge are natural magnets; underlings, like moths to a light, are drawn in. How does this fit into the scheme of things? Find a way inside and it's possible to alter the organization's direction. Yet attempting to alter the direction of the organization implies the leader is wrong and that could have killed the two agents."

Proud of his conclusion, he stood up, thumped his chest, and paraded around the dining room table.

Siegal took his chair and looked at the final item, "Having an idea others wanted to make happen."

"The one trait that makes our terrorist so dangerous. But at the same time, it may be just the one to help develop infiltrators. Don't you agree, Tigger?"

Siegal's back ached from intense concentration. From the corner of his eye, he saw a note taped to the patio window announcing lunch was in the kitchen. His invisible caretakers left fried eggs, potatoes, and a slice of ham in the warming oven. He took his food to the patio and watched a small group of deer in the clearing. It gave him a new sense of understanding about God's creatures and more importantly, why he was there.

Revived from lunch, he returned to his computer. "I think it's safe to assume the leader keeps himself well insulated from direct contact with his targeted enemy. The less his victims know about who or where he is makes him a more terrifying figure. He does not do any of the dirty work. I would also wager that only a select few know him by both name and face. Anyone lower in the rat's rank and file only knows of the party line and how to adhere to it."

Suddenly, as if a lightbulb went on inside Siegal's head, he remembered about the rat cultural interactions at the rat lab. *The rats and terrorist leaders never appear involved in direct hands-on activity. I wonder just how similar the terrorist and the rat cultures are in other ways?*

THIRTY-THREE

THE SUN HAD SET LONG before he called it quits for the night. Sleep came easily. Before long, Siegal was dreaming of a romantic week with Simi along the Mexican Riviera. Still in his dream state, he reached across the bed. It was cold and empty. Simi should be there holding down her side of the pillow. The rude wakening reminded him of the job at hand.

His bladder full of beer from the night before, he said, to no one in particular, "I've got to take a pee."

Someone must have heard because within minutes there was a knock on the door and the distinct aroma of Starbucks extra-strong caffeine wafted through the cracks around his door.

Refreshed and with the morning rituals out of the way, he was back to work. Siegal felt lightning in the air. Everything seemed somehow different. Facts that didn't relate yesterday related today. And those that seemed dichotomous practically jumped together. *Are the similarities between the terrorist and my rat population real, or did I imagine them because I want it so much?*

Siegal taped a new sheet to the wall, drew a vertical line down the middle, and started writing.

On the left side he wrote "Characteristics of a Category III Terrorist Organization." Opposite he wrote," Simi's Observations of the Rat Lab Groups."

Siegal looked at his wall chart. "Hey, Tigger, look at what we wrote. Am I trying to make a fit? No, our list matches Simi's observations exactly. There was always a distinct leader. Then, there was a second level of rats who directed all the aggressive moves of the pack. Submissive rats took positions even further away from the prime rat. They became passive acceptors and carried out any required acts.

"Are human beings as predictable as rats? Is the error factor for predictability of a terrorist group less than twenty percent? The answer has to be yes. I wish I could call Simi and tell her what she uncovered."

Siegal continued thinking of his lab rats. *Prime rats, whether they were males or females, used sexual attraction as part of the equation. The primary reason for living is to procreate the species. That means sex must be a very high motivator for survival. Simi noted when the prime rat was male, there was a harem of females always available at every level. And when the prime rat was female, she maintained a single preferred male rat, but kept other males sensing they had a chance to mate with her. While associates to the prime rat changed slightly from time to time, the prime rat always remained in charge.*

Siegal activated the green phone.

Danielson answered on the third ring. "Sorry. I was on another line. There are rumors our terrorist is on the move. Nothing definite, but that can mean bad things are about to happen. Do you have something?"

"Logic tells me the terrorist organizations must function in the same way as my lab rats. There can be only one ultimate leader." Siegal smiled. "And Tigger's model as head rat is a perfect parallel to our terrorist. He controlled his pack by controlling their motivators. Pick the right motivator and you can get any animal, including humans, to do almost anything."

"Your tinkering with normal research procedures by keeping rat generations together instead of dispensing them after each experiment may prove to be your greatest lifetime achievement."

Siegal felt embarrassed by the rare compliment. His professional colleagues often considered his methods unscientific.

"There's no Nobel science prize material here yet. I think some of the data we reported on earlier to the SOS will lead us to predict very specifically, perhaps even within the zero to five percent error range, who becomes a leader either for terrorism or for good. And who fits the other two levels. The traits are the same."

"Is that all you called me about? You wouldn't have called unless you needed something from me or to tell me something earthshaking."

"Before, it was only conjecture. My current conclusions are a step forward. In our lab, we observed how sexual behavior was the prime motivator luring the other rats to pack around the prime rat. I tried to see what would make humans move and be controlled within any social pack, including a terrorist group. Sex is surely one motivator, but there are others."

"What's your point?"

"I just realized I was lured into this situation to become the worker rat for the SOS. How did it happen? More accurately, how did you get it to happen?"

There was a laugh at the other end. It wasn't so much a, 'The joke is on you' kind of laugh, but more, 'It is about time you asked the question and what took you so long to figure it out?'

Danielson explained how he spent two sleepless nights planning their first meeting. "I needed you and there was no room for error. I studied your personality type as best I could. I determined your strongest motivation was having the opportunity to develop theories and testing them out on your own terms. Once I understood you, the rest was easy. All I had to do was tweak your curiosity."

"You mean, I've been played like a..."

Danielson completed the thought, "...like a rat in a maze?"

Siegal smiled. "Yep, like a rat in a maze. I'm not sure I like that. I suppose if I had realized it sooner, I wouldn't be here now."

Siegal felt Danielson smiling back through the phone line. "Maybe not at first, but sooner or later, you would have volunteered once the danger to the world was explained. Deep inside, you're a humanitarian. And on that point, you were never played. So is there something really important to discuss?"

"Any true leader has an amazing ability to control others by intuitively understanding what motivates his underlings. In most cases the controls are usually healthy. But in more instances than we would care to admit the influences can be very negative, like being attracted to this terrorist group to do unthinkable crimes. I'm beginning to understand terrorist-type group structure more with every minute of my study. Okay, I think I can continue to develop this line of thinking by myself, but I still need information on the two agents who were killed."

"There's been a short delay clearing security. Since I'm no longer the president's chief of staff, I'm out of the CIA loop. But it's done now. Turns out it's too sensitive to send by email; a messenger will be arriving at the chalet early Tuesday. How is your money holding up? Just in case, there will be a pouch full with the messenger, should you need it."

"One more thing," Siegal said. "I have to finish some business with the university and get some more clothes from my apartment.

I can go down Sunday and be back Monday night."

"Do it. By the way, we've been getting scuttlebutt about another terrorist strike, most likely in Europe. We just don't know when. Talk to me Tuesday after you've studied the reports I'm sending."

The phone clicked and went silent.

Siegal was by himself again. Snow outside told him it was late fall. The calendar indicated it was Saturday. He turned to his rat drawing. "This will be my last weekend off. There are things I have to do in Denver. Tuesday, after I get those reports from Danielson, I can determine the type of person who would be accepted within this terrorist group."

Siegal put up another sheet on the wall and wrote:

There are at least three levels within a terrorist group.

Level One is the prime rat and he is omnipotent.

Level Two are the lieutenants, handpicked by the prime rat and who fully agree with that person's purpose. They do work for the leader and not just a cause. Directions given by the leader are carried out without question.

Level Three are cut groups or throwaways. Do all the dirty work. Not allowed to move upward in the chain of command. They work for the cause and not the head person. Any non-compliant behavior is met with severe punishment or death.

Finished for now.

Siegal picked up the house phone and dialed a very familiar number. Before Simi could pick up, he closed the line.

I can't go further without the reports from Danielson. And, I need some primary reward to keep my motivation—like my rats. More than sex, I need her company.

He punched redial.

"Hello, Simi?"

THIRTY-FOUR

CHANNEL NINE WEATHER REPORTED A perfect Colorado ski weekend. Sparse clouds decorated an azure blue crown adorning the whitecapped majesties. Happy warriors of the slopes created stop-and-go ribbons of traffic exiting east down the Rockies toward Denver this late Sunday morning. Ross Siegal relished the snail's pace as he daydreamed the promise of a stolen moment with Simi. He knew his trip to Denver would not all be fun. There was a matter to manage at the university, the final break from his previous life. There was not much time to waste. He needed to be back at the chalet by Tuesday morning to get Danielson's report.

It was two o'clock when he parked in front of his apartment. He entered, and, to his to his surprise, the mess he left in a rush a few days earlier was cleaned up. The phone in the closet also had been removed.

The mysterious hand of the ever-meticulous Tom Danielson paid me a visit. Still, it's good to be home and, once undressed, feel the familiar touch of the pulse shower.

Wrapped in his terry robe, Siegal explored the apartment to see what else Danielson's crew had done. It was as if Siegal had just finished giving it his weekly cleaning, only better. There was garbage waiting to be taken out. The refrigerator had fresh and half-used food cartons stored much in the way he would have done had he been living there. All personal mail was opened and stacked neatly on the kitchen table, ready for handling. The trash mail was exactly where he would have thrown it. Did somebody named Dr. Ross Siegal live here, or was it a clone? He jerked around, expecting a likeness standing there behind him. This was a perfect job of deception, even to having some of his dirty clothes in the hamper.

For whose benefit? Only Simi and the landlord had keys to his apartment. But if there was a fire in the building, my place would be open for all to see. And, I wouldn't put it past Danielson to cause such havoc.

Siegal packed two suitcases in preparation for a long return stay at the chalet and stowed them in the trunk of his car. He finished with just enough time to be at Simi's by seven, as promised.

THE DOOR OPENED before Siegal could ring the bell. There stood Simi, wearing only a hot-pink sash tied in a bow. She kissed him. "I don't want to lose you."

He reached for the end of the bow. It dropped off effortlessly. They lingered at the door for a moment warming each other's lips, searching each other's tender areas, and then retreated to the bedroom. When they finished, it was too late for any movie. They may have continued longer had it not been for Siegal's stomach growling so loudly they had to quit and laugh about it.

As they dressed, Simi asked if he wanted to see BF and Sally.

"I'd like to. But do they want to see me? I feel I've pretty much abandoned them. And I have to be back by late Monday evening."

"It's not too late, we can go to Quandary's for a late supper," she said. "They may still be there,"

Just thinking about going to their team's adopted bar and enjoying a pitcher of ODL on draft instead of bottled at the chalet brought a smile to his face. "Let's go."

SIEGAL WAS SURPRISED how good it felt walking into the familiar sights, sounds, and smells of Quandary's. As his eyes grew accustomed to the dark interior, familiar faces began to emerge. First there was the bartender. *I never did learn his name.* Then the waitress emerged out of the shade. Far across the room, he saw their regular table in the corner. *Shit. It's occupied.*

BF called out. "We thought you'd abandoned us for all time."

Sally jumped in a nanosecond later, "Hey, sweet thing, how's your ass?"

Siegal felt a blush from the surprise. "You guys. Were you expecting me or something?"

"To tell the truth, after you talked with Simi she called me and suggested BF and I might want to see you, so I guess you were set up a little. Hope you don't mind?"

"Mind? Hell no. I've really missed you." He gave Sally a kiss and BF a strong bear hug.

BF waved toward the bar and their waitress brought a fresh pitcher of ODL and filled their glasses. Then BF, in his ever-introspective way, changed the climate of the scene.

"You look tired, boss. Are you okay?"

Siegal wanted to tell them everything. After all, there had been no secrets between them until these past few months. And now all he could do was attempt to change the subject and hope they would understand. Siegal exhaled. "I'm okay. This new job is sticky and hard to get a handle on."

Tears of love flowed from Sally's eyes. "You know I would sell my fucking virginity for you." The trio laughed. Sally's only possibility to do that would have to be in another life. "If there is anything we can do?"

"I know you all deserve an explanation about everything; I'm sworn not to discuss anything. But this I can tell you: our rat studies had enormous impact on what I am now doing. Because of your creative instincts for research, the world has a better chance to be a safer place. Now tell me about what you all are doing?"

Simi did the summary. "We're finishing the rat experiments as you directed and are working on outplacements for the little critters."

BF added, "Your classes are covered and next week starts winter quarter break."

"And our fucking jobs will come, so you shouldn't vorry," Sally added in a bad attempt at a Jewish accent.

Simi interrupted, "Enough business, our beers are getting warm and need our personal touch." The four proceeded to get very drunk.

IT WAS MONDAY morning and Siegal woke with a head only a beer hangover could create. Humpty-Dumpty had nothing on him. Simi fried up some eggs and made toast. Siegal wiped his mouth and placed a call to the dean of psychology, confirming his appointment. He saw a look of shock on Simi's face.

"I'm taking a leave of absence from the university. I don't have a clue on how I would approach Dean Worth. What plausible reason can I give to leave on such short notice? I can't tell her any more than you about what I am doing."

Simi just smiled and gave him a kiss on the cheek. "You'll figure out something. You always do."

DR. ROSS SIEGAL entered the dean's office precisely at 11:27. Her secretary ushered him into the inner office. He had only been there once before, at the time of his hiring. And now this second time for the most opposite reason.

Dean Worth looked up from an inter-university memo she was reading. Her face showed no expression, at least none that Siegal could read. He started to speak, but she took the immediate lead.

"Good morning, Dr. Siegal. It seems a lot has been going on over the past few weeks." She held the up the memo she was reading.

The past few weeks? I made a plan to leave less than a week ago.

Dean Worth continued, "It seems that your full-time services are needed for some sort of internal management problem for the next several months. This memo from our university president asks that I offer you a sabbatical starting immediately. The request came with an extremely persuasive financial argument. Let me tell you, I'm not in favor of losing you midterm. But I have no choice than to honor this request."

The ever-enterprising Danielson again had done his magic.

"I came in begging and you are offering. All I can say is thank you."

Dean Worth stepped out from behind her desk. She offered Siegal a not-too-friendly handshake. "Believe me. I have not always approved of your methods." Then her lips formed a slight hint of a smile. "To tell the truth, I'll miss your unorthodox ways."

SIEGAL RETURNED TO Simi's apartment and said his goodbyes. It was a sad scene. Both felt a certain futility in their relationship.

He got in his car and drove off. He noticed the sun starting to descend behind the mountains. *Just enough time to get back to the chalet before dark.*

THIRTY-FIVE

THE SUN WAS HALFWAY HIDDEN by the north edge of the Gore Range when Siegal arrived at the chalet. There was just enough light remaining for him to make out a small car in the chalet parking space normally occupied by the unseen caretaker's SUV. He would have preferred to see the familiar SUV. Siegal edged next to the car and peered in. It was empty.

Maybe the courier arrived early and is wandering about the open area around the chalet, waiting for me to let him in. Hope I didn't keep him waiting too long. Or maybe it's strangers lurking in the shadows. If so, that wouldn't be good.

Siegal inserted his key to unlock the front door. Surprised, he found it unlocked. He eased his way inside, hoping it was his forgetfulness or the weekend cleaners who left the chalet unlocked. His heart raced.

Siegal imagined different scenarios. Intruders, or worse, burglars who found these empty mountain retreats easy pickings. His other choice was that the car belonged to the terrorist group that he and Danielson were battling.

I need to protect myself.

Siegal looked around for a weapon and lifted an umbrella from the stand by the door. He stood still, weapon cocked overhead, waiting for his eyes to adjust in the darkness. He imagined weird thoughts, not at all thinking that Danielson would never leave the chalet unguarded. The veins in his neck throbbed. His breath shortened. Despite the cool temperature outside, beads of sweat formed on his forehead.

He half whispered, "Is anyone there?"

He could see the form of a man standing outside on the patio. He aimed his umbrella like an assault rifle. "I've got a gun. I will shoot."

The moon was directly behind the person, obscuring his face.

Siegal repeated his threat louder this time. "Come on out. I have a gun and I know how to use it."

The shadow spoke. "Ross, I give up."

Siegal breathed. He recognized the familiar voice; not a robber and not an assassin. "You almost gave me a heart attack. The long ride up here meant I had to pee and almost did it on the spot. Don't know what I would have done if you were an actual intruder."

"Drown him in urine," laughed Danielson as he stepped into the dining room.

Siegal laid his assault umbrella on the dining room table. "Did you get demoted? I hardly expected you to be delivering my information in person."

"I've been feeling guilty leaving you on your own so much. Sooner or later I knew you'd want someone to use as a sounding board. And having nothing better to do except save the world, I decided to make a house call. Besides, the SOS is getting very anxious for results."

"It's only been three days since I've been here. I know the pressure is on, but I wasn't given any deadline to…"

"Right, maybe you weren't, but my years of experience give me a gut sense that something is in the wind. Oops, I'm jumping the gun. First things first."

"Right, then I suppose it'll be followed by the other shoe being dropped."

"I made some coffee. Do you want a mug? Better yet, I made steaks and fries. They should be done about now. Judging by how the pantry here has been robbed of peanut butter and bread, I bet your meals are boring, limited to what your caretakers know how to make. One Chinese dinner with Simi doesn't count."

It always amazed Siegal how much Danielson knew about his movements. He passed it off as a negative of the job.

They exited to the kitchen and retrieved dinner from the warming oven along with a six-pack of ODLs. Danielson carried the hot food tray, Siegal took the six-pack, and they adjourned to the living room.

"We can eat while we talk," suggested Danielson as he set the tray on a coffee table in front of the fireplace. He kindled the logs to break the evening chill.

Siegal's mouth watered as he hardly took time to chew before swallowing. It took a large drink of ODL to clear his throat. "Where do we start?"

Danielson said, "First tell me anything new you determined."

Siegal shared his notes detailing the type of terrorist group they were seeking and the membership makeup. "I've named our group the Rat Pack."

"I like it. So?"

"So I pretty well have the leader type profiled, and even have a good idea of how the lower-level members are managed within the organization. I'm still formulating how the midlevel members make it all work. If the Rat Pack is small, as I suspect, there is probably just one pod. Given time, it will develop several independent acting pods, and more midlevels, all acting on their own. At that point, cutting off the head of the main rat would only slow down their activity. This Rat Pack is still new enough to have only one pod, but probably has two midlevels. The higher midlevel members are the only ones who know the prime rat personally. They probably outline the specific plans and timelines. I think it's the lower midlevel types who lead the missions and control the cut groups."

"And, how do we use this knowledge?"

"It tells us at what level we can best infiltrate the pack."

Danielson asked, "How do you figure?"

"There's only one leader. We can't expect to directly challenge the prime rat for leadership. And as I see it, entry at the second level is just as impossible. We have to plan our attack at the lowest level."

"But we infiltrated the pack by two agents at the lowest level and failed. How do you explain that?"

"Your agents were recruited at the lowest level. Right?"

"Right."

"Their profiles can tell us the most about these members."

"But they were killed. What can that tell us?"

"It gives us the behavioral profile of what the Rat Pack wants for their cut level members."

THIRTY-SIX

A QUICK PEE BREAK AND they were at it again. By the time they returned, their empty dishes had disappeared. A freshly iced six-pack and chips were in their place. Siegal no longer responded to these invisible helpers, accepting them as part of Danielson's effort to make him comfortable.

"Now who exactly were the slain agents?" asked Siegal.

"Que?"

"You know. Not their names, ranks and serial numbers. Why were they unique, chosen to be part of the Rat Pack and then to be slain? It was no accident in both cases."

Danielson thumbed through the case files he brought. "Agent One, born of black, indentured servants mining blood diamonds in western Australia. Father died in a cave-in when he was three. His athletic skills brought him to America on a basketball scholarship at Iowa University, graduating with a 3.8 GPA. The Company..."

"Company?" asked Siegal.

"CIA. They invited him to become an agent and he accepted. He returned to his home country undercover and became associated with anti-government youth movements." Danielson flipped to another page. "His mission in the Rat Pack was to identify the leadership. He became involved in the hijacking at Alice Springs and was later murdered during their escape from Cairo."

"And Agent Two?" asked Siegal.

"Agent Two has a very different background," said Danielson, flipping through the second dossier. "She was raised by her father and grandmother after her mother abandoned the family." Scanning the next page, Danielson added, "Once divorced, then widowed. While in college, she took several classes in Chinese languages, worked at the campus newspaper and wrote many articles on women's issues. She dropped out before graduating. The Company brought her on deck and sent her to China. As directed, she continued writing on women's oppression when accepted into the Rat Pack. She became part of the pod that raided Lijiang. Do you see any comparisons?"

"Slow down. You read what you thought were the pertinent highlights. You're editing too much. I need more understanding of them. It seems, on the surface, the two had few similarities. We have to dig deeper."

"Let's go at it again. Both only knew one parent. Agent One knew only his mother, growing up as a slave. The mother of Agent Two abandoned the family before she was a year old."

Siegal scratched his thinning hair and said, "That could be a common clue. Family lifestyles have major effects on how people react to the world. Simi's observations showed similar behaviors in rats when parents were absent early on and the young were required to fend for themselves. In several instances, these rats became misfits. They had little respect for others in their cage and developed few social bonds with their counterparts."

"Are you trying to say the CIA accidentally put the right people into the terrorist groups without even knowing why?"

"Not exactly, Tom. The CIA didn't do the placing. What really happened is, those two individuals had certain behavior styles fitting the patterns that gained them acceptance at the lowest level. Both insertions were pure dumb luck on your part."

"Son of a bitch. If they were freely selected, why were they killed?" asked Danielson.

"Tom, we have to explore the level for which they were inducted. Your agents had profiles that were comfortable to those who did the recruiting."

"Let me see what kind of student I am. Lowest-level members are inducted as pure followers and are supposed to act that way."

"And the clue here is 'Supposed to act that way,'" said Siegal. "Something about them was inconsistent with the rest. Unlike the other inductees, your moles had a mission that took them out of being passive at different times."

"I get it. Their efforts to get information made them less than passive. But how did the Rat Pack get the passive inductees to perform aggressive acts? That sounds inconsistent. Passive types performing aggressive acts?"

"Passive types and aggressive acts are not mutually exclusive. How often have you read where mild neighbors suddenly take hostages and have firefights with the police?"

"What you're saying is that passive behavior is only the outer coat of a person, and the aggressiveness they are capable of showing is an internal style probably based on pent-up anger."

"And previous experiences, don't forget."

"How predictable do you think these dual sets of behaviors are within animals in general?"

"Very. I see no reason to consider human behavior to be any different than that of any other warm-blooded animal. We need to go back to step one and understand why your two agents were recruited, and their particular behaviors."

Danielson obliged, picked up a paper from Agent One's packet, and read aloud. "Just prior to recruitment, he participated in several counterrevolutionary activities. He carried flags, handed out leaflets, and marched in several illegal parades changing loyalties from one cause or another that focused on any anti-government activity." Danielson flipped to a new page. "He was arrested once for civil disobedience."

Siegal said, "And while often assuming a cheerleading role for different causes, did he ever seek a leadership position?"

Danielson shook his head. "Doesn't seem so."

"That's important. Certainly fits a personality type the Rat Pack would like to recruit. Your young man showed anger but with no specific cause to follow. All he appeared to need was a push. Almost any cause against a government would do."

Danielson concluded, "You're saying it's easy to recruit someone who is out of the mainstream and generally hates authority. What other clues do you think he displayed?"

"Being a political activist is important, but not enough by itself. My guess is he pretended to be a loner, staying on the edge of social groups without actually joining. Maslo, my favorite behavioral psychologist, said, 'Group inclusion is a strong motivator in humans.' It wouldn't take much for a lonely person to alter his or her focus toward any terrorist leanings."

Danielson said, "Okay. Fact: our man pretended anger, frustration, and other similar symptoms about the political problems when he was recruited. Fact: he acted as a loner. Fact: he may have accepted a few perks, possibly sex, money, or recognition. All made him a prime candidate for group inclusion."

The logs in the fireplace had burned and the room cooled. By contrast, two men of differing backgrounds and ideologies welded themselves into a consummate counterstrike team.

It was after midnight and hunger drew them toward the kitchen for any kind of junk food. Instead, they found two plates of hamburgers and fries on the table made by their unseen servants. Taking their bounty back to the living room, they refueled themselves and the fire.

Siegal swallowed a mouthful. "Tell me more about the history of Agent Two. The differences between the profiles of the two were obvious. It's the subtle similarities that will prove more enlightening."

Danielson scanned the second report again. "Agent Two, married twice. First one ended in divorce and the second ended because of a fatal auto-racing accident." He looked up. "We can count the emotional trauma of losing two husbands while still in her twenties."

"Abandonment. We had two actual rebels. They didn't have to fake this part. This second one, besides her Chinese language skills, why did the Company hire her?"

"I'm not sure. It seems she applied to the CIA for training and consistently received high marks. Though without a college degree, they wanted a second look because of her facility in Chinese dialects. They attempted several times to place her in a team with no success. It's noted here that no one wanted to partner with her. CIA was about to cut her loose. Just about that time, intel informed CIA of some antigovernment activity in China. The company took a chance on her to infiltrate the pod. As with Agent One, she was instructed to get involved in some political action groups as a cover."

"Was she able to give you any useful information?"

Danielson frowned. "No such luck. They plucked her off the street the day before the Lijiang raid. My guess is that from that moment, she was never left alone."

"Not luck. Every behavior has an explainable basis. She played a young angry rebel with antigovernment leanings. The Rat Pack saw her that way."

Danielson sat back in his chair and stretched. "I think we've cut the terrorist recruitment guesswork down a lot. Getting new infiltrators should be a hell of a lot easier."

"Now we move to step two," said Siegal. "You want me to make a high-percentage determination in selecting future embeds. That's not possible. We're dealing in probabilities. Have other CIA recruits been killed?"

"Good question. I'll call my sources and see what they have on questionable deaths at or near any youth hostels around the world."

Siegal's mind kept going back to his experimental rats, especially ones that were killed. "Their initial behaviors were acceptable at first. It was only after they were welcomed into the pack that the head rat felt negative vibes."

Danielson asked, "Like what? Our agents were recruited because their demeanor fit the mold. They were trained operatives and should have been able to hide the fact they were plants, but they failed."

Siegal asked, "What was the agents' mission?"

"Our plants were supposed to discover names of second-level members, the leader, and, if possible, find their home base that we could attack and destroy."

"How successful do you think they were?"

"Zip. Nada. They only told us they were accepted. They had no time to tell us much more," said Danielson. "They blew their cover in some way. Just like your laboratory rats when they no longer fit the roles within the pack and were done away with. It's likely any other terrorists were killed for the very same reason. Being an agent or not was of no consequence to the head rat."

Siegal rubbed a cramp in his leg from sitting so long. "Do you feel the reports back to you were intercepted in any way?"

Danielson shook his head. "Not a chance."

"Do you have any information on the slain cut group members who were not your guys?"

"Not at the moment," answered Danielson. "Do you think it's important?"

"Duh. I'll wager they asked too many questions. It follows the old phrase, 'Curiosity killed the cat.'"

Danielson glanced out the window. They sky was getting lighter. He looked at his watch. "Hell. It's morning already. I need some coffee."

Siegal exited to the kitchen. Fresh coffee was on the counter along with some warm, cream cheese-slathered bagels on a tray. Danielson put more logs on the fire and turned on the television to catch the news.

This is Frank Gallow, anchor for MSNBC, reporting. Images of a fiery street scene flashed across the screen. Sirens were evident in the background. "Last evening, President Galdet's limousine and a single armored escort were attacked when a mysterious black van loaded with explosives rammed the escort car and blew it up. We were told that Galdet's car barely escaped the scene by reversing direction and speeding down a side street.

The explosion blew out store windows and injured several pedestrians on the street. The extent of deaths and injured is still unknown at this time. We do know for sure the two men in the escort car were killed instantly in the large fireball. Official word from President Galdet's press office is sketchy at best.

The TV displayed images of emergency personnel treating the wounded.

"All we know at this time is there was no provocation for the assault. No organization as yet has taken responsibility. We will break into regular programming as new information surfaces."

Siegal frowned. "Is this our terrorist at work?

Danielson nodded. "We've been blindsided. I got word of this incident by phone text from Amanda Keyes during one of our breaks. It tells me the clock is ticking."

THIRTY-SEVEN

WILD DREAMS BROUGHT ON BY sitting in one position for so many hours jarred Siegal from his sleep. He woke and heard Danielson's muffled voice in the dining room. "What's going on?"

"After you fell asleep, I made calls to the SOS at the request of President Galdet. I'm scheduling a conference call in your situation room fifty minutes from now. I was just about to wake you so we'd have enough time to clean up and have breakfast. I ordered some grub."

Comforting smells of hot coffee and covered dishes holding eggs, bacon, and fried potatoes produced by the unseen caretakers filled the entire main floor.

The flat screen in the dining room blinked to life as scheduled. The split screen showed all five world leaders ready for the meeting. Danielson spoke first. There was no pretense in his words. "I appreciate that all of you took time to meet on such short notice at the request of President Galdet."

Galdet spent the next ten minutes in Q&A with the others on the screen. He concluded by asking what Dr. Siegal had to say.

Siegal thought for a moment. "Something's bothering me about the attack. I think I understand why the plane was hijacked. And we know why they raided Lijiang to steal a secret virus. But why didn't the terrorist use this V-32 virus against President Galdet? He had the lethal weapon. And he didn't use it."

"And you conclude?" asked Sokoloven.

"Seems as though they have little control on how to use it."

President Cho-Se answered, "I agree with Dr. Siegal. They would have to be in close proximity to their target. Using it like a crop duster or a bomb is too inaccurate for this narrow a target."

Siegal agreed. "My thoughts exactly. As I suggested in our last meeting, an old-fashioned bug sprayer could be very effective. But it would be one hundred percent fatal to the users. Of course, this wouldn't worry either the head rat or his second level leaders. Their cut groups are nothing but throwaways; small collateral damage."

King Ishmere said, "Maybe they needed handheld launcher devices that could dispense the virus to a specific location. I am aware of rocket launchers used for roadside bombings. They can be fired with very little training."

"So they just buy some of these launchers where they get their explosives," said Sokoloven.

"Not so simple," said Danielson. "The ones you speak of are not equipped to handle a gas-borne virus. Such launchers are not easily available. I doubt any are on the open market."

President Russell changed the conversation back to the attack on President Galdet. "Could you determine the attack auto's ownership?"

President Galdet nodded. "To our best knowledge, the van was stolen the day of the raid from a rental agency. There was no license plate on it, but the serial number on the motor helped us locate where it came from. We think the agency owner is not suspect, but we are investigating his employees to see if they in any way assisted in the theft."

King Ishmere continued. "Tell us about the explosive used."

President Galdet answered, "The detonator is a common impact device. They used a plastic explosive, also common."

Siegal made sure President Galdet completed his answer. "Excuse me for breaking in again. I hope I'm not interfering with any protocol. I may be able to help in this part of our investigation. I think being suspicious about the dealership's employees makes sense. I would like more information about them. Chairman Danielson and I have compiled a list of personality factors and personal lifestyles we found common for the two slain agents. You will want to compare all of the rental agency employees with this list of factors. If they were involved, their personalities will jump out."

President Sokoloven asked, "One more time, Dr. Siegal. Do you believe this incident was instigated by our terrorist in question, or just another French malcontent?"

Siegal nodded. "The probability is our new terrorist group, which I like to call the Rat Pack, is involved. Chairman Danielson is right about intel which focuses on Europe. With due respect, President Galdet, France, I believe, is the logical focus based on your political climate and parliamentary style of government."

"What else do you surmise?" continued Sokoloven.

Siegal said, "Our terrorist likes to take small steps at a time. I believe this attack was a small step of something greater. President Galdet's entourage was an unprotected target. If he wanted, the president would be dead now. There is more to his plan than an assassination. He wants you, President Galdet, alive for some greater purpose. I believe he will attack you again and your country. More deadly next time."

The room was silent as if waiting for further direction.

"Does anyone have further questions for Dr. Siegal?" asked Chairman Danielson.

Sokoloven spoke. "I have a question. Dr. Siegal, where do you think that takes us? You tell us to consider this as the third of a series of known acts by this Rat Pack, as you call it. It focused directly on one of us. Let us ponder for a moment that the attack was not directed at President Galdet personally. It could have happened to anyone here equally."

Danielson frowned. "A good thought. Dr. Siegal, do you feel all three attacks have a similar purpose?"

Siegal nodded. "We already know this terrorist has the imagination to draft and execute complicated plans. President Cho-Se indicated the virus, taken during the Lijiang raid, has to be delivered efficiently to affect its full strength and killing capability for a few hours. Putting it in the water supply, for example, would probably kill only the fish in the area. I believe this virus has to be focused directly at the intended target. The good news is that he did not use it on that raid in France. This tells me he does not have the capability to use it as a weapon at this time. Once he has this capability, we can expect a deadly strike, and my instincts tell me he will repeat his attacks in France."

"The terrorist will need sophisticated hand-held launchers to carry the virus, yet simple and mobile enough for anyone to use," added Danielson. "Research and development scientists have developed such a launcher in the United States. The terrorist will need to procure them from one of our armories. This is actually good news. For the first time, we can plan ahead and not wait to react. Using Dr. Siegal's characteristics of people this terrorist is seeking to recruit, we can find several possibles with similar profiles near those facilities. With luck, we can short-circuit the Rat Pack's plans."

The screen went black. The meeting was over.

Siegal felt a lump grow in his throat. "Tom, is there anything else you haven't told me about this virus? Does an antidote exist?"

Danielson shrugged his shoulders. "You know most everything about how deadly V-32 is. And yes, there is a vaccine, but it is only effective if provided by an IV infusion before coming into contact with the virus itself. As far as we know, none was taken during the raid. Which means the Rat Pack doesn't have any of it."

"I don't think that will deter the head rat, who could care less about what happens to his cut groups," said a frowning Siegal. "He's already discovered they're easy to replace. You can bet the cut groups go in unaware of their fate and become suicide squads. That fate may be the same for his second-tier members." He took a deep breath. "And our next step?"

Danielson clapped his hands. "All we need to do is identify locals where our launching systems are stored, train them as informants, and get them to infiltrate the organization. If any of them are tapped, we'll know where our rat is about to attack."

"And you plan to do this, how?"

"Do you remember my headhunters I used to discover you? I can have them onboard in hours. They'll do the identifying legwork."

"And if my characteristics are faulty? Or, if I'm totally wrong about everything?"

"There's no 'I' in 'we.'" If you are wrong, than I am just as accountable."

"Then what happens?"

"Remember the talk we had with President Russell?"

"You said that once I agree, there is no backing out. You said I would have to be reprogrammed or…"

"Worse?" Danielson nodded. "Members of the Summit are not a very forgiving bunch. Some have been known to make their mistakes disappear. You can't be wrong, Dr. Ross Siegal. Our lives depend on it."

THIRTY-EIGHT

DANIELSON ROSE EARLY THE NEXT morning and left the chalet without saying goodbye. Siegal awoke alone with only his thoughts of an unknown terrorist armed with a deadly virus, Danielson's chilling message from the night before, and his one true ally, Tigger.

He punched the remote on his bedroom television to offer some human sound bites as he dressed. The morning news was on. Across the bottom scrolled the local time, temperature, and date. The most compelling number was the date. Siegal realized he had been involved with this project, both as an unwilling soldier and now the lead planner, for almost six weeks.

"Tigger, I remember the good old days when I wanted nothing more than to be a professor of psychology and a behavioral researcher. Gone. It was a wonderful life. All gone. If I proposed to Simi last summer, would my life be any different? No. What is bashert is bashert, Yiddish for destiny. All this would have happened no matter."

The television in the living room blared on:

Elsewhere in the world, follow-up investigation of the suicide bombing in France continues. The French government is downplaying the seriousness of the event. They conclude that an independent group of malcontents who do not favor President Galdet's economic policies are demonstrating their political opposition. In the meantime, a state funeral is planned for the two honored guards killed in the explosion. This is Robert Gallow for MSNBC.

Siegal flipped through the other available channels. *Nothing of interest.* He clicked the power button. The silence was broken by a pair of mountain canaries chirping in a tree just outside his bedroom window. Their peaceful joy was in sharp contrast to the dark thoughts that ran rampant in his mind.

"Tigger, did you hear how they broadcast the bombing? They say political activists did it. Government spin to downplay a national crisis. Another reason why I hate politics. By being associated with the SOS, I am now just as guilty as those spin doctors."

The symbolism of Danielson not saying goodbye impressed on Siegal just how alone he was. To reorganize his mind, he taped a new sheet of large paper on the wall and scribbled the tasks at hand:

1. Wait for confirmation from the headhunters.
2. Wait for a list of military installations that have weapons capable of delivering the virus.
3. Improve upon the profile that will enhance probability of selecting desirable recruits.
4. Put meat on the bones about the Rat Pack.
5. Get my mind out of Simi's crotch.

He pointed to Tigger. "How nice it would be to go over the list with my research assistants. Well, I bargained for this isolation and now I have it, like it or not."

Siegal studied his tasks. Items one and two had to wait for later. He started on items three and four, adding all the subtasks he could think to list.

"Item five is no longer in play, Tigger. Maybe someday when this is all over."

Siegal put up another sheet and wrote "Biological Characteristics."

He stared at the two words for the better part of an hour with no success.

"Brain, don't abandon me now. Maybe my computer can help me." He typed in several key words. Finally, ideas began to flow.

Age: young adult between the ages of 18-33
Stature: average to slightly underweight but not anorexic
Height: men 5'5" to 6'0"; women 5'2" to 5'7"
Appearance: nothing that makes them stand out in a crowd
Sex: orientation not important but probably heterosexual.
    Not important but common
Ethnic: to the youth population of that particular
Location of activity
Health: no noticeable health problems
Intelligence: bright but not attaining potential
Religion: little if any

"Tigger, our list is useless. It fits more than eighty percent of the population in the eighteen to thirty-year age range. Add a couple of years on either side and the possibilities are even greater. The rest of my list better be much more exclusified." He laughed. *Exclusified: not a real word but it certainly fits where I am taking my thinking.*

He typed socio-economic factors of terrorist members. He post-ed results on a new page.

Parents: probably a single parent background
Financial: usually enough money to not be concerned
    with survival
Education: at least some college education and majoring
    in humanities areas. May also be a continuous college
    student with no degree prospects
Home: raised in a middle to lower-upper class value home
    setting
Work: almost none as a youth as an adult usually not
    working or only part-time employment

"Now we're getting somewhere, Tigger. I can pare our list of recruits down to maybe twenty-five percent of the world. Not good enough yet. But it's coming."

From the data he collected and the profiles of the two dead agents, Siegal started a third list to include mental aspects of cut group prospects.

Political: came out of a conservative family background
Thinking: wants to change the world for the better
Organizations: supports activist groups against any
    government no matter who is in power, anti authority
Causes: often global in nature but also can become
    concerned with local issues
Criminal: may have some arrests but only for minor
History: civil disobedience, shoplifting, loitering and drugs
Involvement: usually a follower and never a leader
Motivators: being accepted without being challenged

free love or no love, money is not a primary
motivator
Socially: probably a loner or part of a very small
social circle

Siegal backed away from the wall. His neck was stiff from star-ing. He wiped his forehead with his sleeve, now wet from concentra-tion. He had stood the entire day, not even sitting for lunch. Was he missing anything? He felt confident that he was down to five or ten percent of the world population. His error probability was equal. He had accomplished what the SOS had set for him. It wasn't enough for him.

"Now, Mr. Danielson, it's up to you so find enough people to identify in all the possible attack sights. Find agency people who both fit the profile and are clever enough not to get caught."

Siegal went into the kitchen and reached in the refrigerator for a fresh ODL. The six-pack he started yesterday was spent. He started a new one.

Siegal gazed at his calendar. It was Thursday. He called Danielson to report his refinements to selecting possible imbeds.

"I'll get back to you," responded Danielson.

AT TWO A.M., a ringing in his ears woke Siegal's uneasy sleep.

"Hello?"

"Be ready to be in Washington as soon as possible. Your driver will take you to the airport. I will pick you up at Dulles International. Bring all your notes."

PART FOUR

LET THE SOLDIER BE ABROAD if he will, he can do nothing in this age. There is another personage—a personage less imposing in the eyes of some, perhaps insignificant. The schoolmaster is abroad, and I trust him, armed with his primer, against the soldier in full military array.

Lord Henry Peter Brougham, January 29, 1828

THIRTY-NINE

SIEGAL SAT AT THE DESK, sorting his notes for his trip to see Danielson. A knock on the door broke his concentration. He opened it to see his favorite linebacker standing a full two inches above the jam.

"We have to leave now to make your flight, sir. Sometimes the traffic gets pretty heavy and with increased airport security, better to be a little early than miss the plane."

SIEGAL SHOWED DISAPPOINTMENT as he read Denver International's lighted departure schedules.

Not again. Rain delay.

The last time this happened, it was a command performance by Danielson under the guise of a secret funding agency for his research grant. Siegal attempted to avoid that trip. This time was different. Today he was totally aware of the stakes. He had to wait.

Almost every chair at Gate 45 on Concourse C was taken by people awaiting the delayed takeoff. He found a seat and opened a Jeffery Deaver thriller bought at the bookstore. His inner instinct caused him to look up. A bearded man stared his way.

I'm being watched. Someone's here to assassinate me? Or is it an SOS member's death squad?

The stranger activated a cell phone and spoke into it. Siegal wished his linebacker was here instead of driving away after dropping him off at the departure door. The stranger rose from his seat and moved toward him. Siegal readied his briefcase as a shield.

You're not taking me easy.

From behind Siegal, a woman and child stood as the mystery man joined them.

False alarm. *Next I'll be imagining the Red Baron dropping bombs on the tarmac. Another 9/11.*

Finally, an announcement over the loud speaker, "Nonstop flight to Washington is now boarding at Gate 45."

AT DULLES INTERNATIONAL, Siegal retrieved his luggage at the revolving carousel and went outside to the passenger arrival area where Danielson waited. They drove directly to the Marriott and checked in.

"I'm very glad you made it so quickly. I know it's late, but would you like to share some dinner?"

"I'm tired. Maybe a sandwich in the room. That is, if you don't have any surprises planned."

"No special agenda for tonight. Have your sandwich. We'll meet in your hotel for breakfast. Say, eight o'clock. We can talk then. I've scheduled a late lunch at this nice little restaurant I know. The house specialty is tuna casserole. The next day you meet my head-hunters," added Danielson. "See you tomorrow."

SIEGAL RETREATED TO his room, undressed, put on a mono-grammed bathrobe and lay down on his king-sized bed. He spotted a late edition of the *Washington Post* on his nightstand. One head-line followed by a short blurb caught his attention.

TWO MEN WERE APPREHENDED LAST NIGHT IN FRANCE FOR THE ATTEMPTED ASSASSINATION OF PRESIDENT GALDET

The French secret police carried on a high-speed firefight with two suspected political activists as they were attempt-ing to cross into Italy. Both were shot and killed.

"Nice spin, Galdet."
Ross turned to the business pages, which put him right to sleep.

THE ROOM PHONE rang. He answered and listened to an auto-mated message. "Good morning, Dr. Siegal. It is seven o'clock." A quick shower, shave, and then breakfast with Danielson.

Siegal picked up his briefcase crammed full of notes and walked to the elevator. Downstairs he was led to a private breakfast room. Danielson was already there.

The hostess greeted Siegal and directed him to the empty chair across from Danielson.

"Good morning, Ross. You slept well?"

Siegal nodded. "Thank goodness there was a wakeup call. This sea-level air makes me tired."

"I get the same feeling in Colorado. Hungry?"

"You bet. Any suggestions?"

"I have been told their pancakes and waffles almost float off the plate."

"Then waffles with strawberries it is."

Danielson nodded and picked up the phone on the table. "We'll have two orders of waffles with strawberries." Turning to Siegal, he asked, "Do you want bacon or sausages?"

"Sausages."

"Put a side order of link turkey sausages on each, please."

Ten minutes later a waitress brought their breakfast, refilled their coffee, and left them to their privacy. This was the first time Siegal had ever had breakfast ordered by phone in a restaurant. He tried not to act impressed, but his smile told it all.

After cleaning their plates of every last morsel, Danielson called the waitress, who promptly picked up the dishes, scraped leftover crumbs from the tablecloth and left.

Breakfast was over. The business meeting started.

"Tell me what we have, Ross?"

Siegal opened his briefcase and extracted his notes on descriptive characteristics of possibles for the Rat Pack.

Danielson looked them over. His experienced eyes absorbed the information in moments.

"Looks good. How do you feel about them?"

"Well, I think from this list we can identify candidates with reasonable accuracy."

"How much is reasonable?"

"Offhand and without field-testing my conclusions, I would say between seventy and eighty percent."

"Not good enough. How many possibles would you say we would need to assure one will be chosen?"

"Don't really know. I would imagine six or eight would raise the success rate pretty high."

"Still not one hundred percent, Ross?" Danielson frowned. "Putting eight agents with the desired characteristics in our focus locations in such a short time can be tough." Siegal felt like Danielson knew the logistics were next to impossible.

"Remember what your original embeds were doing when they were picked?" asked Siegal. "Our terrorist will most likely pick their recruits the same way. All we need to do is to plant the right people in the right places at the right time, and we have it made." Siegal snapped his fingers. "Simple."

Danielson nodded. "I have a plan that involves my headhunt- ers. I need to have your notes duplicated first." Danielson made a call on his cell phone and a messenger from the hotel picked up the notes, was given instruction, and left without a word. "It's about eleven. Would you like to see the city?"

Siegal nodded. "If we have time."

"Our next meeting is for late afternoon. We have a little time." Danielson signed the restaurant tab and the two walked outside and climbed into the rear seats of a black SUV. Danielson played tour guide.

"I think of this city as America's Mount Olympus." He pointed to Washington's Obelisk, Lincoln's Memorial, and Jefferson's Tomb. "These I think of as memorials to our greatest gods. The large of- fice complexes are sites of our lower gods. And that pink marble structure," he pointed to the DAR office building. "I think of it as the Temple of the Vestal Virgins. What do you think? Isn't it all so beautiful and magnificent here?"

"What? Sorry, I wasn't listening. I was thinking about something else."

"And?"

"Every time you attempted to embed agents, they were killed before providing useful information. What makes you think that, even with your headhunters, you'll do a better job? Whoever you choose, they will be easy to spot."

"Where is this going? You mean we are doomed to failure?"

"Of people living in the area, many will have level-three Rat Pack characteristics. The problem will be in training them to be our informants. Remember, one of their common characteristics is their dislike for government authority. I think they would refuse to cooperate with you."

The dialogue continued well into the afternoon with only questions and no answers.

"There has to be some way," pondered Danielson.

FORTY

AT PRECISELY FOUR P.M. EDT, the SUV driver maneuvered through a series of iron gates, each protected by military guards, and stopped at a side door to a large building.

Siegal turned to Danielson. "The White House?"

Danielson nodded. "We're about to have lunch."

A guard opened their door and greeted them by name. "Follow me, sirs." He led them through a maze of corridors stopping at a small elevator. "This will take you to the Oval Office." He unlocked the cage door and left.

EVELYN KEYES, THE president's secretary, looked up as they entered. "Good afternoon Mr. Danielson. And you too, Dr. Siegal." She touched a button on her intercom and waited for the white light to blink. "You can go in now."

"Ross, it's good to see you again. I trust the weather in Colorado is still something to yearn for. I keep telling my wife we should move there after I leave office."

Tom waited a respectful amount of time for the comments by the president to run their course. "Let me bring you up to speed, El. Our plans have been going forward. We are embarking on a two-pronged move. First, a plan to get some possible recruits into the Rat Pack, as Ross calls them. We're also starting to put a head on our terrorist and on his goal."

"First things first, Tom. I feel we need to discover their next target or targets and attempt…no, not attempt. We need to stop their next action."

"I just thought…"

Turning to Siegal, Russell asked, "What does the good doctor have to say?"

"Well, I have tried to understand the gestalt, the big picture, of the entire organization. There are three discrete levels. Level three is the cut groups who do all the dirty work. Level two is the tellers collecting cut group inductees and directing them. Level one includes the king rat, who remains unknown to all but his innermost circle."

"I like it so far, Ross," replied the president. "Tell me more."

"It is impossible to infiltrate level one and almost as impossible getting into level two. Our concentration is on level three as the most logical entry point."

"I agree," said Russell, "we have to put out the fire first before looking for the match that started it. And hopefully not get any agents burned in the process. Where are we now?"

"Excuse me just a minute, gentlemen," said Danielson. He left the room and asked Ms. Keys for some papers, the ones he gave the messenger at the restaurant. He returned and handed the president a copy of Siegal's notes.

"These are the characteristics of possibles our terrorist likes to recruit. Ross gave them to me at breakfast, and I had them sent over to the most confidential secretary I knew on short notice for duplication."

President Russell laughed. "You used my personal secretary? However, under the circumstances, Evelyn is the best choice for maintaining confidentiality."

As Russell examined the notes, a gentleman in a white coat brought in a rolling table containing their late lunch. The main course was predictable, tuna casserole, the president's favorite dish. The white-coated gentleman silently set three places and served out healthy-sized portions. As a topper, he opened three bottles of Old Dog's Leg and poured them into tall, frosted flutes. He left as quietly as he came.

Siegal, not having eaten since early morning, was hungry. He visually measured the remaining portion on the tray to see if there was a possibility for second portions.

The president laughed. "Don't worry, Ross, if we run out of food, I can order some more. I know the maitre d'."

They ate in silence. At the same time, the president reviewed the notes.

"Is this list any good? We can't afford the luxury of a mistake. We have to jump in with both feet and hope it's water and not quicksand. How do you feel about this set of attributes, Tom?"

"Ross is the person we chose for determining them and we have no better option than to go along with his thinking."

"I agree. The Summit placed their trust in this starving man here who is now on his third plate of tuna casserole and second bottle of beer. Ross, continue."

Siegal swallowed, "Well, sir, as I told Mr. Danielson, if we selected six to eight people and placed them in the recruiter's area, the chances of one of them being selected is pretty good."

President Russell asked, "Then why don't we identify fifteen or twenty instead?"

Danielson responded, "We can try for more, but we just don't know how many good choices we can find. Most of our agents are older than their most-likely recruits."

"Where do we go from here?" asked President Russell.

"El, we need to determine locations in which to focus our attention and see if we can cut down our options."

"I can help you there. At the last SOS meeting, you suggested the terrorist needs a handheld device that can launch V-32 at close range, one that's easy to use. There are two locations where we store them, plus one secret place where we keep one-of—kind prototypes, all in the United States. If the terrorist is thinking of needing a whole arsenal, the third site is an unlikely target."

Danielson said, "Good. Focusing on just two sites makes our job a helluva lot easier."

President Russell asked, "Any suggestions?"

Two pairs of eyes turned toward Siegal. "We need recruits from the community. Not Company agents. But we can't have them contact us in any manner."

"How do you propose we make it work?"

The question came from both the president and Danielson in almost a rehearsed fashion.

Siegal continued, "Is there any way we can identify possibles already in the area without them ever knowing they were selected by us?"

The president grinned. "I like it. We locate likely candidates almost as if we were the Rat Pack and put a tail on each one."

"Forget it," interjected Danielson. "We don't have enough of a time window. And besides, being antigovernment, they would never work for us anyway. Also, too many strangers at one local could alert the Rat Pack."

Siegal added, "Maybe once they're recruited, we identify the level-two recruiters and track them instead."

Danielson said, "Seems like a stretch. We knew when our agents were recruited and we still couldn't track them to anyone higher."

"Maybe we need to track them in a different way. For the rats in our lab at the university, we implanted electronic chips in their brains and read changes in their activity levels. Maybe we could install some sort of emotional monitoring device on the recruits without having them know. We could determine when they were being called into action."

"Nice try, Ross," said Danielson. "I just don't think we can implant something in their brains without them knowing."

President Russell concluded, "Maybe we don't need electronics that sophisticated, Tom. Maybe all we have to do is place a simple tracking system on them and keep following the signal's whereabouts. Then when they're called upon to move to a unique location, we use that as a clue that something is about to happen."

Siegal scratched his head, "Electronic surveillance and implants on humans? Like Star Wars technology."

"Have you forgotten," said Danielson, "how we can hone in on anyone's privacy, including yours?"

"I remember. But just how do you plan to put probes on these recruits without them knowing about it?"

"That'll be my problem, Ross," said Danielson.

President Russell took a final swallow of his drink. "It sounds like this meeting is over." Turning to Siegal, "Oh, yes, Tom tells me you will be meeting with his headhunter team tomorrow. Believe me, they're pretty good. They found you. By the way, do any of you have plans for tonight? I am having a few guests over to hear a jazz concert in the main living room. You're both invited."

Danielson begged off. Siegal accepted, due more to his curiosity about who gets to be a guest at the White House than in listening to the concert.

THE EVENT PROVED an enlightening evening for Siegal. He was introduced to several visiting dignitaries from countries he didn't even know existed. Jazz was his favorite and the late dessert was excellent. He was back at the hotel by midnight, left a wakeup call at the desk, and had one thought before falling asleep. *Tomorrow's meeting will be very different.*

FORTY-ONE

DAYLIGHT DIDN'T COME EARLIER ON the East Coast. It only seemed that way to Siegal, who lived two time zones west. He tried to stretch his morning sleep a little more. Not knowing exactly what Danielson had in mind for him made him uneasy. A knock on the door at seven-fifteen eliminated the last chance for any respite.

"Room service, Dr. Siegal. I have a fresh pot of coffee, pumpernickel bagel, cream cheese and lox for you, sir."

Siegal put on his initialed bathrobe, a courtesy extended for the hotel's celebrity guests, and lumbered to the door.

A white-coated server from catering entered and placed the food tray on the desk. "A table in the private dining room is available if you choose to eat there."

"This is fine. Thank you…" Siegal eyed the server's name badge and added, "…Miguel."

Turning on some piped-in music, he relaxed by the window as he ate, but the time change was his enemy and his eyes closed.

The room phone rang again. "It's ten-thirty, Dr. Siegal. Your transportation is here."

He hurried. Previous experience reminded him how Danielson hated to be kept waiting.

Danielson sat in his personal car, no limousine. They exchanged short salutations and were off.

After an hour's ride through the city and into Maryland, they arrived at the Smoking Musket restaurant. Only a few cars were parked in the lot.

"Is this some special place of historical significance that I should have had in my tour guide?"

"Actually, most of us in Washington have developed these special private meeting places. It's good for the restaurant business, but more importantly, it helps to keep security at these meetings. The headwaiters usually know everyone who comes in and can spot unwelcome visitors. This little place is my hideaway."

"Let me see. You have a private chalet in Colorado and now a restaurant. To just how many places do you claim ownership?"

"I don't own any of them, not even a piece. From my time in the White House, I have hideaways like this all over the world. Besides, the food here is excellent."

They left the car with a valet and walked into the restaurant. It appeared smaller on the inside than on the outside. Siegal guessed that the space concealed several private dining areas.

The headwaiter nodded to Danielson as they came in. "Your table for six is right this way, sir." He led them to one of the several private rooms.

Impressed, Siegal sensed the immensity of Washington's complex insider agencies and how easy Danielson flowed through them. Up until now, everything he experienced seemed detached; this super-spy involvement, definitely surreal.

Siegal perceived there were many more sides of Danielson to discover. He began to develop an earned trust for the person, and didn't understand why. This man who looked so ordinary could easily disappear in a crowd, but was on a first-name basis with the president and who else? *Just how powerful is he?*

"Have my friends arrived?" Danielson asked the headwaiter.

"Not yet, sir."

To Siegal it was like a movie. Only this was in real time.

"Is everyone always this accommodating when they deal with you, Tom?"

"Usually, but remember, I'm the one paying the bill. In this city, everyone bends over twice for the green stuff." He changed the subject. "Do you want a drink or something?"

"Coffee."

Danielson signed a coffee-pouring gesture, a letter "C" on his lips, and their waiter brought a freshly-brewed pot of the house private blend.

The light from the front entrance glared into the subdued ambience of the restaurant. It blocked the facial features of the group coming in. In a moment, four figures approached the table.

Danielson spoke, "Good afternoon, everyone. Please sit down."

A waiter brought everyone water and coffee.

"Let me introduce all of you," said Danielson.

Siegal recognized two as visitors to Quandary's. The same two he saw in the ID office at least twice.

"For security reasons, I prefer we leave last names out. Ross, meet my infamous headhunters, Jamie, Doug, Kevin and Tim." Each nodded after their names were mentioned.

Siegal reviewed his past encounters with them. Their dress code had not changed. The woman, Jamie, dressed the sharpest. Doug wore inexpensive-looking clothes that didn't quite fit. Kevin and Tim could easily have been lost in a crowd of three.

Danielson continued. "Ross and I have a problem, and you four are the best in the business for solving it."

The lady, as in Ravid's office, spoke first. Siegal thought she must be the leader. "What do you have in mind, Mr. Danielson?"

"Here it is in a nutshell." Danielson leaned forward for emphasis. "We need you to locate a few special people in two locations here in the U.S."

"That doesn't sound too difficult. How many is a few and what's the catch?" she asked.

"The catch is time and accuracy. Yesterday is my deadline. At least one of the few in each location has to be selected for membership by an organization we would like to tune into."

Doug, Mr. Odd Clothes, as Siegal nicknamed him, said, "Tell us about the organization; this doesn't sound too difficult."

Danielson shrugged, "We don't know the organization yet or what their exact plans are, but it is absolutely essential that we find them."

Mr. Odd Clothes continued, "It sounds like you're trying to infiltrate a terrorist group of some kind."

The statement went unanswered.

The conversation continued. Siegal sat amazed at how much the five of them understood each other and the shared understanding that the headhunters know as little as possible. It was not in Danielson's game plan for them to know too much at any one time, and they accepted that.

After a few moments, Jamie asked, "How do you want us to proceed?"

Danielson said, "You all remember when you selected Dr. Siegal for us. His special skills have been very valuable. One of the things he has done is to develop a list of characteristics that should help you identify these individuals."

Danielson opened his briefcase and handed each of the head-hunters the same set of Siegal's notes the president received. The headhunters each took a copy and internalized every word, comma, and period. For the next few minutes, the table was in complete silence save for the clinking of ice cubes in water glasses and sips of coffee.

When the four had finished studying the notes, Danielson explained. "The two locations we want to place your efforts are Dallas, Texas and Rock Island, Illinois. We want you to identify some, let's call them possibles, who fit Ross' mold."

She asked, "Not the places I would choose for my dream vacation. No matter. After we find them, then what?"

"We'll take over from there."

"Fine," joked the woman, "just when it gets to be fun, you deal us out."

Danielson added. "There will be other steps where you'll be included again, I promise."

Clarifying how to proceed with identifying the possibles, the headhunters raised many questions. Danielson and Siegal answered them all. They spent the remainder of the afternoon going over the notes again until every detail had become clear.

"Anything else you want to add, Dr. Siegal?" asked one of the silent two.

"I have only one addition. I think the possibles must be regulars in the community where you look."

"Good point," agreed Danielson. "So how do you think you'll proceed?"

Jamie touched Mr. Odd Clothes. "I'll take Doug and we'll go to Rock Island. Kevin and Tim will go to Dallas. By splitting up, we can cover both locations at the same time."

The business part of their meeting was over. Danielson closed his briefcase and stood to leave. He motioned for the waiter, "Anyone for late lunch? It's on my tab."

FORTY-TWO

"WELCOME TO DAVENPORT AND THE Quad Cities, home of the Rock Island Arsenal and other points of interest," announced the flight attendant.

Jamie, leader of the headhunters, and Doug stepped off the airplane.

"Landing in Davenport gives us an opportunity to take the toll bridge across the Mississippi and drive past the guarded entrance to the Rock Island Arsenal," she said. "Or, we can stay on the Iowa side of the river. What do you think?"

"If I was a terrorist recruiter and didn't know much about the area, I'd guess lower downtown Rock Island is the best bet for us to set up camp. According to my internet search, it's where disenfranchised youths would likely gravitate."

"Agreed. We can start there, then work our way back over the river if we come up dry."

DOUG DROVE THEIR rental to their target location and found a garage about a block off the main street. "I don't expect we'll need the car, but close enough, just in case we have emergencies."

Carrying their light luggage, they checked in to a hotel. Their choice was an older brick five-story brownstone. The bed linens were clean enough. Neither expected a mint on the pillow at night. In the small lobby sat two salespeople sharing a six-pack, and a threesome of monthly guests reading the free newspapers. It seemed a perfect cover.

"I'll be ready to start just as soon as I take a shower and clean off some travel scum," said Doug.

"Careful. We don't want to look too sharp or we'll be made as outsiders."

"Good point. Meet you in the hallway in twenty minutes."

"WHAT'S THE PLAN?" asked Doug as they descended the stairs from their second-floor rooms. They passed the people in the lobby with a casual nod and went out onto the street.

"I thought we'd window shop for a while to get the lay of the land. Maybe have a couple beers in one of the taverns on the street. There's a lot to choose from in this part of town. Later we can go to a local diner followed by an evening in some place that has live music, or at least a jukebox."

"A beer sounds good right now," said Doug, feeling his dry throat from the plane ride. He pointed to a small bar across the street from their hotel. In its single front window hung a neon beer sign, Drink Pabst Blue Ribbon. "We can try that one on for size."

The King's Roost was not as royal as its name suggested. The décor was vintage 1950s. The smell of old beer and body odor filled the room. The clientele, a thirty-plus crowd, didn't fit Siegal's criteria.

One beer without a glass to protect against germs of the realm and the pair were on their way to the next pub two doors away.

Inside, Jamie said, "This place looks more promising. The people are younger, far less shopworn. Care for a game of pool? "I'll order the beers and meet you at the table."

A lone coin-operated pool table, worn from years of abuse, stood at the rear of the room. One person controlled the table as king of the hill and, like a shark, was waiting for any prey. Several quarters lined up on the cushion waited their turn to be taken by him. Doug meandered over, put down three quarters and waited his turn. Thirty plus minutes later, it was Doug's turn at the slaughterhouse.

"New around here, man?" asked the king, chalking up his cue.

"Yeah, sort of. I just got into town. Waiting to become a new CEO or something. Just wasting some time before my appointments tomorrow."

"Okay by me, man. Your business is your problem. Eight ball's my game and since it's my table, I call it. I'll match your three quarters if that isn't too rich for you."

"Eight ball it is then. I'm not that good at it."

The king broke and ran the rack. It was Jamie's turn. She set her drink on a nearby table where Doug placed his earlier.

"Are you with him or do you swing separately?"

"I don't swing, if that's what you mean, but I do like to shoot pool."

"I'll rack 'em up, babe. Ladies first. You break."

Jamie beached the shark in a single turn and stayed king of the hill until dinnertime. It was about seven when they left.

"Did you spot any possibles?" asked Doug.

"I saw several. We definitely have to go back there again. And not just to shoot pool."

"We have an expense account. We don't have to earn it. Where do we want to eat?"

"My gourmet dining guide of downtown Rock Island identifies this dive, Mama's Diner, as a four-star grease bowl," she said, pointing to an eatery a few doors down from the bar. "Wonder what's their house specialty?"

Mama's, one of only a few restaurants still open after eight, was smallish, eight tables and a counter. Even given the hour, it was still busy. Only two seats were available at the counter. The headhunters took them. A menu, scribbled on a chalkboard, hung on the wall behind the counter. It said "Daily Special," but it was easy to see it had not been changed for some time.

"Oh good," said Doug. "Chicken-fried steak with mashed potatoes and white gravy."

"We better find our recruits fast or this kind of diet will clog my arteries before I'm forty," responded Jamie.

A fat, unkempt woman wearing a food-stained apron with 'I'm Mama' embroidered on the bib came over and placed both elbows on the counter. "New here, aintcha?"

Taking a redneck approach, Doug answered. "No choice. We usually stay in Moline at the Hilton, but our suite was canceled. So we're stuck at the fleabag down the street."

"No skin off my back. What'll you have?"

"Any recommendations?"

The fat lady wiped her nose with her apron. "We have filet mignon with caramelized mushrooms on a bed of lightly toasted French baguette bread. Or you can have our whole Maine lobster served with clarified butter."

Doug said, "I think I'll have a hamburger…lettuce and tomatoes, no onions. Make that burger well-done."

"Fries or mashed potatoes?"

"Fries."

"I'll have the same," added Jamie.

"Two orders of old shoe soles with weeds and crisps," Mama called to the cook in the back.

Doug leaned over and whispered to Jamie. "See any candidates here?"

"There is a loner at the other end of the counter. She seems to be pickier about her food than anyone else in the place. We should keep an eye on her and see where she goes after dinner. My bet is she won't be going home to mother."

"Nor having a date either," added Doug.

After finishing as much of their meals as they could stomach, they sat at the counter toying with coffee refills until the girl left.

"I'm glad she's finally leaving," frowned Doug, "I don't know if I could stand another cup of this so-called coffee."

"Me either. I have to pee so badly, but I wasn't ready to sit down in this place. Maybe we can find a gas station and I can use their ladies' restroom."

The girl immediately entered a small tavern on the corner. A Shell station was across the street.

Jamie said, "Follow her, I've got business to attend to."

The tavern appeared to be an after-sunset meeting place for youths not going anywhere in particular. In the center of the room was a small dance floor where several couples gyrated to Sonny Rollins from a jukebox. In the corner was a pinball machine in use, with a couple of watchers standing by. A back booth was in use by a girl giving head to a moaning youth. In another corner was a bumper pool table. The pool shark from the afternoon was holding court.

Jamie, much relieved, followed Doug into the tavern a few minutes later.

"Given Dr. Siegal's criteria, it looks like there's more than a few people we could select. Any suggestion on how to move on them, Doug?"

"I think the dancers are out because they're too social. The pinball players could be possibles; it takes a certain amount of intelligence to beat those machines. The lookers don't seem so viable. They seem out of touch and not aggressive enough to challenge the machines. I like the odds on those at the pool table because they have enough loose money to gamble."

"And the two in the back booth?"

Doug nodded. "Maybe."

"I think we just watch for a while. We shouldn't be too pushy. Where is our counter girl?" asked Jamie.

"She's sitting at the end of the bar sipping a glass of wine. So far no one has talked to her. She seems like a prime candidate to be sure. Fits our age and appearance dimensions. Her clothing shows definite taste, indicating at least an upper-middle-class upbringing. On one hand, her attire looks pretty much like everyone else's, but on the other hand she seems put together more like she's wearing a costume."

Doug watched the pinball players. Jamie offered her quarters on bumper pool, letting the shark win his share of games. About ten, the counter girl decided to leave. She paid her small tab with a twenty. Doug followed. She waved down a cab and got in. Her getaway surprised the headhunters.

"Don't worry," said Jamie, coming out of the bar. "She'll be here tomorrow or at least the next day. Let's go back to the hotel. I spotted at least one other possible we can talk about later."

THAT SAME AFTERNOON, Kevin and Tim arrived at the Dallas-Fort Worth Airport. Once checked into a hotel in lower downtown Dallas, they changed into their casual clothes and began walking the area near the armory.

Nearby were a number of cheap motels and hotels, lots of taverns, a few adult entertainment centers, several pawn shops, and a small green open space. A good collection site for possibles.

Kevin located an empty bench in the green space and the two sat down. "This looks like as good a place as any to hang and people watch."

Both pulled out paperback novels from their shoulder packs and read. It was early winter; however, Dallas was experiencing a heat wave. Afternoon temperatures topped eighty degrees.

"See anything interesting?" asked Tim after a while.

"Just the usual joggers and Frisbee players. Oh, and one couple rolled in a blanket, oblivious to others," said Kevin.

"What do you think about the ones playing basketball, Kevin?"

"Too athletic."

Tim added, "I cut out the couple gyrating under their blanket."

Kevin totaled possibles in his head. "Not many to choose from. There are two guys playing portable computer games, a girl reading a cheap paperback novel, and three others laying out catching some rays. I'm not sure any fit enough of Dr. Siegal's criteria. I think we need to see where they congregate. Maybe more will pop up later."

About seven o'clock, people in the green space thinned out. The basketball and Frisbee players left in cars or rode off on bicycles. The lovers and loners stayed on foot, walking to nearby diners, an adult movie theater down the street, or to the bars that lined the green.

"I don't see any worth following. Kevin?"

"I say we just go back to our hotel and see who shows up tomorrow. No sense becoming visible too soon. No one really jumps out at me."

An early exit to the hotel suited both men. Getting ready for this job on short notice and the long cross-country flight from

Washington had slowed their energy, but not their enthusiasm for the challenge given to them.

"Early to bed and early to rise, mate," said Kevin. "I'm eager for a fresh start in the morning."

FORTY-THREE

AT MIDNIGHT EASTERN, THE PREDETERMINED time, Danielson made a conference call to both teams. "Anything to report?"

Jamie said they had a few who fit Siegal's criteria. Kevin and Tim were less enthusiastic.

Danielson gave one piece of advice: "Keep going."

THE ROCK ISLAND team woke early. The previous day led them to feel they were on the right path; one possible, a girl, was already earmarked and several others were in the ballpark.

The phone in Doug's room rang. "Ready for breakfast?"

"I've been ready for over an hour. Any suggestions?"

Jamie answered, "I think we should try Mama's again. If it attracted one possible, it could attract others."

"Got to pee first. See you in the lobby."

Jamie took the moment to survey the lobby before Doug appeared. *Not exactly a model for House and Garden.* Four armchairs, a two-cushion couch dented by many years of use, and a cheap, stained pine end table. A local morning newspaper, still folded by the carrier, lay on the table. A plastic cactus, the only non-beige decoration, guarded one corner.

Doug eyed Jamie by the door. "Ready," he said. "These cases always make me hungry."

"It wouldn't hurt to shed a few of those pounds," joked Jamie. "It's a good thing we don't do much chasing on foot or you'd get an early heart attack."

"Don't worry about me. I was on the soccer team in college."

"Girls or boys team?" She gave Doug a playful nudge. "Let's go visit Mama."

The sun just peaked over the tallest building on the block, warming the street. The few people on the street wore only light jackets or sweaters.

Doug peered through the unwashed window. "Look. That girl from last night is sitting in the same chair at the counter, reading something."

"It must be her regular spot."

Two stools immediately next to the girl were empty. The pair sat down.

Doug, taking the adjacent one next to the girl, said, "So, what are you reading, girl?"

The sudden question gave her a surprised look. "The *New Voice*. Ever read it?"

"Nah. I don't usually read those kinds of rags. Their editorials are so liberal. I prefer science-fiction novels. You got a name?"

"Susan."

Soon the two were in a friendly argument about search and seizure. Jamie pretended not to be listening, but she was impressed by how easily her teammate engaged the girl in conversation.

"Can I buy your breakfast?" Doug asked.

"No way, man. I carry my own weight."

"Hey, just being friendly. Wasn't trying to come on to you or nothing. A $3.99 breakfast ain't no big thing."

There was no more conversation. They all paid their tabs and were soon out the door. The possible turned to the left and the headhunters turned right.

"Doug, while you were getting to know your new girlfriend, I was looking around. The couple sitting in the corner was at the nightclub last night. One or both of them could be possibles."

"That makes three. How many do you think we need to identify before eliminating anyone?"

"Our orders are to collect, not eliminate."

The pair spent the day observing who was on the street. It wasn't until late afternoon they decided to barhop and focus in on specific people. Their first stop was the same tavern where the shark held court the previous afternoon.

"There's something about the shark that puzzles me, Doug. He's more than he pretends."

"He does seem more together than most of the other patrons. If he's really trying to make a living from playing Eight Ball, there are better places than this. And yet he doesn't seem to be doing anything else."

"I think I'll go one-on-one with him again," suggested Jamie. "I'll lose a few times, you know, to get his interest. Did you notice anything special about his accent?"

Doug nodded. "Sounds European."

Jamie won the first games but then pretended to fall into a slump and lost the next four.

"Hey, girlfriend, what happened to your touch? Are the bright lights in here blinding your dead eye?"

"Dude, I think maybe I was just a little lucky yesterday. Or maybe you were just laying back on me."

"No way, babe. I play this game straight. I don't take advantage of pigeons and I don't set up the better players for higher stakes. Not my style. It's strictly recreation for me."

She wanted to ask what he did for a living, but thought better. "That's enough pool for me." She joined Doug at a side table. The remainder of the afternoon went by with no new possible nominations.

"Eat at the same place?" asked Doug.

"I think we should try another gourmet café. I noticed one around the corner."

"Okay by me. I still have a little stomach lining left from yesterday."

The second café was almost a carbon copy of the first. A half dozen two- and four-top tables lined against the long wall. At the back were two wooden booths. The counter was covered with a cheap beige vinyl, and six of the eight red plastic-covered swivel stools needed major rejuvenating. Many of the patrons were among the target crowd they had seen earlier. There was also a mix of older street people who had begged enough extra change for both their booze and some food.

In the middle of their meal of fried greased leather made to look like a steak with brown gravy potatoes, Shark sauntered in and took one of the back booths.

"Hey, chick, I see you and your loser friend found the best restaurant in town." Then pointing to a booth in the corner, "Care to join me at my private table?"

"No thanks, we're fine here at the counter," answered Doug.

He looked directly at Jamie, avoiding eye contact with Doug. "I didn't ask your fuckin' friend. I just asked you."

Jamie called back without looking up, "Forget it, asshole."

Jamie's experience as a headhunter told her this kind of language only served to turn on people like Shark. She knew he only read it as a temporary put-off with future possibilities.

"Next time, chick, we play for a date instead of a buck."

"In your dreams, lover boy."

The conversation ended, but Jamie's curiosity about Shark's character stayed unabated. And, for other reasons, Shark's interest in Jamie got stronger.

After dinner Jamie and Doug walked the streets to see more of the local geography. Both felt very sure this area held promise.

With looks and pointing hand signs, the duo spotted several other possibles.

Doug asked, "How do you think we can determine if our possibles are what Danielson wants?"

"We're only to identify possibles. Choosing is above our pay grade."

"Let's find a bar. To tell the truth, I can use a beer to cut the grease after that dinner. Same one or try a new place?"

Jamie said, "I think we should stick to the same place. It'll keep us from looking too inquisitive, just in case anyone's watching us."

Within the hour, several possibles came in. Two stood behind the pinball players, looking on. Another silently watched the pool players. A fourth sat at the bar drinking a bottled beer. The couple who was first listed as possibles started to socialize and even danced with other partners.

Then the surprise of the evening happened. About an hour later, their friend Shark came in with another man who could have been his clone with the same style of clothes and haircut shaved high on the neck. They ambled to the bar and ordered a pitcher of beer. The clone found a table and Shark moved to the pool table. Both men acted overly deliberate as they scoured the room.

Doug's focused in on their actions. "Are you getting the same vibes I'm getting?"

Jamie, her headhunting antennae working at full speed, answered, "You mean about Shark and his buddy?"

Doug nodded. "I think they're more than just hanger-outers."

Jamie responded, "I get the same sense. They don't hang out during the day like the others. And they don't fit our profile. But they sure do have my attention. We can keep one eye on them, but remember, our real job is to locate people who fit Siegal's level-three profile. Still, Danielson needs to know about them."

"Gotcha," responded Doug. "Just looking around makes me feel we have at least four more to add on our list."

"That makes five or six," said Jamie. "But ten would keep us on the safe side of error. I say we don't worry how many we get. The more the better."

Two more beers and the headhunters headed back to their hotel. On the way, they passed the bar where they first spotted their female possible. They stopped and looked in through the unwashed front window.

"There she is, alone and sitting at the end of the bar drinking wine," remarked Jamie. "What did you nickname her, Street Sue?"

Doug smiled at his own cleverness. "Yep. Well we won't have to worry about keeping track of her. She's very predictable."

KEVIN AND TIM started on the same park bench, eager to have more success than the day before. They pretended interest in their reading material. Kevin scoured a free press publication and Tim immersed himself in a paperback novel.

Tim said, "Nothing's happening. Do you see anything more than I do?"

"Not really. Hope Jamie and Doug have better luck."

Being the professionals they were, they chose not to abandon their efforts too quickly or until told to do otherwise by Danielson. They passed the day, hoping their luck would improve.

At dinnertime, they opted for a local convenience store and

picked up some sandwich meat, soda, and chips. The stop was the most fruitful of the day. Two young adults were setting up to do some shoplifting.

Tim looked at Kevin.

Kevin nodded.

DANIELSON MADE HIS midnight call as planned. He wanted both teams online at the same time to keep them on the same page.

"How's it going?"

Jamie, as usual, spoke first. "Mr. Danielson, I think Doug and I are doing very well."

"How well?"

"Doug found a girl he nicknamed Street Sue."

Doug interrupted, "Her nails are manicured and her hair looks well-groomed. Too many things, even her mannerisms, are not part of the cesspool you want us to identify. Still, she's worth watching."

"Careful, Doug. Don't get caught up into making it personal. Jamie, continue your report."

"It seems too easy to find several possibles. At first, we thought Dr. Siegal's notes would disqualify almost everyone. And the problem would not be to cut down from our list, but rather to scrounge in order to find enough candidates."

"Is that a problem for you then?" Danielson asked.

"Not really," answered Jamie. "It would be better if we could identify each person by name and then research their backgrounds for the finer points of their personality profile. Siegal's criteria are really very good."

Jamie fully expected Danielson to indicate some displeasure. Instead he just took in the information like a sponge.

"How about my Dallas duo?"

"Well, sir." It was Kevin on the phone. "We've come across a dilemma. We have identified two possibles. Most youths around us don't fit even a few of Siegal's observable criteria."

"The goal was to find at least six possible recruits at each location," said Danielson. "I wanted both locations covered. Kevin, can you find a more fertile spot?"

"We can try the other side of the Dallas armory or better yet, a different park near there."

"I know it's not that your skills are lacking. It just may be a dry hole down there. Give it a go for one more day. Move to other locations to see if that will help. If your efforts still look dry, I'll send you up to help Jamie. My intuition tells me it's the more likely spot."

Jamie said, "You never told us why we were looking for these particular individuals. We're just traveling on your energy without knowing where it leads."

Danielson said assuredly, "I can't tell you anything more yet. I hope to have Plan B working by then. Anything else?" Not waiting for an answer, he hung up.

"We didn't get to tell the boss about Shark and his friend. Next time be sure we get that in," said Doug.

Danielson reached across his desk for the red phone. It was after midnight in Washington, D.C., but the person at the other end of the line picked up the phone on the second ring.

"Amanda, can you arrange an early morning meeting with him?"

FORTY-FOUR

"I TAKE IT YOUR LATE-NIGHT call is serious," said President Russell as he offered Danielson a chair in the Oval Office. "As chairman of the Summit, I expect you to handle everything. We can't have one-on-ones or we'll lose credibility with the others. I'll listen, but after today, you're on your own." President Russell picked up a folder marked "TOP SECRET" from his desk. He put a hand on Danielson's shoulder and led him toward the door. "Walk with me. I have to meet with my executive support people in the situation room. Seems we have to break in a new chief of staff. My last one left me suddenly."

Danielson smiled humbly. "El, I'm wondering if I bit off more than I can chew. When I was a Navy SEAL, attacking an enemy submarine base was easy pickings compared to this. I feel like I'm alone and need a friend."

"Then, as a friend, I'm all ears."

"Why has our rat terrorist not used the virus as a weapon?"

"And the answer is?"

"My gut tells me he needs an effective way to use this virus as an attack weapon. He would have used it on Galdet or somewhere else with certain impunity. Which reminds me, didn't you say we have the exact weapons he needs stored in our arsenals? If we shore up our defenses on these arsenals, he'll either back off or wait us out. Siegal and I know he'll use local cut group people as his troops on the ground like he's done on his other assaults."

"Sounds like you already solved the hardest part. Using Ross's characteristics, find the people he inducts as cut groups and stop them in their tracks."

"Any intervention, providing we have time to act, would have to be without their knowledge."

"A catch-22."

"I don't have enough resources to cover all my bases. You said there are two locations where the launchers are stored. I have two of my headhunters in those locations, Dallas and Rock Island. If he's found another way to use the virus, I'm shit out of luck."

"They're house chips. Lose and you're expected to pay back the SOS in blood. How's your chances?"

"I think my odds are a little better than even."

"Then I say go with your gut. What else?"

"I told my headhunters to identify at least six possibles in each locale. In one, we've already identified several."

"You're betting a lot of lives on this gamble."

"My problem, how do I get that many to work for us? I can't actually induct them or we will be setting them up for the same fate our embedded agents experienced. There has to be some way to have them work for us without them ever knowing."

"Tom. Where's the holdup? You didn't come here without an idea or two. I know you better than that. What do you think will work?"

"It's a harebrained idea, but feeding off Siegal's ideas he used in his lab, we could use some sort of homing implant on them; we could follow their moves and determine when any action is forthcoming."

"Maybe a few technicalities need to be ironed out. I know you. You'll work it out."

Danielson said, "This is so different. Before, when I was working for you, I could afford to make mistakes because you always had my back."

"And now you're working without a net."

"I have to figure a way to place implants on them without their knowing. They're just amateurs. We can't just ask them. Word will get around and our cover'll be blown. If these fucking terrorists could see through our trained agents, these guys will be sitting ducks. By the time we discover one has been recruited, it will be too late to act. They'll be under the constant eye of second-level pack members and on the move."

"Then do it first. Place these homing devices on all your possibles. If you know of ten or so, place an implant on each one. It certainly isn't an issue of cost. You're already using my discretionary fund as your personal expense account. Why back off now? Just because it may be a little illegal hasn't stopped you before. This is my stop. Time to get off the bus. Good luck, my friend."

DANIELSON SPENT THE remainder of the day walking around the great marble statues and monuments of the Capitol. Their size and beauty gave him a feeling of awe. They were erected to the country's greatest thinkers. Men like Lincoln and Jefferson all had problems to solve that kept America strong throughout history. They had always helped him make intelligent decisions. He hoped they would inspire an answer now.

"I have it."

FORTY-FIVE

ELEVEN P.M. DANIELSON HAD WORKED all afternoon and evening in his office putting together what he knew had to be the winning plan. Feeling his bladder bursting, he yelled into his computer screen, "It's your job, headhunters, to determine a final list of possibles. I've got to go pee."

Danielson punched his speed dial after returning from a trip down the hall to the floor's only bathroom. Phones rang simultaneously in Jamie's Rock Island and Kevin's Dallas hotel rooms. Echo feedback told Danielson Doug and Tim had plugged in their earphones so all could hear.

"Good evening, team. Any news on the streets of America?"

"You sound unusually upbeat," said Jamie.

Tim answered in a not-so-upbeat fashion. "Not much luck on our end. We tried several other locations. At the most, one possible."

"And you up north?" asked Danielson.

"We're at seven or eight strong candidates plus a couple of others," responded Doug. "We could be more specific, if we could dig more deeply into their backgrounds. And the problem with that..."

"I know, the problem with that is you just don't have the luxury of time," responded Danielson. "I'm pulling the plug in Dallas and concentrating our assets on the Rock Island Arsenal area."

Jamie said, "Can always use the extra help. Maybe if we knew more how you plan to use these possibles, it would help."

Danielson continued. "Just remember that you all are involved in a very high-level and potentially explosive international problem. Our best intel is that this group is about ready to start a new phase, which promises to become deadly."

Jamie asked, "How much more can you tell us? You know, without letting out too much sensitive information."

Danielson hesitated. "Your involvement is not our first attempt to learn more about this gang. All previous efforts to infiltrate the organization went sour, leaving us two dead federal agents. There are three distinct levels of this particular terrorist organization. Your job is to focus on identifying the lowest level of the terrorist Rat Pack. They're called cut groups. Dr. Siegal says they will come from locals living in and around the point of attack. They're inducted to do the dirty work for the organization."

Doug broke in, "So identifying all these so-called cut group recruits is just step one in the process. How do you suggest we size down the number?"

"You don't. The more you find makes the odds of identifying who gets recruited that much better. Logically there has to be some mid-level people in the area as well to select the recruits."

"Are you suggesting we should also have to identify these middle guys?" asked Kevin.

"Slow down, friends. Lowering the odds of exactly who will be recruited is impossible, which is why you need to identify more. Determining who are the mid-level people is just as improbable. One thing, the two are more like oil and water and would never interact with one another under normal social situations. When the oil and water start mixing, then maybe, just maybe, it can be the yellow flag something is about to happen."

Jamie asked, "So how do we make your plan work?"

"Keep your eyes on all possibles, adding others as you find them. I feel the real clue is when someone who doesn't fit Siegal's characteristics approaches one of your possibles, you will want to follow that up."

"Up to now we weren't looking for any second-level people," responded Tim. "Now you want us to double our observation efforts and wait until oil and water start interacting together. Right?"

"Wrong. Steer clear of anyone who seems to be a second-level terrorist. They are cold-blooded killers and you are not trained to deal with this kind. They'll spot you in a second. The two levels will not connect unless something is about to happen. They are two exclusive types of people and have nothing in common with each other. I'm only telling you this for your knowledge of what we're dealing with.

The lines clicked off.

THE ROCK ISLAND team was more upbeat than before. They were getting all the action they could handle. And Kevin and Tim were coming to help.

Tired of the greasy spoon cafes they ate at during their observations, Jamie and Doug went to a little grocery to find a healthier breakfast. Jamie bought a small pot and some premeasured bags of coffee. She started the water boiling, then knocked on the common wall between her and Doug's room.

"I'm up."

"Coffee's on," she offered. "Bring the food you bought. Come on over when you're ready."

In a couple of minutes Doug came in with a large bag. He emptied cookies, two varieties of Hostess Cupcakes, and some bagel chips with a small container of lox-flavored cream cheese.

Jamie had to laugh. "You're certainly the original junkman when it comes to eating habits. I thought we were going healthy. But this morning, you have competition. I need a sugar fix today." Then her voice changed. "Let's review what we have. Our original mission was to locate at least three possible recruits for the Rat Pack. We now have seven."

"But," interjected Doug, "we may have accidentally come across another level in the pack. I think Shark and his clone buddy may be part of the second level. I think we can remain invisible to them."

"Nice try, Doug. You're getting fat and lazy in your old age. Our job is to identify possibles. We need leadership from the boss before changing our mission. Danielson has always been very specific in the past and I doubt very much he would like us to rechannel our energies without his blessing. He said to identify possibles and that's what we'll do."

FORTY-SIX

MORNING IN DOWNTOWN ROCK ISLAND started normally for the headhunters. Their seven possibles were all out as usual. Kevin and Tim were headed north. There was one difference. Shark and his clone, for the first time, were on the street in the open.

"I wonder what they're doing?" mused Doug.

"Something'll happen today," said Jamie. "I get that feeling."

By afternoon the jackals began their prowl—almost imperceptible at first. It would have been missed, unless you were Jamie and Doug, experts in people-watching and looking for the interaction.

Jamie nudged Doug. "Look there, in Mama's Diner. There's Shark sitting next to your girlfriend, Street Sue."

They watched from across the street to avoid being spotted by Shark or his clone, who the headhunters guessed was nearby.

"Clever way to make a connection," said Doug. "He's just sitting there, not saying a word or even looking at her."

Shark and Street Sue finished eating, paid their tabs and left in different directions.

THE PHONE RANG simultaneously in Jamie's and Kevin's rooms precisely at midnight Eastern.

Danielson said, "Call it an itch, Jamie, just have a feeling you had some things you might want to mull over with me."

Jamie spoke, "Good scratch, boss. We've been observing all day. Our possibles came out and did their usual things. But then something else: two men in their late twenties or early thirties keep showing up. One I nicknamed Shark because of his eight-ball skills and his clone buddy. They don't fit the general street population but they're around. We think they may be your second-level members."

Doug added, "They're just different from the rest of the street people we've been watching."

"They always stayed in the bars till now. Today was different," said Jamie. "We saw them on the street for the first time."

Doug added their observation at the café.

"This can be important. Anything about their appearance that drew you in?" asked Danielson.

Jamie said, "Their clothes are a little less shopworn than our possibles. Other than that..."

Doug broke in. "Both have foreign accents. I think Polish or German. Anyway, Eastern European."

"You don't know how important that can be. One of our terrorists has been heard speaking with an East-European accent. This is a major break. Be ready for Plan B."

The next day, Shark and his clone were again in the open, arranging themselves into closer proximity with some of the team's other possibles. That night they reported this to Danielson.

THE REGULAR MIDNIGHT call from Danielson came. This time, all four headhunters were in the same city but at different hotels.

Doug asked, "Boss, we were wondering why it's still important to keep a sharp tab on each of our possibles if we already suspect we have located two second-level members?"

"We don't know what level Shark and his clone are. They may be small role players and unaware of any plans other than selecting cut people. Maintaining everyone on a need to-know-basis at the lower levels is the strength of any terrorist group. It keeps it safe from erosion within as well as discovery from the outside. Like the four of you. If you were caught and forced to talk, you wouldn't be able to tell the whole picture."

FOR THE NEXT day, the headhunters converged upon the possibles while keeping an aware but wide berth of Shark and his clone. Kevin and Tim stayed in their rooms and worked on the internet, using facial recognition technology to research backgrounds of the identified possibles.

Without an exception, each possible had some kind of money flow allowing them the freedom to be street types. Two earned money soliciting for sex. Four earned extra money by putting leaflets on car windows, collecting glass bottles for refunds, and generally panhandling for change on the street. Two lived at home and the rest resided in cheap boarding houses. All were loners. None were what anyone would identify as leaders. Each was easy prey to anyone offering simple pleasures like food or extra money to play the pinball machines. The one thing they had in common? They all fit Siegal's criteria.

In contrast, Shark and his clone always had more ready cash than would seem logical when they apparently did nothing to earn it. They always had money for better food, clothes, and entertainment. They lived in an inexpensive hotel nearby with windows facing the outside in easy view of the street below without themselves being seen. Using Danielson's connections, the team checked with the local phone company and discovered there were several cell calls made to them. Each call was from burner phones, making it impossible to trace their origins. Whoever was masterminding the organization knew how to cover his tracks. At best, the team could determine only that Shark and his clone were recent arrivals to the area.

During a day when Shark and his clone were on the street, Kevin and Tom checked out their rooms. Luggage tags bore names from national and international locations. There was a passport with Shark's picture. Danielson checked with immigration and found it was false.

Circling like great whites after a meal, both Shark and his clone started interactions. The clone took Street Sue to a movie one afternoon. Shark invited two others to play pool with him without requiring their quarter donation. It all seemed innocent enough. On Friday night, Danielson called to get a report.

Doug began the conversation by asking, "So what's next? How do we get our possibles on the side of the good guys?"

Danielson smiled. "I got that covered. The answer is, we don't. I'm sending in a group of dental folks. They'll offer oral exams as part of a free clinic for all street people in the area. We'll get a local radio station to advertise the effort and put an article in the local paper like the one your girl possible was reading. Notices will be posted in business windows. They'll need your photos to identify each possible for the dental clinicians. Email them to me."

Doug asked, "How is that going to get them on our side?"

"As the dental clinicians are examining their teeth, they will be placing micro homing devices in their mouths. I will be bringing in a team of electronic surveillance specialists to track your possibles' implants. Movement by any one of them will be closely monitored.

Without knowing it, they will be working for us but never in danger of being identified. The personality quirks of being too aggressive and inquisitive that identified and killed the two CIA agents will be eliminated. If all goes as planned, we will be able to stop this rat in his tracks."

Jamie asked, "What's next for us?"

Danielson said, "Your work in Rock Island is over. As always, you did a great job. You're all the best."

FORTY-SEVEN

ISOLATION FROM OTHER LIVING SOULS played on Siegal's imagination. Every blast of wind, the cooling creaks of the chalet, even the changing cycles of the dishwasher made his muscles tense and blood pressure rise. Regular updates by Danielson were not enough to relax his nervous energy. He looked across the dining room patio into the early twilight.

Wait. I see it. Movement in the undergrowth. He rubbed his eyes. *There it is again.* He grabbed the cast iron tool from the fireplace and ducked behind the dining room drapes to hide.

The bushes moved again. Then parted. A dark form emerged. *A bear. Only a goddamn bear.*

It was yesterday when he thought he heard muffled voices whispering in the next room. It was only the television he had forgotten to turn off. Every day, Siegal hoped the green phone would ring, telling him it was all over and he could return to the university and all his old friends.

"Dr. Siegal?"

Siegal, weapon in hand and staring out the window, jerked back. He swung toward the sound of the voice, hitting a lamp and crashing it to the floor.

"Dr. Siegal, you have been staring out the window for the past hour." It was his linebacker caretaker, Ben Goldberg. "Mr. Danielson was concerned that your isolation is taking a toll on you. He thinks you may want some company and asked me to join you in the main part of the chalet. He also thought you may also enjoy reading to-day's article in the *Washington Post.*"

TERRORISM ON OUR OWN SOIL

The United States met the challenge of terrorism yesterday and won. Last night the Rock Island Arsenal was attacked by a paramilitary force. The raid focused on the rocket or-dinance building. But unlike most paramilitary supremacy groups active in the country, the attackers wore no badges or uniforms. Three attackers were captured. One attacker was killed, a young woman carrying an identification of Susan Benson. The Armory guards reported that no sensi-tive area was breached. The attackers were halted before gaining access to any buildings. President Elwin Russell congratulated the CIA for their very exacting work.

Siegal couldn't help but smile. "My theories actually worked. Ben, they worked."

Ben responded calmly, "We always knew they would, sir."

On cue, the green phone rang in the dining room.

TWO DAYS LATER, the Summit of Six met again via their respective situation rooms.

Chairman Danielson spoke first. "Not long ago we asked Dr. Siegal to develop a profile, one we could use to help us infiltrate the terrorist organization. His input has been invaluable. His theories about terrorists have allowed us to collapse the guesswork we had to work with in the past and approach a level of near perfection."

The members lifted their water glasses as a toast. Siegal felt humbled by these men paying such a tribute.

Danielson continued, "Using Dr. Siegal's criteria, we narrowed our target to Rock Island. To that degree, we were at one hundred percent accuracy. Using implanted electronic tracking devices, we tracked these cut group recruits wherever they went. When they started going to unpredictable places, we activated our defensive forces. The recruits were working for us and never knew it."

"Mr. Chairman," President Sokoloven spoke. "Mr. Chairman, this sort of news could easily have been sent by courier. We are not, I believe, a high-priced group of cheerleaders for the work done by Dr. Siegal."

"You are correct, sir," responded Danielson.

"Then why exactly are we here?" asked an impatient Sokoloven.

"As I stated before, Dr. Siegal's work included two responsibilities. The initial purpose, identifying lower levels of terrorist groups, has proven to be very successful. We are now tying this kind of information with the next level of their organization. In time, we should be able to identify even the leader as well."

"Mr. Chairman, you are what you Americans call beating around the babushka." Danielson smiled at Sokoloven's attempt at humor. The rest remained silent, waiting for the real purpose of the gathering to come out.

Chairman Danielson went on, "We determined the United States would be the focus of the terrorist group to access a delivery system for the virus. On that point we were accurate. But on our decision to decide which arsenal they would attempt to target, we were only half correct. A second location was also targeted. The Rock Island Arsenal was a smokescreen, a false lead. Their real target was one of our more secret weapons storage installations. The arsenal at Biloxi, Mississippi was attacked that same evening. We did not expect the terrorists to know of its existence. We were caught totally off guard. They captured our prototype weapon capable of delivering the virus with pinpoint accuracy. Even the most inexperienced personnel should be capable of using such equipment with a minimum of training."

Shock waves evinced on the SOS members as they heard this revelation.

President Russell rose. "Gentlemen, we are in a war unlike any war we have ever witnessed before. This war will not be fought across clearly-defined lines, but asymmetrically. And worse, our enemy's weapons of choice are unannounced attacks and virus warfare."

President Galdet spoke next. "How do we fight an enemy that has no permanent military body, no actual military ordinance, and no territory to defend?"

"First you say we did well and stopped an incursion on one of your military arsenals," interrupted King Ishmere. "Then you say you allowed a second target to be overrun by a troop of nonmilitary misfits. We know for a fact they have a virus that can kill millions. And now you say the enemy has not only this virus, but the ordinance to discharge this virus wherever and whenever they wish. I only hope it is not a time for international mourning."

"We are not exactly at ground zero," said Siegal. "We know a good deal about this terrorist organization. We know how they recruit their workforce. We can even identify likely workers when they are on a mission. But…"

"But you don't know who they are, their next move, or what their overall intent is. And worse yet, you have no idea where to start looking," interrupted President Cho-Se. "How many people will have to die before you stop them?"

Siegal felt all eyes on him, expecting…no, hoping for a simple answer. He cleared his throat, "Gentlemen, there has to be logic in every situation. Nature is totally organized and predictable. Human beings are part of nature, and therefore must be predictable."

"Where is this discussion taking us?" asked an impatient President Cho-Se.

"We need to examine what has happened. So far our terrorist has carried out three actions, each for a designed purpose. Several days ago, he gained the means to deliver the virus. Gentlemen, he is fully prepared to strike. There must be one more intermediate step before he lets his intentions become known. He has to try the weapon out in real time. He still has not tested the full force of his power to kill."

"You're telling us, Dr. Siegal, that he will begin killing people without apparent cause?" asked Sokoloven.

Siegal nodded. "I believe so. And at this point, we do not know who or how many. We don't know where. And just as puzzling, we still don't know why."

Galdet said, "I do not like this wait and see. We need decisive action."

Siegal pondered his next words very carefully. "Then I believe France, or maybe Italy, will be his next target. Both countries are subject to major regime changes because of their method of selecting a ruling government. But he will attack some other place first to test his skills in the use of the virus.

How many terrorists does it take to turn off the world? thought Siegal. *The answer is one.*

"There will be casualties," said Danielson. "We are at the mercy of the terrorist who has the power to choose when and where to attack."

Siegal added, "We have three points in our favor. He thinks he is smarter than us. Second, once a pattern is established, he will not deviate from his direction. And third, we already know our enemy uses a new set of troops for each effort. Once we learn the focus of the attacks, the sooner we can begin looking for possible recruits in similar fashion to what we did in Rock Island."

Danielson added. "These next days are going to become extremely stressful for all of us. It is important for each of us to remain resolute, maintain unity within your respective nations, and with each other. All your intelligence gathering resources must be on high alert twenty-four/seven. When any of you become even remotely aware of any attack, you will need to feed the information to me." He paused to give each the opportunity to add their thoughts. No one spoke. "This meeting is adjourned."

FORTY-EIGHT

SIEGAL HAD AN EMPTY FEELING, an itch that couldn't be scratched. His mission was to understand this terrorist's motivation and behavioral style, thus making him vulnerable. He hoped he was up to the task.

He turned to Tigger. "Most of my speculations has been right, but not all. For instance, I theorized the terrorist required an entire arsenal of handheld launchers to arm his organization. That was wrong. This rat sought only one. The attack at the Rock Island Arsenal was a clever diversion while Biloxi was always the planned target. The terrorist rat had outfoxed me. I think he will repeat this diversion scheme in other attacks. In fact, I know it." He banged his hand on the dining room table. "Ouch." He rubbed his sore hand. "I need to take a walk."

When he returned, Goldberg had his favorite thinking tools, large sheets of blank paper taped to one wall and two fresh marking pens on the buffet, laid in perfect marching alignment. Next to them were two cups and an urn of coffee.

"Thought you would like something to take off the chill from be-ing outside, sir. I wouldn't mind having a cup myself, if that's all right with you."

"Having you to bounce ideas off is appreciated. I'm sure, you being so close to Danielson, there are no secrets I need to hide. All Tigger can do is listen."

Goldberg avoided the obvious probe. "Thank you, sir. It will be my pleasure to be of any help I can."

"Just in case anything has been left out of your knowledge, this is what we know." Siegal picked up the black felt marker and began writing.

WHAT WE KNOW ABOUT THE RAT PACK
A MULTLEVEL TERRORIST GROUP
HEADED BY A SINGLE LEADER
BRINGS IN CUTGROUP WORKERS THROUGH LOCAL RECRUITING
EACH ACTION USES A NEW SET OF WORKERS RECRUITED
WEAPONRY FOR HIS MAJOR ATTACKS WILL BE THE DEADLY VIRUS (V32) DELIVERED BY A SINGLE HAND HELD LAUNCHER
THE RAT PACK IS READY TO KILL

"Ben, What am I in the middle of? If I fail, millions will die."

"Your information stopped the attack at the Rock Island Arsenal. You didn't fail then, and you won't fail now."

"But we can't stop them if we don't know why he's doing it. What is this head rat's motivation? And the biggest question, why is he content to acquire only one hand launcher? Help me, Ben."

"Sleep on it. It'll come to you, sir."

Ben picked up the empty coffee cups and disappeared into the kitchen. Siegal retired to his bedroom, hoping for a divine thought to come in his sleep.

GOLDBERG WAS WAITING for Siegal when he came downstairs for breakfast the next morning. Bagels and coffee were on the buffet. Siegal's petroglyphs were hanging on the wall, waiting for his pearls of wisdom to be translated. The black and red felt pens lay patiently on the buffet like well-trained dogs ready for their commands. And Tigger stood guard to one side.

Siegal taped an adjoining sheet and added two lines, one in black and the other red.

THE GOAL: STOP THE RAT PACK
LEARN MOTIVATION OF THE RAT LEADER

He turned to Goldberg, "Do you have an idea?"

"It's your show, sir."

Siegal was beginning to understand why Danielson put so much trust in this supersized man. He had that unique sense on where to be and what to say. He knew his job and never stepped on anyone's responsibility.

"What do you think, Ben? Is he really after land and material acquisitions?" Silence from his companion. Siegal knew not to expect any. "I think not. If he wants land at all, then it would be the entire planet."

Finally a response, "If you want me to clean out a nest of these rats when you find it, I could do that. I just follow orders. Your kind of thinking is above my pay grade."

Siegal baited Goldberg for more thoughts. "How about gaining control of a water supply? History is full of water wars. But then, we're talking about a small pack of terrorists. They could supply themselves with a weekly supply of bottled water from the neighborhood supermarket with pocket change. Water control isn't a motivation. Our choice of munitions control is probably just as illogical. An unending supply of Virus V-32 is already in their possession at the desire of the head rat. The system they captured is reusable. So that's out. What else can there be?"

Goldberg said, "Maybe he's just a bully. You know, like you talk about with your rats in the lab."

"You're right. I'm being too complicated." He picked up the red marker and wrote "Human Domination" under "MOTIVATION OF THE RAT LEADER."

"Of course. It's so simple. His greatest pleasure would be to make everyone a personal slave, do his bidding without question, the super-master over an inferior world. Why hadn't I thought of it before?"

"Sounds logical to me."

"Okay, so how does he plan to accomplish this domination?"

Siegal scanned through the resource books he brought with him from Denver. "Listen to this, Ben. Power, by its definition, is something a person has over another. One does not take power; it is given. But this isn't always done freely. One person can force another to give up freedom by sheer strength, but it is the body and not the mind that is being controlled. The way to gain power over another is to control his feelings...his mind. Put dreaded fear into the equation and this can be accomplished."

"Is fear the only way?"

"Good point," said Siegal. "Fear is one end of the behavioral continuum; pleasure is on the opposite end. Both fear and pleasure are equally strong. But fear is easier to maintain because it can be used intermittently and still keep its full power to bring on bad things at any time. Pleasure works best as a short-term control procedure, like using sex and drugs for his cut groups. His prey is much more significant. Understanding is one thing, but setting forth a plan to combat this enemy who chooses to attack and hide at will is something entirely different."

Siegal added to his wall sheets, "ONE METHOD OF DOMINATION IS TO CONTROL BY FEAR."

Then, turning to his new student, he said, "Just what kind of fear would control you?"

"Well, sir, I have been assigned to protect certain individuals, including the president. I am trained to stand and take deadly fire to carry out my mission. I am willing to die if duty demands me to do so. But it is my choice."

"Then, maybe it's how to die, rather than if."

"Sir?"

"I fear a slow death rather than something quick. I could be killed from lack of water, or maybe die from too much water while drowning. Both would be slow and agonizing. But a bullet to the head would be quick and not too painful. So maybe, Ben, the fear of the pain preceding a death is the prime motivator in controlling people and not the threat of death itself. Living with fear can be worse than death. The question now is, how does this rat terrorist strike fear so great his target can be controlled?"

Just then the green phone rang.

Siegal answered. "I take it this is not a social call."

"Sgt. Goldberg suggested I call."

Siegal was right about Goldberg being in Danielson's loop. "For a while I was pretty much braindead. But today, things are starting to click."

"What did you come up with?"

"It may not seem like much, but to me it's a giant step forward. Our rat leader's motivation is human domination; just a few people at first, but inevitably the entire world."

"How do you propose he'll do this?"

"Not sure, but he will accomplish this through some manner of fear control."

"Are you suggesting this little rat leader, who only has a few followers and minimum dollar resources, plans to control the entire planet?"

Siegal grimaced. "Yes."

Danielson asked, "And how do you think he can accomplish this?"

"If our terrorist using V-32 can completely devastate the animal and human population of any nation, and this ability becomes common knowledge, the people of that nation could revolt against their leadership. And, Tom, what do you think is the greatest fear of a national leader?"

"I think it is evident now that you put it that way. They fear their followers will revolt against them."

Siegal agreed, "Exactly. Waiting to determine his target is the hardest part, isn't it?"

"I think we're through waiting. I received a phone call from intel a few hours ago. Turn on your TV."

THIS IS ROBERT GALLOWS reporting. Evangelists on a humanitarian mission came upon a small village in Ghana, South Africa. They experienced total silence save for a few birds in the distant forest. No dogs barking, no children playing lion hunter, not even the sound of women scraping roots for food. At first they thought the entire population had just migrated to another encampment. Or worse, that perhaps a neighboring tribe had slain everyone or taken them prisoner. Then they discovered the ghastly truth, a dead dog twisted in grotesque agony. Next, they saw a man slumped over his unthrown spear. Inside grass huts were women and children huddled together as if trying to protect each other. The entire village population, including animals, was dead. A medical team from a United Nations health unit was dispatched to the area. They discovered every living thing, humans and animals alike, all had rashes covering their bodies. No contamination source was found. There seemed no answer for this sudden plague. It was as if this complete devastation happened in a matter of minutes and then disappeared .

"What do you think?" asked Danielson.

"Ugly," answered Siegal.

"Worse than anything I ever saw in my stints overseas," added Goldberg.

Danielson continued, "Every soul, including animals, was covered with the ulcerated rashes we expected from the stolen Chinese virus. Our terrorist definitely did this."

"Tom, were any attackers found dead in the village?" asked Siegal.

"None."

"Then he used second-level terrorists and not cut groups to test the virus and delivery system," said Siegal.

"Why would he attack an innocent village?" asked Goldberg.

Danielson said, "To observe V-32's killing capability firsthand."

Siegal replied. "It tells us that he's a creature of habit. If something worked once, he will stick with it. He chose Africa for his training ground like he did in the hostage takeover of Flight 234."

"Ross, you don't expect him to attack an entire country using only one V-32 launcher as the weapon. Its scope is too limited."

"True. The virus will not be used to kill his enemy, but to instill controlling fear. He is ready to make his move for power."

Danielson said, "If that's true, we need a plan and we need it fast. We have to checkmate the direction of this head rat."

The phone clicked.

FORTY-NINE

"IF YOU WERE A TERRORIST and wanted to control people, how would you use fear?"

"I suppose, sir, I would have an army and attack. I would give my enemy the choice of giving up or dying."

"Or," added Siegal, "giving in."

"I get it. You don't want to become the supreme leader but you want their leaders to be so fearful they would submit to your demands."

Siegal continued his thought. "Political leaders must maintain enormous self-esteem. Their biggest fear has to be losing face with their constituents. Controlling the leadership and remaining invisible to the rest of the world could be accomplished by challenging a leader's self-esteem, the ultimate coup."

Goldberg asked, "How do you defend against a ghost? Traditional defenses are useless against this enemy. What happens next?"

"I believe the next attack will be on his target country. Many innocent people will die in this next attack. I only hope we can stop the assaults quickly and before too many innocent victims are slaughtered."

Siegal returned to his sheets on the wall:

OVERCOMES DEFENSES
REDUCES LEADER'S RESPECTIBILITY
HIS ABILITY TO LEAD/RULE

Siegal continued. "Okay. How would I become afraid if I lived in a threatened country?"

"That is easy, sir. Vulnerability. If people or communities around me were dying without anyone having the power to stop it, I would be vulnerable."

"Helpless to counter. It's fitting together."

"You need your private thinking space and I have to tend to other matters. See you at dinner."

Siegal added another sheet to the wall:

POLITICAL LEADERS   GENERAL PUBLIC
OVERCOMES DEFENSES   BECOMES WARY OF LEADERS
MAKE THEM VULNERABLE
REDUCES RESPECTIBILITY
ABILITY TO LEAD/RULE

It so simple in theory. Now what?

FIND THE NEST OF THE RAT PACK:
DETERMINE ITS LEADER
ELIMINATE ALL SECOND-LEVEL PEOPLE

Siegal opened the dining room door to the patio and yelled, "I'll get you, Rat. You will make a behavioral mistake and that will be your end. I promise. No. I swear it."

FIFTY

THE WALL CHARTS, REMINDERS OF the seriousness at hand and hanging like hastily-applied wallpaper, now covered two walls of the dining room. Siegal stared at them over and over, looking for missing pieces. He was consumed by thoughts of the heartless slaughter of innocent people in Africa—and his responsibility to save others.

Siegal never considered himself a gambler. But winning this pot meant discovering answers that would save lives. Losing meant destruction of the free world. With his special behavioral knowledge, he knew the odds were on his side, yet he felt frustrated with no results.

"When will the next shoe drop, Tigger?"

The morning passed with no progress made.

Goldberg entered the room with lunch. "Why don't you call Mr. Danielson, sir?" Goldberg's straightforward military training manner was Siegal's link to sanity. "I believe you need someone to talk with."

He handed Siegal the green phone. It was answered on the second ring.

"ROSS, I WAS expecting a call from you."

"This job is getting to me. What if my ideas are not good enough? Or maybe wrong and this rat terrorist wins?"

"Relax, pal. Ben has been keeping me current. Your theory stuff is not just a fantasy. We're further along than you imagine."

"Then why haven't you called me? At least to let me know what's going on."

Danielson responded. "The reason the phone hasn't rung is because there's no one crying wolf at this end. My gut tells me Africa was the final step in the rat's preparations. His next step is the real war."

"In that case, no news is not good news."

"It means that things are about to break. Get your gray matter working and give me a clue where."

Siegal responded, "Okay. How about this? He's too small for a worldwide attack. He'll go after the weakest national power he can determine. Not by size, but by political structure. And it won't be a direct assault, but a glancing blow."

"Say, Ross, have you ever considered a military career in charge of strategic command forces? Just kidding."

Siegal did not feel the humor. "This assault has to be fast and capable of being easily repeated if necessary."

"Whoa," blurted Danielson. "I thought you said you haven't gotten anywhere. What kind of attack do you see? Will it be at some base of operations crucial to the control and running of a country, like a power facility or a munitions dump?"

"Remember, V-32 kills people. If I was the head rat, I would try to determine where one or two strikes would cause public panic; freeze a nation and its leaders."

"Can you get closer?" Danielson asked.

"I don't have enough political information to hazard a guess. I can only react if I hear a suggestion."

Danielson paused. "Could he attack us in this country?"

"You're thinking too conventionally. Remember, the only weapon the rat pack has is V-32, one launcher, and some untrained recruits. This terrorist has no real territory to defend nor interest in land control. Strong military might would be overkill. A small strike force is all you need to be effective. You could probably chase down the Rat Pack on bicycles."

"Okay, pitcher. Three strikes and I'm out. What do you suggest?"

"He wouldn't attack our homeland. We have so many lines of succession. The missed heartbeat would hardly be noticed. If all the people around the president, but not the president were killed, that might be more devastating. Think about how he would react if members of his own family were slain or at least put in mortal danger. What would that do to the man's thinking? How would that affect his ability to resist? Would you be able to resist, Tom, if it was you?"

"Whew," breathed Danielson. "How many attacks do you figure we have to rebuff?"

"My guess is maybe two, but no more than three. Remember, this rat has limited resources. He can only attack one nation at a time before stopping to reload his virus. I think the United States is too large a nut. I figure one or more of the weaker governments are more legitimate targets. It still think France is a logical choice. It has a type of government that can change its privileged by calling for an election whenever the current political mood of the country changes. There are many others who fit the political profile, but France is part of the European Union, and an attack there can have a great impact."

"Okay. Assuming you're correct. How does he make it work?"

"Maybe I'm thinking too simply, but all world leaders are major egotists; self-importance is part of their nature and motivated them to become national leaders. Once their leadership is challenged, they can be blackmailed into accepting the rat's control over them if only to remain in office as the country's symbolic leader."

Danielson knew this terrorist was a threat, but Siegal's analysis made him feel heavier than he had imagined.

And Siegal, on the other hand, surprised himself at discovering what had been an itch inside him.

"It sounds as bad as it can get."

"It can be worse. Ordinary citizens might pick up arms and attack their own leaders. Military force cannot stand up to them. It would be like a pride of lions no longer accepting leadership by the alpha male."

"Similar to the revolts in Egypt and Syria," said Danielson. "Almost anyone can take over."

"It wouldn't be difficult to lay a blanket of fear through terrorism and never even involve the national leaders until they become powerless to control it."

"And then?"

"And then the terrorist comes in without a bullet being fired, armed only with the promise the threat will stop."

"We just witnessed a village in Africa completely laid to waste with no forewarning," said Danielson. "Entire cities could be attacked anywhere and at any time. A few well-publicized events and many populations of the world will be on their knees."

Siegal continued, "Can you imagine it? Once the threat is established, even a simple flu epidemic will be perceived as a V-32 attack."

"Thanks for being the harbinger of such good news."

"HOW DO YOU feel now, Tom?"

Danielson frowned. "I can't say I'm feeling very comfortable, El. You heard him on the speakerphone. Our playing field has no sidelines and no boundaries. Attacks using V-32 can happen any place in the world. How do we guard against that?"

President Russell speculated for a moment. "You just have to narrow the limits of speculation. It means risking some lives, but if you guess correctly, you will save millions of others. The strategy is to reduce collateral damage."

They replayed the message tape between Siegal and Danielson.

Danielson spoke, "So far we've trusted Siegal's theories and they have been on target. His first inclination is to put France on guard. And remember, the rat already attacked Galdet's motorcade to test the president's reaction. Ross thinks these attacks will continue, but on France's civilian population. The more I think about it, the more logical it sounds. Citizens of a country are more likely to react when their own kind are killed. Military personnel are expected to die."

President Russell said, "It's a media-friendly world. Any news can quickly become big news. This rat leader is no dumb cookie. He never does anything by chance. The SOS put you in charge. It's your call, Tom. Case closed."

"I'll send each SOS member Siegal's speculations and see if they have any suggestions. But I can't wait for them to respond. I have to move on my own. I have to depend on Siegal's theories, wherever they take me."

President Russell asked, "And where does that take you?"

Danielson answered, "For one thing, we know all the grunt work is done by new recruits. We have to determine where in France is the most logical place to look for them."

"Galdet, in respect, has to be told before telling the others. Do you want me to contact Galdet?"

Danielson responded, "No, it's my job as chairman. I'll do it personally."

The President pushed a button on the intercom, "Amanda, will you please get President Galdet for Mr. Danielson?"

THE PHONE CALL between President Galdet and Chairman Danielson was amicable enough.

"And where do you suggest we begin?" asked President Galdet.

"If Dr. Siegal's information is accurate, the terrorist will attack one of your small villages. You will probably get a message from the terrorist claiming responsibility shortly after," said Danielson.

"What is he going to demand?"

"I doubt he will ask for anything at all. This attack is intended for its shock value. He is only showing he can do it. Neighboring communities will be frightened and demand protection from you. I'm sure the news will quickly spread across your nation, putting people in full panic."

"And, Mr. Danielson, you think this one attack will be all?"

"Dr. Siegal believes he has plans to strike one or two more times after that. Sometime after the second attack he will start making demands."

"Demands for what?" President Galdet asked, but he already knew the answer.

Chairman Danielson was guessing. But the more he talked, the surer he was that everything was going to come off exactly as he described. "At first it will be something simple, like extortion If this succeeds, he will ask you to perform some sort of political action. It will first be something you will have to do within your own country.

When he thinks you will do whatever is asked, then do not be surprised if you are expected to do something economically against your allies, such as changing trade treaties. After that, he will have you in his power and may ask anything, including all-out attacks with your military."

"Never. I have been threatened before." Then almost discounting the threat, President Galdet concluded, "No little person, the head rat, as you call him, will force me into anything I do not wish to do. Chairman Danielson, I thank you for the warning. I will stay on my guard and let you know if anything unusual takes place."

Danielson hung up the phone and immediately made a second call. "Jamie, have your team pack some clothes and update your passports. You're working for me again. The four of you are going to France. I want your team to set up in the southern wine regions, a place where youths tend to congregate. Enjoy the scenery for a while. but be ready for action when it starts. Your task will be similar to Rock Island."

"We're on our way."

FIFTY-ONE

THE LATE MORNING SUN OFFERED premature warmth to the region. Children in shorts played in the streets. Women enjoyed the weather to dry their clothes on the line. Fathers and older sons were in their sheds, repairing plows, preparing for spring planting. A French flag waved in the city square.

Two canvas-covered trucks parked near the edge of a small village in northern France. Four men in each truck dressed in hazard gear eased out from under the canvas coverings. The drivers remained at their wheels. One man in the lead vehicle, also dressed in hazard gear, got out carrying a bazooka-like device. Without a word, he gave hand signals for the others to fall in to an umbrella formation several yards apart from each other. He waited for a breeze from behind, then fired his weapon. A light mist exuded from the weapon's muzzle. Air currents carried the mist toward the village. The attack was over in minutes and the trucks left before the first effects of the virus took hold.

Within minutes, all humans and animals were either dead or dying in agony. People shielded inside their homes from the toxic vapors were stricken as they left their shelters to help. An angry rash covered everybody it touched. Birds were silent, flailing helpless on the ground.

The French National Observer was the first paper to pick up the news.

CATASTROPHE

A mysterious event took place last night in northern France. A small community of two hundred residents, too small to be found on most maps, was hit by what appears to be a highly toxic poison that slaughtered every human being and animal.

Local scientists are at a loss to explain the phenomenon but speculate it was caused by some extraterrestrial event such as a meteor strike. The people of France viewed this early report as a secret government test gone awry. President Galdet did not comment, only adding to the public speculation over what really happened.

Other syndicated newspapers followed with speculations of their own.

"Did you read the papers today, Ross?" asked Danielson, calling on the green phone.

"Yes. Definitely a V-32 attack."

"It seems the reign of terrorism has begun. You guessed right about it being in France. You're also right about the size of the community the terrorist would attack. What other theories do you have, this time to save lives?"

"The attacks will continue in France until the rat feels in complete control of the country. This one was in the north of France. I think the next ones will be in the south. Our terrorist wants to show off his ability to move at will and at the same time keep our investigative strengths divided. I think a beachfront location where youths like to hang out is the logical place for your headhunters to set up shop."

Danielson asked, "Do you think he has already recruited his cut group?"

"No. Too soon after the last attack. The terrorist rat has to evaluate his level of success."

Danielson breathed an audible sigh of relief. "I was hoping you'd say that. Do you want a closer shot at this? I still have one more plane ticket to Europe."

"No thanks, Tom. I can do better work from here. Just tell your headhunters to look for a beach where lots of youths congregate. The next point of attack will be near that area. Why don't you come out here and we can double-team it."

"Good idea. I can use a change of scenery. I'll be on a plane tomorrow."

TWO NIGHTS LATER as the two men returned from Blackhawk, they saw the light on the green phone blinking.

Danielson opened his briefcase, withdrew a small code book, and flipped some pages. Taking a pen from his pocket, he scribbled different letters and numbers. Using the house phone, he punched the code and waited.

A person on the other end answered, "Bonjour. This is President Galdet's personal secretary. My I ask who is calling?"

"This is Tom Danielson. I received President Galdet's request to call." And then cupping his hand over the mouthpiece, mumbled some identifying words from his code book. After a short delay the other end of the line sprang to life.

"Chairman Danielson? This is President Galdet."

"I am here with Dr. Siegal. I want him to hear the conversation so he will get your input firsthand."

Expecting the worst, Danielson touched the button for the speaker. "Where did they attack this time?"

"That's just it, Mr. Danielson. They have not yet attacked again." There was a short pause. "You thought they would carry out at least another incursion before contacting me. Instead, I received a short message sent by courier this morning."

"It's not like the terrorist to rush an action," said Siegal.

Danielson shook his head. "On the other hand, it is a bit of good fortune in that fewer people will have to die before some form of counter can begin. Please read the message, Mr. President."

Galdet began:

As you may expect, the incident in the north had to happen. However, no other incidents have to happen if you follow my lead. I want you to know I can kill as many French people as I wish. Believe me when I say I can make you totally ineffective to stop me. I will be in contact shortly. Be prepared to follow my demands or you can expect more deaths, this time in the south of France.

Galdet paused. "What shall I do? You are chairman of the SOS and selected to protect us from this madman."

Galdet was not the only one who was scared. Both men at the chalet looked at each other. They dared not speak; the phone was on the loudspeaker. All they could do was shake their heads.

"Mr. President," Danielson began, "we expected our terrorist to make another attack before contacting you. This letter is very beneficial for us. He is laughing at our inability to stop him."

"His brazen, cannot-fail attitude may be his weakness,"

suggested Siegal. "Something we can use to plan against him."

Danielson continued, "This letter confirms our suspicions that your nation is the target. I have sent my operatives to southern France waiting for my instructions. And, as for your question about how I can protect you, the answer is not simple. The only way we can protect anyone is to capture the terrorist and put him out of business. Mr. President, there is one more thing. I need the letter for investigation. I know you have excellent forensic experts. But if this threat leaks, there will be a panic situation you cannot control. In the meantime, trace the letter through the messenger service used to deliver it. If we can determine the origin of it, at least we could shorten the world search for our terrorist's nest."

President Galdet spoke, "My secret service is doing that as we speak. I will do as you request, send the original document by currier."

The conversation ended.

Siegal sat back in his chair. A man who impressed him so at their first meeting at the chalet was caving in fear. *The first part of the terrorist plot is working. Humbling behavior, a sign of fear, is a step toward being dominated. Can I, you, or anyone else stop this madman?*

Siegal moved his lips silently.

"What?"

"Just thinking."

Danielson looked at Siegal. "Don't you panic yet. I think we're in offensive mode. My headhunters are on point." He dialed a number and waited.

"This is my cell number. Although I am not at home, your message will be forwarded to me. J."

"Contact me the first chance you get."

FIFTY-TWO

NOT WAITING FOR A REPLY from his headhunters, Danielson thumbed through his cell phone directory and speed-dialed Labs Plus, a highly secret forensic research facility.

"This is Tom Danielson. May I speak with Dr. B?"

A pause. "Good. No elevator music.*"*

"Yes, Mr. Danielson, this is Dr. B."

"There will be a letter in my mailbox at the White House in two days. You have my identification number on file for authorization to retrieve it. Find out everything you can about the contents ASAP."

"You continually amaze me," said Siegal. "Among other surprise connections, you're also on a first-name basis with a secret research lab. I pity anyone who becomes your enemy. I wouldn't be surprised if you have your own little army as well and Ben is head of that force."

Danielson winked.

NIGHTS AT THE chalet were always cool, no matter how warm it was during the day. Danielson lit a fire in the stone hearth to warm the living room. Ben, no longer the invisible man, always left a large bowl of hot popcorn on the table and cold Old Dog's Leg in the refrigerator following their after-dinner walks. Tonight, Danielson invited him to join them. He did.

"Now what?" asked Siegal.

"We wait, both for my headhunters to position themselves in the French Riviera region, and Labs Plus's work on the message. I hope the Rat Pack gives us enough time to find some answers."

"All dressed up for the dance and no date," said Siegal. "We have always been so busy with one crisis or another. Tell me about yourself. You never mention it. Are you married, have children, all the usual stuff?"

Danielson surprised himself at how private he was. He knew everything about Siegal and Siegal knew nothing about him.

"Married, yes; children, no. But being a Navy SEAL and the White House Chief of Staff never allowed much time for a private life. Ultimately, my wife found a male companion who could give her the affection I held back from offering. We parted as mutual friends and occasionally see each other at official events. That was several years ago. It is the one part of my life I could not manage."

"I'm sorry. Do you miss that part of your life?"

"I had to make a choice. It's like wanting pie a la mode with two scoops of ice cream when you're on a strict diet."

THE FIRE IN the living room hearth burned brightly. Goldberg brought the bowl of hot popcorn and the beer and took a seat with the two men.

"You've been unusually quiet all day. What's eating you, Ross?"

"I'm trying to get a more complete behavioral profile on the head rat. We know what he wants. But we need to discover a trait, you know, a subconscious weakness we can exploit besides his never-can-fail attitude."

"I'm no psychologist," said Danielson. "One thing for sure, he's no Robin Hood doing things from the goodness of his heart. I don't think he even has a heart."

Siegal said, "I agree he's power hungry. Only there's a stronger driving motivation. He has to prove something. That is his payoff."

"I'm not following."

"All animal behavior has motivation. It can be food, sex, warmth, love, acceptance, or a myriad of other things. We need to discover our terrorist's motivation. With his superior problem-solving capability, he could be almost anything else."

"Is that your ground-zero answer for what to attack?" asked Goldberg.

Siegal nodded. "One trait we know is his unusually strong charismatic personality. He can get almost anything out of anybody. It's common to all world leaders. I remember the first time I entered the dining room and saw all the Summit members looking at me. The power of these individuals even just sitting there and saying nothing made my body parts revolt. I almost peed in my pants."

Goldberg responded, "How do we use that?"

"He has to lead; he can never be second. And this can be double-edged."

Danielson looked puzzled. "I'm not following."

"He sees himself as being invincible. This may be his Achilles heel, the weak link to get at him. It will cause him to make a foolish mistake. And we need only one mistake."

"You may have something there. I read while getting you on board that the larger the size of one's self worth, the less that person really knows about themselves. They feel omnipotent and believe they can never be stopped."

"Right, a blind spot."

Coughing out a husk, Siegal continued, "I think we can lure the rat out of hiding by playing on this blind spot. Once he's in the open, his best defense, invisibility, is diminished. We need to find the cheese to draw our rat out of his hole or, even better, find his hole."

Danielson jumped up, spilling the popcorn bowl. "Yes. That threatening letter to Galdet before attacking a second city."

Siegal finished the thought, "A very big mistake. He's successful every time he has tried so far, starting with his base of operations, still an unknown factor to us. His second-level leadership is working well gathering cut groups. His intel, in learning about the V-32 virus and where it was stored, was truly amazing."

"But we stopped him in Rock Island," said Goldberg, returning with more popcorn and beer.

"Did we really? Remember, his real target was our secret munitions depot in Biloxi. And now an attack in France, creating fear in President Galdet. In the parlance of behavioral psychology, the response to a positive reinforcement has been a one-to-one ratio without even the slightest hint of failure. We are dealing with one hell of a super intellect."

"Whoa. You're way past me, Ross. What do you mean by this one-to-one ratio?" asked Danielson.

"It works this way. If you get success five times in a row, then your best expectation for your next effort is a win as well. And, every time success comes after each try, the anticipation is maintained at a one-to-one ratio. Our hope is that he keeps working at this level and expects his successes to continue every time. His sense of omnipotence means he'll start putting in less planning and start getting more careless each time he acts. Sooner or later foolish mistakes will show up. Ergo, his sense of a bulletproof self-image will lure him out of hiding."

Goldberg asked, "What happens if we stop him one or two times in a row?"

"That's when he can become most dangerous. As long as he gets positively reinforced for every effort, he will continue to use his same planning style. For the present, his basic MO is always the same. He uses a cut group to carry out his attacks. Whenever he starts a new action, he collects another set."

"Even the one in northern France?" asked Goldberg.

"Even that one. I believe the cut group membership was collected from one of the nearby communes and given purpose in their action. He will need another group for his next action."

"Do you think he'll change his methods? You know, to fool us or something," said Danielson.

"He'll continue the same way until we stop him or he has achieved his ultimate plan."

"We need to plan so that his first failure will be his last," added Goldberg.

"And the warning letter to Galdet before a second attack, that was something new in his plan, wasn't it?" asked Danielson.

"A major mistake. A chink in his armor," said Siegal. "His conceit interfered with his common sense. He believes no one can stop him and is daring us to do so."

Goldberg said, "You know, we have to get this bastard before he causes too many deaths. He may just kill a few thousand people outside of France for the sport of it."

"He did that in Africa," reminded Siegal. "But his focus is France. He won't leave there until he's done. Once he gets Galdet into his power base, we no longer will have just one man to deal with. We will be adding one of our allies as an enemy. Once this rat gets that far, other nations will fall in line."

FIFTY-THREE

DANIELSON, RETURNING FROM HIS MORNING run, spotted Siegal coming down the stairs.

"How many beers did we drink last night? It seemed like a whole case," Danielson remarked. "I'm beginning to get a taste for your favorite brew."

"Only a few. Altitude does that to you," laughed Siegal. "Care for some scrambled eggs and salami? I've got the hot plate going on the buffet. It's the one thing I'm better at than psychology." He set two plates on the dining room table while Danielson poured coffee from an urn on the buffet. "Anything new?"

"Labs Plus tells me we should have their results regarding the message to Galdet in no more than two days. With any luck, we'll learn where the letter came from and the language quirks giving us the nationality of the person who sent it. Taking a large serving and adding hot sauce, he said, "I've been looking over your wall charts. Do you always do this sort of thing?"

"It helps me to think. Whenever I come up with something new, I either fill in the gaps or start another sheet."

Danielson thought for a moment. "And this funny looking rat?"

"He keeps me sane. I talk with him instead of to myself. At least," Siegal continued, "I did before Ben came to my rescue."

Danielson pointed to one notation. "Single generational?"

Siegal cleared his throat with a swig of coffee. "It tells us something about tyrants and probably terrorists as well. Historically, only during the Roman Empire did control over others last longer than one generation. Again, most lasted only through the life of one leader."

"You're saying we defeat this guy and another, not remotely related, pops up to take his place. It means our rat is not developing another to take his place. You're talking a new terrorist and we haven't put the goddamn damper on this one."

"There's always another waiting in the wings."

Danielson said, "Sounds like a lifetime career for both of us. Getting back to today's business. We've got a fucking terrorist out there who has his claws on France. Okay. Tell me again, why France?"

"Why not? Our Rat Terrorist has his choice. France just got the short straw."

"I get it. But, if he follows despots of the past, he knows his power is time-limited. Right?"

"Right. Our head rat is not an idiot. He's likely a student of history. And he developed his nefarious plot with full knowledge of others before him. I just don't think he cares who follows him."

"I get that, too. He itches, we scratch. Okay, next item. You believe one can control people through fear with very little oversight."

"Right again. He can control many leaders, ergo nations, with very little oversight."

"And thirdly, you think he can maintain control by challenging targeted leaders' self-esteem."

"And, right for the third time."

"It's just that simple to you?"

"Human behavior is not that complicated once you break it down into its elements. That's why you can predict much of human behavior just by studying motivation, or, as we behaviorists say, reward verses punishment.

"Eat your salami and eggs before they get cold. And then you need to get your headhunters to work right away."

Danielson picked up the phone. "The eggs can wait." A few moments later he said, "Done."

FIFTY-FOUR

LATE WINTER SNOWS PILED HIGH, trapping Siegal in the chalet and doing their best to cover most of the United States. By contrast, the warm sunny weather in southern France was a welcome change, greeting the headhunters as they stepped off the plane carrying only backpacks as luggage. Doug leased a four-door compact from one of the discount car rental booths, and they were soon out of the airport and headed toward the beach.

"Any suggestions where we hang our hats?" asked Jamie as they looked at the map of the French Riviera.

Kevin, who enjoyed streaming the internet more than the other three, suggested, "I was checking out several spots that should make our cover look good." He read from a brochure on his iPad. "The small beach community called Saint-Aygulf, known for its open way of life. Teens to young-at-hearts are drawn to this avant-garde community offering styles of swimming and sunbathing apparel from full coverage to complete nudity. The waves are friendly and provide novice body surfers easy rides."

Tim said, "Sounds good to me. I like the idea of the beautiful exposing their bodies to the sun."

"And to you," joked Jamie, "I suggest a cold shower."

The conversation remained casual, no talk of business during the twenty-minute beachfront ride from the airport. Doug rolled down his driver-side window to enjoy the warm and unpolluted air, so different from D.C. mired with auto exhausts. Jamie checked the local airport map for possible locations to set up shop. Kevin closed his eyes and was asleep in moments. Tim continued his stare out his window, enjoying the bikini-clad women jogging and riding bicycles.

In the beach village of Saint-Aygulf, the temporary population outnumbered permanent residents four-to-one. The main street faced the Mediterranean and was dotted with many boutique hotels catering to short-term renters. As luck would have it, two adjacent hotels for younger singles displayed vacancy signs in their lobby windows. Doug found a small parking garage about a block away and stowed the rental. The four split into pairs. Jamie and Doug went first, opting for the hotel to the right. Kevin and Tim took the other to avoid anyone making them as a group of four. It was still a little early in the season and neither pair had a problem getting rooms with windows facing the coastline.

In her hotel room, Jamie gave directions via her cell phone. "Kevin and Tim, I suggest the two of you patrol the beach area. Look for possibles like you did in Dallas. I know this will be hard for you, Tim, but try to keep your mind on what you're supposed to be doing. Doug and I will reconnoiter the local bar scene."

THE BOYS, IN swimsuits, wraparound glasses, and sunscreen, settled under a tree that offered a panoramic view of the beach.

Doug and Jamie, dressed in shorts and T-shirts, moved through the many small bars on both sides of the beach. Everyone enjoyed the unusual heat wave for this time of year.

From the semi-darkness of one bar came a voice. "Hey, chickie babe, haven't I seen you somewhere before?"

Jamie turned. The accent was all too familiar. It was Shark.

She whispered to Doug. "This has to be more than a coincidence."

Doug tensed. "Fantastic. We struck the motherlode on our first try. I'll text an alert to Kevin and Tim."

Jamie went into her act, pretending not to recognize Shark. "Could be, lover boy. I've been to other places before."

"No, for real. I think we even played some eight ball once. As I recall, you beat me up pretty good. Care for a rematch to avenge my bruised ego?"

"I do remember you now. I think you tried to come on to me. I told you then I just go in for table sports. If we do play some pool, don't get any other ideas."

"No problem, babe. There's plenty of skin all over the beach if I want some of that. Do you have anything going on later? There's a decent pool table over there." He pointed to a little bar on the edge of the sand. "It's a great hangout for people like us."

"Maybe I'll see you there later. I just got into town this morning for a short vacation. Besides, I have my friend here who I came in with. I'm not a ditch bitch."

"Hey, again no problem. As I said before, I just like a good game of pool once in a while and the competition here isn't so great. And you have more going for you than all these other beach-loving deadheads. I'll be busy until about nine tonight if it interests you. Later, sweet cheeks." With a wave of his hand, he was out of the bar and off running down the beach toward the surf.

Doug said, "That guy is slick. I believe he had you blushing a little. Play your cards right and I can fix the two of you up."

"In your mother's dreams, Doug. He's definitely not my type. That man is scary. I swear he'd just as soon kill you as make love to you. There's no way he gets me in a room alone. Keep an eye out for his clone. I suspect if something is going down, that guy has to be around somewhere. I don't want that rat sneaking up on us."

THAT NIGHT, THE headhunters met for a takeout dinner in Jamie's hotel room to map out their strategy.

Jamie shared a cell phone picture she took of Shark in Rock Island. "Danielson sent us here because he suspects things will be happening here."

Doug added, "Shark is not here by chance. My gut tells me something is happening right now. I hope we're not too late for Danielson's sake."

"And for the world, for that matter," chimed Tim.

FIFTY-FIVE

KEVIN SNAPPED HIS FINGERS. "GOT an idea. Tim and I can be bait and be selected as cut group possibles. This Shark already knows the two of you; we're unknown assets, and the right age."

"Too dangerous. Mr. Danielson reminded us when we were in Rock Island that we're not trained as spy types. They'd spot you in a second," responded Doug. "Our skill is surveillance, not counterterrorism."

Agreeing with Kevin, Tim suggested, "But on the other hand, it's simpler than identifying others and having dental implants done on them. We already know the types this terrorist wants for his cut groups. We can act the part."

Jamie thought for a moment, then reluctantly agreed. "We'll try it while still looking for other possibles. Just remember, protect your backsides at all times. And don't get nosy. If it begins to look the least bit edgy, you're both out of there. And that's an order."

"Yes, ma'am." They saluted.

"I'm skipping any pool game tonight. It will just make Shark work harder to entice me. And if I am a good judge of his type, get him to drop some of his protective armor."

THE MORNING SUN offered another warm day of sunbathing and other forms of leisure for most of the people in Saint-Aygulf. The ploy was to act the part but to remember their serious mission— thwart whatever plans the rat terrorist had. With Shark in the area they knew there was little time to waste.

Tim was on the beach first. He discarded his spandex swimsuit and pretended to spend the day taking the sun in the full Monty. He carefully chose a book on political/art revolution of the twenties and thirties in Europe, when young activists stood on boxes in nearly every park's open space reciting poetry and damning their particular governmental leaders. Kevin followed in cutoffs. He took a table in a shaded area at a nearby coffee house to protect his light skin from the sun's rays.

By plan, Jamie and Doug came out an hour later. They decided on breakfast in a small, sidewalk café on the edge of the beach just across from the bar with the pool table suggested by Shark.

"Hey. Small world, ain't it. Mind if I sit down?" Shark did, not waiting to be invited. "Their English muffins with homemade grape preserves are the best thing on the morning menu. Say, sweet thing, do you have a name?"

Guarding against any subtle slip, she decided to use her actual name. "I'm Jamie and this is Doug. What's yours? I sort of pictured your name as Shark."

Whether it was truly his name or not, he said, "As a matter of fact, that's exactly what most of my friends call me."

"Say, where's your sidekick? You know, the one we saw you with in the States?" asked Jamie.

"You must mean Snake."

"Shark and Snake," said Doug. "What an interesting combination of names."

"Yeah, kind of funny, ain't it. He's around somewhere. Last night he was with some rich chick. For all I know, he's still banging her. When I see him, I'll tell him you asked."

There was no need for subtle looks or signals. As experienced headhunters, they knew Shark and Snake were there to round up possibles.

Shark was the first to get up. "I've got to go. You know the drill, people to see, places to go and all that shit. Here are some Euros. It should cover breakfast. My treat. You can buy tomorrow."

Once Shark was out of earshot, Doug asked, "Do you think he's on to us?"

Jamie shrugged. "Can't tell for sure. I know he's a great judge of character. I say we keep our cover of just being a couple here for a vacation break. Any prying and he'll make us in a second."

"That leaves us to let Kevin and Tim do their thing and cover their backsides as best we can," said Doug.

"Right. Tonight I think I'll be playing some pool. And you?"

"I think I'll wander around a little, maybe do a little tourist shopping. I'll drop in at the bar later as if I was coming to get you. Meanwhile, I'll let the boss know what's happening."

FIFTY-SIX

IT WAS JUST AFTER SUNSET when the weather abruptly changed. Severe lightning and a sudden shower forced all the nighttime beach revelers indoors. The covered cafes and beach bars were jammed with half-bikini-clad moon bathers and nude nature lovers.

Tim hung out at one of the beach bars playing pinball. Kevin sat nearby at a two-top table reading his book when Jamie arrived as planned. They displayed no visual recognition.

Shark camped at one of the two pool tables, pretending to let some locals win at his favorite game. Snake was there walking in and around, making general conversation with different young adults. He approached Kevin's table.

"Is this chair taken?"

Kevin pretended to be uninterested and kept reading.

"The place is full tonight," continued Snake. "Mind if I sit down?"

Kevin continued his act but he could feel his heart beating. He gave an uninspired hand motion.

Looking at the book title, Snake said, "I read that book once. It has some pretty interesting shit in it. I like the way common folks stood up against the government. The rich get richer and the poor get an old bone, like us." Snake was indeed living up to his name, using his well-rehearsed conversation opener. If Kevin was a true cut group candidate, he would have been sucked into Snake's coils.

Kevin, acting the naïve reactionary, looked up. "You read this book?"

"It's like my Gideon Bible that I keep by my bedside."

I have a nibble, you bastard. Now take it slow and easy.

Kevin looked up. "I used to think only unimportant people like us think this way. But this book tells me that some of the most famous writers and artists of all time felt the same. That includes the likes of Dali, Monet, and Picasso."

"Man, you got it. What's your name, dude?"

"Kevin. And yours?"

"I don't have a regular name. Some folks around here call me Snake." He pointed to a tattooed reptile wound around his bicep. "Pretty cool, huh?"

"Too bad for me. My skin's too sensitive for tattoos."

Careful, not too fast, but not too slow or Snake will bolt.

"I just got here. So far I've been to exactly two places. The coffee shop down the street where they let me read and my one overpriced room from the beach. Tonight I decided to come in here for a change of scenery."

"This can be your lucky night. Let me tell you, this bar is a good place to socialize if you're in to it."

"I'm not into the social thing. I like to keep to myself."

"Are you one of those guys who doesn't like girls?"

"It's not that. I'm just shy I guess. Don't like noisy crowds."

"No big deal. I'm that way, too. Hey, man, you know, if you're interested, there's a small group of us that hang over at the park. There're plenty of trees to protect your fancy skin from the sun. Just joking about your skin."

Snake waited for a response from Kevin to judge his interest. Kevin, a trained interviewer as a headhunter, acted neutral to Snake's suggestion. It became a scrimmage between two battle tested warriors.

"No offense taken, Snake. I burn very easily," said Kevin. "Did you say the park?"

"Sure. It's on the edge of town. You know, away from all these government-loving tourists. If you want to try it out, just follow the main drag away from the ocean. You can't miss it. We usually get together in the late afternoon. Someone usually pitches in and buys the beer and pizza. After that, it's whatever you're smoking that makes you happy, if you get what I mean."

"Sounds good to me," said Kevin. He reached into his pocket for change. "Let me buy you a beer or something."

"Don't worry. The beers are on me. I already set it up with my friend the bartender. Say, why don't you come along with me and I'll introduce you around the room. There are a couple of chicks here who enjoy an intellectual like you."

Kevin got up with Snake's arm around his shoulder.

JAMIE TOOK HER turn shooting pool with Shark while watching Kevin and Snake out of the corner of her eye. It took her attention off the game. She missed an easy bank shot and scratched.

"Something bothering you, girl? That's two out of three for me."

"What? Oh, I must have been daydreaming or something."

"Come on," Shark played at begging. "Play another. We'll use my Euros."

"No thanks, I'm too tired. Maybe tomorrow."

She exited the bar just as Doug was coming in the door. She shot him a quick thumbs-up sign. At the same time, Tim nodded his head in the direction of Kevin and Snake.

Doug eased up to the bar. "Bartender, do you have any wine that won't sour my insides?" He sat at the bar a few stools from Tim.

Kevin left with Snake. They talked for a while outside the bar and then parted in different directions. Shark stayed on the pool table, playing all comers.

About eleven o'clock, Doug and Tim left the bar, staggering their departures to avoid any connection.

AT ELEVEN THIRTY, the team convened in Jamie's room to review the day's events.

"We're on target," stated an elated Jamie.

"Right," added Doug with a wink. "and our leader is setting her target on Shark."

"That's not at all true. Women are not crotch-watchers like men. Don't worry about me, guys. Under other circumstances, I might be tempted, but this guy is one bad apple and he is going down. I was married once and I really do date men now and then."

Her comments quieted the good-hearted bantering. The team had been together for several years and worked in some of the closest confines. And suddenly each realized they knew almost nothing of each other's personal lives.

Doug got them back on track. "I noticed the other guy hung onto you, Kevin. How did it all go down?"

"Snake slithered over and started a conversation. Seemed he had already read my book and acted interested in my apparent feelings regarding ruling powers in general. He invited me to join his like-minded friends at the edge of town for some beer and pizza tonight. I begged off. I figure he'll ask me again. I'm betting on tomorrow."

Doug warned, "Don't put him off too long. I think he's collecting cut groupies as we speak."

Jamie nodded. "I agree. If he doesn't contact you, you'll need to find that place in the park yourself. Now it's late. Enough for today."

THE RAIN STOPPED about midnight and morning brought back the warming sun. Tim spent the day pretending to enjoy some body surfing. Doug stayed on the beach, watching over the others like a guard dog. Jamie redeemed herself at the pool table, taking Shark in eight of ten games. That afternoon Snake found Kevin and guided him to his private party in the park.

THAT NIGHT THE headhunters gathered in Jamie's room, anxious to get Kevin's report.

"Snake and I walked about a half mile to a wooded area. He introduced me to four young twenties. We shot the breeze for a couple of hours, talking mostly about dirty politics and social class issues, including the high prices team owners pay their professional athletes. One of the guys left and brought back pizzas and beer. We lit a couple of joints. Excuse me if I still act a little high. I tried not to inhale too deeply, but that weed was really high quality."

"Any talk about killing anybody?" asked Doug.

"None at all. It was all social."

Jamie joked, "Be careful about fitting in too much. We wouldn't want to lose you to the other side."

"Hey, girl, from what I'm hearing, you shouldn't be so concerned about me."

Jamie gave a finger sign back.

"Don't act too sold on everything," warned Doug. "Let Snake and Shark sell you when they're ready."

The headhunters didn't need Doug's advice. They were a seasoned group and knew their covers to perfection.

"I guess I'm the leper," frowned Tim. "No one wants me."

"Don't get too down-hearted. It's still early in the game. If they want more recruits, you're still in the mix. But if not, you're an unknown to them, which may come in handy later," said Jamie.

Jamie's cell rang. It was Danielson. The events of the past two days were relayed to him. Danielson congratulated them on their creativity to get involved. "Shark and Snake are no dummies or the head rat would not give them so much leeway. I don't need any of you ending ten toes up. Good headhunters are hard to find."

THE NEXT TWO days were uneventful. Tim was left alone. Kevin finished one book and started on another about the early hippies of Germany just prior to World War I, when young men and women paraded around the countryside in their birthday suits singing tunes of revolution accompanied by others playing guitars. Jamie and Shark spent time together talking, sipping wine and playing eight ball. Doug and Tim stayed in the shadows, ready to move if needed. On both days at about five, Snake would meander over to Kevin and escort him to the park. Things were moving well. Neither Shark nor Snake showed any signs of mistrust.

Then things changed.

FIFTY-SEVEN

AFTER MUCH URGING DURING A pool game, Jamie agreed to a casual dinner at one of the beachfront restaurants. Just before desert was ordered, Shark excused himself, saying he had to call his mother before she went to bed. That was the night Shark joined Snake and the recruits at the park.

A mission was imminent.

The team put themselves on full alert. Jamie called Danielson and got permission to follow through with their plan as long as it did not entail any deadly force. As part of their plan, Kevin bought an electronic locator device from the local pet store and taped it just under his left armpit. The team tensed, hoping their efforts would save lives and neutralize a part of the terrorist organization.

THE ATMOSPHERE AT the park resembled the 1960s. About a dozen hippie-looking young men and women, dressed in recycled clothes, sat around a campfire spouting anti-government slogans. Wine and hash pipes passed freely. The only thing missing was acts of free love. Out of the darkness, Shark approached and sat down beside Snake. Everyone identified Snake as their leader and when he stood, all talking stopped.

"Tonight we have a very special guest at our campfire. This is my friend Shark. Some of you may have seen him around the beach."

Shark started to speak. "You all are enjoying the beach. But is it free?"

"No," chanted the group in unison.

"You're right. The beach, the sea, and the air around us have been here before man inhabited this area. Who owns it now? Is it you or me?"

"No."

"Is it fair to be under the ruling dominance of the oppressive French government?"

"No." chanted the group even louder.

"We need a change. Are you afraid to stand up for freedom?"

"No."

"Are you willing to cower back and continue to be slaves of this republic?"

"No, no, no," chanted the frenzied group.

Alcohol and drugs loosening everyone's minds and Shark's effective words of persuasion were a lethal combination.

"Soon, very soon, it will be your turn to act for freedom."

The crowd split up about midnight. The damage was done and a new group of recruits had been inducted to follow the head rat's plan.

DANIELSON CALLED PRESIDENT Galdet. "Our terrorist is ready to strike. He recruited about a dozen followers in Saint-Aygulf. I expect they will attack tomorrow. Can you have your special forces outside the town and intercept them?"

"They will be ready in three hours," said Galdet. "C'est la Guerre."

Donaldson continued. "One of my operatives is embedded with them. He will look like the rest. He can be recognized by a white beret. Don't shoot him."

"He will be safe."

THE RECRUITS GATHERED in the park. Two canvas-covered trucks were parked nearby.

Snake called out, "All right everyone. This is your chance to prove how you feel about the oppressive French government. Each of you take a rifle and climb into the trucks."

It was the signal for the French Special Forces to attack. Bursts of gunfire exploded into the trees, sending a rain of leaves and branches on the recruits. The shock effect stopped them in their tracks. Most threw down their weapons and raised their hands in terror. Three, including Snake, chose to return fire and were killed in the abbreviated firefight.

The green phone in Danielson's office rang. It was Galdet. "Our mission at Saint-Aygulf was successful. The French Special Forces were able to stop them before any civilians were killed. The terrorist your headhunters call Snake was killed along with two recruits."

"And my headhunter?"

"He was hit in the shoulder by a stray bullet from one of the recruits."

"Damn. What about the other recruiter called Shark?"

"He was not part of the raid."

"Still, not only did we stop a deadly attack but took a second-level member out as well. Did they have any V-32 in the truck?"

"No," answered Galdet, surprised at the revelation. Then Galdet's message sobered. Danielson listened as his smile disappeared. "Thank you, sir. I'm sorry." He replaced the phone in its cradle.

"THAT'S THE GOOD news, Ross. The bad news is there was a second simultaneous attack on a village five miles down the road. Devastation was complete. All were killed with V-32. We fucked up, you and I," said Danielson.

Siegal sat stunned. "Of course. The rat used a two-pronged attack on the weapons depot. It was successful then, so it was logical he would use a two-pronged attack on the villages. There had to be at least another team of second level people gathering recruits. I missed that entirely. These deaths are my fault. As your behavioral profiler, I should have known that."

"Don't be so hard on yourself, Ross. He set us off with a single raid in the north of France. Why wouldn't we expect a single one in the south as well?"

"We can't let him do this to us again. I'm fucking angry. This rat terrorist has made it personal."

FIFTY-EIGHT

BEN GOLDBERG CAME INTO THE chalet dining room with an envelope. "This just came by special messenger, Mr. Danielson." He put it on the table and stepped back waiting for any other order.

Danielson recognized the security wax seal on the flap. "Let's see what the laboratory has for us, Ross."

Inside was the original message to President Galdet and a thin packet labeled "FINDINGS." Siegal remembered the voluminous reports they always had to provide at City University and ID. Here was information that could save the world in three pages total.

"Interesting," said Danielson digesting the information silently. "The type of paper used is of low quality. Comparison studies of the petroleum used in the process rules out Asia and Middle Eastern countries. The fiber length is short, suggesting it did not originate in the United States. The lab techs feel strongly that the origin of this paper is European. The ink used is a cheap generic. Its origin can't be traced. The language syntax is European, probably Teutonic in nature. They narrowed the author as being Eastern European, probably German. Ross, can you add any inferences to their report?"

"Sounds complete to me. A rat with a German history is intriguing. If that's his background, then it may answer questions of motive. It's something I have to mull over" Changing the subject, he asked, "Did you get any report about the trace on the courier from President Galdet?"

"None. The president put his best men on it. They found the message didn't come directly to Galdet. It was first delivered to the Swiss embassy. When they opened it, there was a sealed letter with forwarding instructions."

"That means you can forewarn the Swiss embassy, should another message be sent to them."

"Sounds nice, Ross, but don't put much store in that. Paris is loaded with foreign embassies. As clever as our rat is, he will send his next message through another embassy. We could never cover them all."

"I wasn't thinking that."

"So my psychological friend, do you have any thoughts about where this rat has his hole in the wall, besides, of course, somewhere in Eastern Europe?"

"Try this on for size. A German despot attempted to conquer the world through armed force and it became known as World War I. A second unsavory character, also a German, wanted to control the world through armed domination and even attempted to do it with the help of Italy and Japan. Both were successful to a point, ultimately failing. The world has changed and time has passed, but I am not so sure the personality of world domination has left the mindset of the Germans. His strategy has changed, but the wishes for world domination has not."

"Good focus from my favorite behavioral profiler."

"Does that help you with a plan?"

Danielson glanced over toward Goldberg and thought of his headhunter assets in France. "Maybe."

FIFTY-NINE

JAMIE LAY IN BED WITH a smile on her face that seemed to reach from ear to ear. It was the first time Danielson used her team as part of the action instead of their usual role, locating people with certain profiles. She thought of Kevin's success as a recruit by the terror- ists. Her team had helped to avert an attack that saved many lives.

Sleep came easy.

"What the hell?"

Jamie rolled over and looked at the illuminated hands of her travel clock. "Two thirty?"

She was not expecting a call. As far as she was concerned, her work in France was complete except the wait for Kevin's release from the regional hospital so they could return to the United States as a group.

Danielson's voice at the other end was sober, not at all what Jamie would have expected. He filled her in on both the success and failure of the rat's actions.

"We didn't plan to put you and your team in any real danger. I'm sorry."

"You mean having Kevin wounded? He'll heal."

"No, I mean even more than that." Danielson paused and then went on. "Jamie, I need your help to find this rat's den. At this time, we believe his home country is Germany. But that's as close as we can pinpoint."

"What do you want from us now? We'll do it. You can bet on that."

"It isn't the team I want this time. I need you to go it alone. Our best lead is Shark. I hate to ask, but you know him best and according to your reports, he seems to have a thing for you. And…"

"And you think my relationship with him can help lead to the head rat's home base."

"Dr. Siegal thinks the failure at Saint-Aygulf may have shaken him up and expects he will be calling his second level members together for a powwow. We need to know where that is. Shark has to be one of his sharper guerrillas, possibly even a part of his top tier. He would easily catch on to any normal form of surveillance. Dr. Siegal thinks his attraction to you can blind his suspicious nature."

"Tell me, do you always woo your agents in this manner?"

"Never. But, the stakes are high and we're out of choices. And we think you can do it."

"Then I have no choice."

"You can walk. You'll still be my main headhunter. But I was betting you'd say yes. The money isn't great and the hours are worse. And, oh by the way, your life may not be worth a plugged nickel."

"The second shoe hasn't dropped. Give me more details."

"You'll have to do things that go against your grain. But if you trust your natural instincts, you should come out of this okay. Lie, steal, or whatever. There is no training for what I'm asking. Just remember, whatever you do is strictly business. My quick-strike force will keep in close contact should you need to be extracted quickly."

"I'm a big girl now. I can handle it. As you say, I'll have to trust my instincts. How will we keep in touch?"

"Check your message box in the hotel lobby. I sent you a mid-range locator beacon. It's about the size of a nickel. We'll be able to track you from fifty miles away. It includes a variable sender beacon, making it difficult to trace. Find a safe place to hide it. If you get caught with it, we can't promise to…you know…"

"Protect me?"

Jamie was wide awake now. She imagined several scenarios. None pleased her.

"Yes, sir, you want me to become Shark's main squeeze. I've done one-nighters in the past, sometimes not even knowing the person's last name. It's not like losing my virginity. All I have to think of is that it will be a small price to pay in exchange for saving many lives. I'll keep him interested in me, I'm a woman. It shouldn't be too hard."

"Few people will ever know what you have to do. I promise."

Jamie smiled, "I just decided where to hide the locator beacon. I hope your beacon doesn't transmit pictures. In case you're curious, it'll be attached to my diaphragm. Be sure your little tracker is moisture proof."

DOUG AND JAMIE sat in one of the numerous coffee shops having a late breakfast. After all, the Riviera was a vacation mecca where nobody gets up early. Kevin, healing nicely, was being transferred to a military hospital for further observation so far as anyone else knew. Officially, he was under house arrest.

"Sleep well, Doug?"

"Yeah sure." Jamie never started a conversation this way.

"Okay, what's up?"

Jamie went over her conversation with Danielson.

"You're not going to go through with it, are you? You could find yourself in a compromising situation too sticky to climb out of."

"Don't worry about me. Its business. I can damn well keep my personal feelings separate. All those deaths he's already responsible for makes it easier. This asshole is going down and I want to be a part of that."

"About the team? Do we keep doing, you know, hanging out or what?"

"Kevin will return home for recuperation soon. Tim is still an unknown to the enemy and will disappear for now."

"Good. That leaves me to protect your backside."

"Sorry, you can't do that. My role will be to lure Shark into a relationship. Your presence interferes with that."

"Interfere? What the hell, Jamie. We're talking about your safety. I'm sticking around."

"No you aren't. You take orders from me. You're flying back with the others. Danielson already ordered your ticket.

You leave on the six o'clock tonight. I need your rapid departure to convince Shark we had a falling out and that he and I can become an item."

Doug, with tears in his eyes, gave Jamie a warm hug. "Good luck, girl. Take care of yourself."

"I will. I will."

AROUND NOON AND two cappuccinos later, Shark wandered by.

"Hey, sweet cheeks, where's your shadow?"

"We had a fling for the week, but he had to leave and go back to his wife, I guess. It was fine while it lasted, but if I ever want to get serious about someone, that guy would have to be…"

"Let me guess. Single, entertaining, and probably a little mysterious to keep your interest."

"Single was what I was going for, but the other points are definitely a plus. Sounds like you're talking about yourself. Are you putting a sell job on me?" teased Jamie.

Shark changed the subject. "Want to go for a swim and some dinner later?"

"Are you sure you're available? Or do you have to check in with your mother?"

"She's fine."

"I have to go back and get my swimsuit." She winked. "I hope it fits."

"I'll walk with you, if you don't mind."

Once at the door to Jamie's hotel room, the mood got heavy. Shark was moving as if to be invited in, but Jamie blocked the door. They kissed and she slid into her room but left the door open a crack to let the conversation continue.

"No rush, we can continue this evening."

"Not tonight. I just broke up, remember? I'm not completely over it. I think I just want to be alone. You know, I have some postcards to mail back to the States. Let's skip the swim and the later dinner. I'll see you tomorrow." She closed the door and latched the security chain.

Shark, acting the smooth poker player, raised his voice. "Then tomorrow it is. I'll see you for brunch. Wear your swimsuit. We'll go sailing."

LATER THAT NIGHT the usual call from Danielson came to determine how things were going.

"Your plan is working. He's interested all right. It'll be like Ulysses, and I'm the Siren."

"Just take it slow. This man plays everything for keeps. He'll kill you in an instant if he suspects anything. What's going on with the guys?"

"They'll be on the plane tonight. Everything is a go. I'll call you again when I can. In the meantime, you have me on your waterproof locator beacon."

"I wish there was some other way to trap these terrorists."

Jamie knew what he meant, Danielson was suggesting that Jamie keep away from sex, but he knew this was wishful thinking. There could be no soft spots in their plan.

SIXTY

THE PAPARAZZI WERE RELENTLESS. CAMERAS clicked in rapid succession. Reporters and correspondents from all over the world tried to get the latest word. On the garden steps of the Elysee Palace, Galdet's residence, the president faced them in a futile attempt to defuse their feeding frenzy.

A personal spokesperson for President Galdet came to the podium first, speaking in both French and English. "Attention, the President is about to make a statement regarding the incidents in two rural provinces. He will not field questions until there is more information available."

Galdet started slowly, "Thank you for being here today. You are all aware of two serious accidents to several of my fellow citizens. One week ago there was a deadly incident, possibly an unknown viral epidemic, which attacked a small village in the north. Because of the remote location, we were not able to bring in proper medical support before every man, woman, and child died. We were at first concerned that this was some highly contagious disease, one that would travel from city to city. Then two days ago, a village near Saint-Aygulf contracted what we believe is a similar deadly strain. Our medical teams are investigating every clue at this very moment. Thank you very much. Vive la France."

Questions were shouted from the press corps.

"Is this the beginning of the end, as some soothsayers predict?"

"We were told there are mysterious fumes leaking through the mantle of the earth's crust, is that true?"

"Does this coincide with recent UFO sightings?"

"Are you experimenting with some radioactive chemical?"

"Is this an outcome of global warming?"

"Is it true that Frenchmen everywhere are demanding your resignation?"

That night, several syndicated newspapers carried graphic images of the devastation in the two villages along with President Galdet's verbatim comments.

WITHOUT HER TEAM support, Jamie sat alone at the usual coffee shop. Shark, acting casual even with the thought of a blooming relationship, came by about noon.

"Hey, sweet cheeks, what's shakin'?"

"Nothing new, just the same old, same old," responded Jamie. "I like you, Shark, but I much prefer to be called Jamie rather than sweet cheeks."

"I'm a quick learner. From now on, you are just the wonderful and beautiful Jamie."

It wasn't so much that Jamie did not appreciate Shark's pet name, but taking control was crucial to their relationship. She sensed that Shark needed a woman with strong character. Anyone weaker, he would have chewed up and spit out.

"You know, I keep looking around for your friend Snake. The two of you have been inseparable. Or am I taking him out of your space?"

"Not really, but you could do that without half trying. He became ill and had to return home to Canada."

Good. She was checking if Shark identified her with Kevin or anything having to do with the raid that went sour. She felt in the clear.

"What would you like to do today?" Without waiting for a response, he said, "I thought maybe you'd like to go deep-sea fishing and after a late dinner, spend some private time together."

"Fishing and dinner sound great. We'll see how the day goes before promising anything more."

He paused. "I have to take care of some unfinished business. Why don't you catch some rays? I'll be back about two."

AT TWO ON the dot, Shark returned. Jamie was enjoying a nap in the sun. Shark leaned over and kissed her on the neck.

Jamie awoke with a start. It was not so much the surprise of being awakened by a kiss, but that the warmth of it countered the expectation from a heartless killer.

"Is it two already?" Jamie asked, trying to collect herself. "Did you take care of your business?"

"It looks like my company wants me back on the road tomorrow. This will be our last day together. I will miss you, Jamie. Really miss you."

Jamie heard his remarks as sincere. She had to take the next step. There was little time. "Well, at least we can enjoy this afternoon and evening. Shall we charter a boat?"

"I already did. There's a small ketch at the pier. I talked to the captain and he's waiting for us. He promised me that if we didn't catch any fish, at least we would enjoy his cooler stocked with wine and oyster dip."

True to form, no one caught any fish, but the wine and oysters did their thing on the only two passengers on board. Shark tried all his moves and they seemed to work. He started to untie her string bikini.

"Not in front of the captain," whispered Jamie. "Later."

They returned to shore about eight.

"Are you hungry?" Shark asked.

"Famished. I didn't realize how hard it is to fish with only wine and oyster dip for bait."

"I know a little restaurant in town that serves excellent lobster."

"Isn't that sort of expensive?" Jamie asked.

"Not to worry, love. My company pays me very well."

"I have never asked what you do. So far I haven't seen you do any work. Are you on vacation?"

"I'm between jobs right now. But I'm still on an expense account."

Dinner passed. Jamie was on the verge of losing her opportunity. Once back at her hotel room, she took the last chance she had. "Do you want to come in for a while?"

No words were exchanged for the next hour. Only animal action.

Shark finally broke the silence. "Jamie, I know it sounds like a line, but you are a special person. I leave tomorrow and we'll be like two ships passing in the night. I will miss you."

"Don't say anything. I feel the same about you."

"I know this is short notice, and I don't know if it will work out. Will you come with me tomorrow?"

She nodded. *The plan is working.*

She handed Shark his clothes and almost pushed him out the door naked. "So leave now and let me pack!"

She took a cold shower to regain her composure before reporting to Danielson. She checked her beacon. It blinked, indicating it was waterproof as advertised.

"Are you okay, Jamie?" Danielson asked.

"Yeah, sure. Why do you ask?"

"According to my watch, it's almost three o'clock in the morning your time. It's either very early or very late for this call."

"Shark is being called away and has to leave in the morning. Either he is setting up for a new raid or he is being called back to the rat's nest. I think it's the latter." She paused. "And he asked me to go with him."

"Do you want to tell me how you did it?" asked Danielson.

"Don't ask. I'm a big girl."

"The ball is in your court. If things get out of hand, we can always extract you quickly. All you have to do is destroy your beacon and we'll come in. All I can say is good luck and be careful."

I'm in control. It's all business.

SIXTY-ONE

JAMIE SAT ON A SALTWATER-AGED bench outside her hotel. She made arrangements for an early checkout and was enjoying the midmorning sun. For her, the weather and ocean view made what was a difficult work week a wonderful dream vacation. She made a mental promise to return one day on her own time.

Her thoughts were suddenly interrupted by a classic air horn. She looked up to see Shark turning the corner.

He put his muscular arm on the passenger headrest of his red BMW convertible. "Morning, sweet...I mean, Jamie. You look ready to go. Good. We have a long drive ahead of us. Put your stuff in the backseat."

Jamie loaded her backpack and patted her door. "Nice. Red BMWs are my favorite means of transportation when I have a choice. I never saw you driving this before. Is it yours or did you just borrow it from your company?"

"It's mine. I like to keep my car handy in case I need to take a quick trip or something. I store it in a rented garage at one of the beach houses down the coast."

How many cars does Shark own, or does he buy and sell them wherever he is sent? Being a prized employee of this terrorist rat must pay pretty well.

Shark reached over and opened the door. As Jamie sat down he leaned over and gave her a warm kiss first on the cheek and then on the lips. Jamie obliged.

"And where to, my fine chauffeur?"

"I'm not exactly your chauffeur, but I think breakfast first is high on my priority list. A long trip is always more pleasant if you start on a full belly."

"Who said that, Shakespeare?"

"No, I did."

They laughed. He drove to their favorite café for a sendoff breakfast. Within the hour, they were highway bound.

"Is this going to be a long ride? Last night tired me out and I could use a little nap."

"This part of the ride is boring. Go ahead."

Jamie tried to read the road signs through her half-closed eyes, but her French was lacking. Her only reference to their direction of travel on the winding road was that the sun remained on the right, giving her the sense of going north. Shark, on the other hand, seemed to know exactly where he was going and changed from one highway to another without a road map. By noon, they were heading northeast.

"Where are we?"

"Never you mind. I told you before, I had to make this business trip, and you are just a guest." Feeling her thigh, he added, "A most welcome guest."

"You know women's curiosity," she said in a flirty manner. "It really doesn't matter, but I've never been to Europe before except to fly in and out of the major cities. Seeing the countryside up this close makes me realize how beautiful this part of the world really is. And maybe I'd like to come back here one day."

The topic was dropped. Soon Shark drove off to the right and parked by a small roadside market.

"I'll be just a minute." Shark got out and returned with a bag of groceries. "I bought some wine, cheese and bread. There's a quiet stream nearby where we can enjoy lunch."

The sound of the water rushing over some rocks and the privacy of their picnic spot offered additional opportunity for Jamie to reinforce her cover.

AROUND FOUR IN the afternoon, the sun was at their backs. The two had reached the border between France and Germany. Jamie was grateful she had used her real name so her passport was acceptable by the German entry patrol. By nightfall, they reached the borders of the famed Rhineland Forest region. They checked into a gingerbread-looking farmhouse turned into a bed-and-breakfast hotel.

"This is the finest inn around," said Shark. "We can check in, rest a while, and have a nice late supper. One room or two?"

"I see no sense in wasting your money."

They approached the check-in desk. "One room. Make it your best."

Later, in the small dining room, the innkeeper approached them. "Sie essen (You want to eat), ja?"

"Ja, danke (thank you)," Shark responded.

"I'm impressed. You speak English and now both French and German. Where did you get so worldly?"

Sharked avoided the question and just smiled. "Just a few words to get along in my business."

The sauerbraten and perfect wine of choice were excellent. Following a leisurely supper, they retired to their room. Jamie collapsed on the antique canopied bed and was asleep in minutes.

IT WAS MIDMORNING when she awoke. Shark was gone without a goodbye. She looked out the window. The space where Shark parked the BMW was vacant.

Did I blow it? Did Shark drive to this out-of-the-way place and then abandon me to carry out his mission? Damn. I was so close and now so far. No sense in feeling sorry about myself. This is not the time to panic. Maybe if I have some breakfast, I can clear my head.

She dressed and went downstairs. A buffet of cheeses, deli meats, and breads greeted her. The dining area was empty. It appeared she and Shark were the only guests.

Is this a terrorist safe house? And is this innkeeper part of the terrorist gang?

She spent the remainder of the day wandering about the lobby, searching for clues to her whereabouts. There were many German collectibles displayed about the inn, but no maps or sightseeing pamphlets common in American bed-and-breakfasts.

THE SUN WAS setting below the forest tree line and Shark had still not returned. Jamie retreated to her room and dug a cell phone out of her duffle.

"I think I blew it, boss. Shark left me at this inn somewhere in the Black Forest and hasn't been back since. I don't know if he is coming back or not."

"I can't talk to you right now. I'm having an important meeting. Give it some time. Shark will not leave you in the lurch unless he's on to you. And if he were, you'd already be dead. Call me tonight if he doesn't return."

She felt both stupid and adrift.

SIXTY-TWO

THE TWO HORRIFIC ATTACKS IN France prompted a hastily-called Summit meeting resulting in a detailed report from Danielson. Split screens lit up in each SOS member's situation rooms. They all waited for Danielson to begin, but a pleading Galdet spoke first.

"Please, Monsieur Danielson, tell us things we want to know. Tell us we are winning the battle."

"Let me assure all of you we have made a great deal of progress in our war with this terrorist."

"So, Mr. Chairman," interrupted Sokoloven, "does that mean you are close to capturing this fiend?"

Danielson hesitated. "Not yet. But…"

"What is this 'but?'" questioned Sokoloven.

"With due respect, let me review where we are," responded Danielson. He opened his briefcase, removing a packet of papers duplicating the ones he emailed to the SOS members. "We know for a fact that the two attacks in France were accomplished by our targeted terrorist. There was a prior attack in Africa by the same group. Dr. Siegal and I believe the African attack was to test the virus's effectiveness and the accuracy of the handheld rocket launcher taken from the U.S."

King Ishmere said, "Mr. Danielson, what else must we know about this virus?"

"We know from Cho-Se that it's stored in airtight containers at zero degrees centigrade. This means it must be stored in a permanent location and only moved when used for an attack."

"On the surface, this virus seems very easy to manage," said King Ishmere. "But what kind of chemical degree would one have to have to safely discharge it?"

President Cho-Se responded, "Anyone could maintain it and even duplicate it with a minimal technical background."

"Very interesting," continued King Ishmere. "So who can tell us about the weapons delivery system?"

President Russell answered. "The rocket launcher taken from our base is as simple to manage as the virus itself. The firing device is similar to a handheld antitank weapon with a range of over half a mile. Besides the launcher, ten cases, each containing twenty hollow-core shells, were also taken. These shells are airtight and can be safely loaded at temperatures below freezing and taken to the location of a raid. Any questions?"

"President Russell and President Cho-Se, it seems the duplicity of your two countries have created a weapon that anyone can use to destroy the world. Yes, indeed," concluded King Ishmere.

President Sokoloven asked, "Is there any good news you can report, Chairman Danielson?"

"Yes, we are certain the terrorist home base is somewhere in Germany. And like his German predecessors of World War I and II, he is after complete domination. But his method is different. Instead of attacking in the historic way of killing off most of his enemies and taking over their territory, his method is control by intimidation."

"And just how do you think he can do this?" President Sokoloven asked. "No one can force me to act by intimidation. We Russians invented intimidation. Once I get my hands on him, he will not last a minute"

"His plan is to select a country with leadership which can be removed from office at the whim of its people. Once in control, he will continue to another country, and so on."

"Continue, I don't fully understand. This terrorist can control me without controlling me?" asked Sokoloven.

"Exactly. He has selected France to start with because they have a government chosen by a coalition of smaller political factions. A few factions can call for an election and remove current leadership from office. The leadership of this form of government requires compromise from different elected party members to remain in power."

"So," said President Sokoloven, "how does this intimidation work? As I've said, I could never be intimidated."

Siegal entered the conversation and continued the explanation. "In France, he sent up a trial balloon with the attack on President Galdet's motorcade to see how his nation would react. Then he carried out raids on two unsuspecting villages. He didn't need an entire army of mercenaries to do this. He spread the killer virus and was well out of the area before the effects of it took place.

Danielson continued the explanation. "Once the level of threat is established, the terrorist will make requests for minor favors, such as releasing criminals from prison or maybe asking for a small ransom, harmless on the surface, but setting precedence for something more compelling. As time goes by, these demands will turn military in nature. The country can evolve into a police state with an ever-increasing army and will be told to take over weaker nations."

President Cho-Se spoke next. "Chairman Danielson, you believe this terrorist rat's nest is in Germany?"

"Yes. The two previous major world takeover attempts originated in Germany during the World Wars. The ideology of an Aryan 'super race' has deeply permeated the German psyche for over a hundred years. Two defeats have not cooled their fervor. This arrogance has spawned our terrorist."

"Good," continued President Cho-Se, "now all we have to do is find his base of operations and, as you say in America, take him out."

"Do you have a plan?" asked President Cho-Se. "Mr. Chairman, you always must have a plan."

"I do," responded Danielson. "We have an operative in the area that has close contact with one of the terrorist's mid-level people. Just minutes before this meeting, I received a call from this agent. As you know, our terrorist has already killed two of our previous agents and would not blink at killing another."

King Ishmere entered the conversation. "How will you proceed, Mr. Chairman?"

"Our plan is based on this operative being able to help us locate the terrorist's home base. We'll know in one day, two at the most, if our effort is successful. But just in case it fails, we are moving other elements into place. My special strike force is on the ground. If the surprise raid on the rat's nest is effective, we will be able to recover planning documents, the stockpile of V-32 virus, and our head rat as well. Our takeover must be at the highest level of secrecy because we have only one chance to succeed. Should the head terrorist escape, he will disappear into the countryside and start over somewhere else."

Chairman Cho-Se abruptly changed the subject. "I expect you intend to return the virus to us since it was originally taken from Lijiang. We created Virus 32 for the peaceful purpose of making our inner cities habitable for our citizens. Only this time, of course, we shall protect it more carefully."

"Collecting all the available virus will be difficult enough. I would imagine its disposal should be the result of an agreement between all of you," said Danielson.

"I would be honored to provide manpower to invade your rat's nest," suggested President Sokoloven.

"Deciding who goes in is premature," said Russell. "I think that should be something we determine once the logistics of the attack are a known."

"Thank you, Mr. President," said Danielson. "If time permits, I will be contacting each of you with the finalized plan before we carry out the raid. If not, it shall be my responsibility. The number of troops defending the rat's nest is small and my specially-trained quick-strike force is more than adequate to do the job. You entrusted me to take this responsibility and I am up to the task. Is that still acceptable to everyone?"

Danielson had no intention of letting his plan be known in advance. "And now I ask all of you to have patience. Remember, his only weapon is fear." He paused. "I believe this meeting is over. Good luck to everyone. And especially President Galdet who, for the moment, is shouldering the burden for all of us."

The screens went black.

"YOU WERE VERY quiet today, Ross."

"Something about today bothered me. I can't put a label on it. I think some members of the SOS are developing their own agendas," said Siegal as they took their coffee and tray of cookies into the living room. Danielson lit the fireplace.

Settled in the soft chairs around the warming fire, Siegal continued. "I have never been comfortable with these world leaders. I noted you were not all that sure yourself, wanting to use your own special forces instead of a multinational team. These power brokers of the world have come together. They perceived a common problem they could not solve. But they allowed two relative lightweights, you and me, to lead them. This is not consistent with their strong personalities. It just doesn't fit."

"I don't see anything unusual in that. These men often delegate jobs to their lower echelon. They have a problem and we are instructed to solve it. Once it's all over, everyone goes back home. And then they can go back to being their original egotistical selves."

"You just hit the phrase that pays."

"I did?"

"Yes. Egotistical selves. As a behaviorist, I don't use the Freudian term. I call it a sense of self-importance. That's the same phrase I used in profiling our terrorist rat."

"I'm seeing your point. You say that one, maybe two are no better or worse than our terrorist. So?"

"I don't know. If they're no better or worse, than maybe, they're more of the same."

SIXTY-THREE

IT'S AFTER TEN A.M. AND he didn't come back last night. Have I failed? I need to clear my head. Maybe a walk in the woods will make me feel better. I hope there aren't any wolves out there. I've already been bitten by one wild animal.

It was almost noon when Jamie returned to the inn. Shark's parking place was still vacant. A call to Danielson was in order, then making a quick exit.

Damn, I left my phone in the room.

Jamie opened the door to her room. She felt goosebumps. One of her dresser drawers was slightly ajar. Then she noticed the clothes in her closet were rearranged.

Those bastards tossed my room. What were they looking for?" *The frau innkeeper has to be working for the rat and was checking me out.* Then she smiled. *Good thing I forgot to take out my diaphragm from last night, or they would have found my locator. Am I really suspected as a spy or is this routine? I think better after a reviving shower. Then I'll call Danielson.*

Shark arrived as Jamie stepped out of the shower.

"Sorry, I had to work late so I stayed over." He kissed her cheek. "Hope you were not too worried."

"Here I am, stranded in a strange place. Damn right I was worried." Then she softened her tone. "I thought you left me for your mother or someone younger and more beautiful than me."

She chose not to discuss her mysterious visitor, not knowing whether Shark planned to have the room searched or if it was the head rat's doing.

During their lunch, Jamie decided she had to find the rat's nest and decided to push the issue.

"Is this adventure of ours going to be the same every day?" Jamie asked. "You leave me alone without any forewarning. Do you ever get the day off so we can go sightseeing or something?"

"It can't happen right now. This is the way it has to be. I'm falling for you in a very big way. But for now, work is the most important thing in my life and we just have to fit our private time in as we can."

Jamie pouted like a teenager. "You know, I thought maybe there was a city or something near here where I can at least spend the day shopping. It's just one of those girl things I have to fulfill. I have a couple of nieces who I like to buy touristy things for."

She patted her groin area, feeling comfort knowing her locator beacon told Danielson's men where she was. But she wanted to know real places for her own comfort. Right now all she knew was that she and Shark were staying at an inn somewhere in the Rhine Forest in Germany. Her walk in the woods didn't help. Her line of sight, even in the small clearings, was less than a hundred yards.

"Sorry, honey. There are no towns between here and my work. My job takes me to a remote little cottage just a few kilometers from here. Maybe in a couple of days we can leave and spend some time playing tourist together." He gave her a kiss on the neck. "You'll hate this, but I have to go back this afternoon."

AS SOON AS Shark left, Jamie got her cell phone and sneaked back into the woods behind the inn, hoping the hausfrau did not see her.

"Yes?"

"Let me bring you up to date while I have a chance. I can't talk much; I think the innkeeper is on the terrorist's payroll or a sympathizer. Last night I thought our plan was blown when Shark didn't come back to the inn. When he did, I urged him to have some lover's time sightseeing. When he said that can happen in a couple of days, I felt things were beginning to move. Each day he leaves in the morning for a place, he says, that is near here. I tried to get him to drop me off into a town on the way. No luck. He said there were no towns nearby. I feel like a failure."

"You are doing great, Jamie. You brought us this close to the rat's nest. A little bit more and you get us all the way."

"I just feel like I keep coming up blank. Do you think I subconsciously want Shark to get away?"

"Not you, Jamie. You're doing your job. You won't change allegiance and go over to the dark side. I'm betting on that."

"I know what I'm here for."

"This can put your mind at ease at least a little bit. You know the locator beacon you have? We've been tracing you ever since you left the French Riviera. We know exactly where you are and we can come in and extract you in less than thirty minutes."

"Oh wonderful," responded Jamie sarcastically. "That makes me feel much better. Oh, I almost forgot to tell you. My room was tossed yesterday. It was a good thing I didn't take the time to get the beacon out or I would probably be a dead lover right about now. Just dumb luck, I guess."

"Luck is never dumb. It's skillful awareness of a situation."

"What do you suggest I do next?"

"If you can't get him to take you, then you have to let him take part of you. Your beacon. You've got to get it on him somehow."

THAT NIGHT SHARK parked his Beemer at the inn shortly after dark. Jamie felt both nervous and relieved at the same time. She had to make her move before he left the next morning. Following dinner, they took a walk around the inn, enjoying the crisp night air.

Shark took Jamie's hand and announced, "Our vacation is almost over. I have one more day here and we will be off. Have you had a nice time so far?"

"Yes and no. Our time at night has been wonderful; my days are a bore. Where will we go next? Will we finally get our chance to do some sightseeing?"

"I'm afraid when we are through here, you and I will have to go our different ways. After a time, if you wish, we can connect again."

Jamie pretended to make an excuse. "My time with you has been wonderful. But like you, I have my own obligations and need to return to the States."

Hope Shark doesn't see through my words.

They spent much of the night caressing each other's bodies and making love. Before going to sleep, Jamie asked a question. "I know your mother did not name you Shark. Do you have a real name?"

"Alexander Rose."

"Alexander Rose. I like it," said Jamie, thinking this is probably the last and most honest thing she would ever know about him.

AT BREAKFAST, SHARK announced he had to leave right away. There were some very important things to finish and he would be home early to help pack.

"I suggest we spend a day in the Swiss Alps and you can catch your plane to the United States from there."

"Sounds wonderful, Alexander Rose."

"I like the way you say my name. It's been a while since anyone used it."

"I'll walk you to the car. Then I can kiss you goodbye. I can't wait till you get back."

Shark climbed in the driver's side. Jamie came around and planted a long and warm kiss, first on the neck and worked her way across his left ear reaching his lips. Her right arm draped around the bucket seat. As the kiss ended, Jamie's hand opened and a small item dropped to the floor behind the seat.

The engine roared to life at the turn of the key. Shark cruised out of the parking lot and down the road into the forest. The locator was on the move. So were Danielson's special forces.

JAMIE HEARD AN automobile engine break the silence as the sun made its daily ascent. She peered out the window expecting to see the familiar red convertible. Instead, a black Mercedes SUV pulled into the space normally occupied by Shark. Three men got out of the car. It was Kevin, still with his arm in a sling, Doug, and Tim. She rushed out and gave them a hug.

"I thought Danielson sent you all home."

Doug explained. "Sending us home meant we were off the payroll and Mr. Danielson no longer controlled what we do. Jamie, we're a team. You going solo felt wrong. We convinced the boss to let us stay nearby, undercover, in case you needed us. When he told us of the plan for your extraction, we insisted on being here."

"Hell, Jamie," said Tim. It was the first time any of them heard him swear. "We'd fight this terrorist with slingshots and pea shooters if need be."

Tears of happiness and hugs of joy followed.

Kevin urged, "Now get in. Danielson's soldiers are following Shark to the rat's hideout as we speak. He wants you safe should anything go wrong. You don't have time to pack. We're out of here, stat."

SIXTY-FOUR

DANIELSON'S SPECIAL FORCES FOLLOWED JAMIE'S beacon in two assault helicopters, carefully staying just out of sight of Shark's BMW. Forty minutes later Shark pulled up to a small acreage surrounded by an eight-foot electrified, razor-wire fence. An armed guard opened the gate and directed him to proceed.

The choppers landed in a small clearing out of earshot of the compound. The first person exiting out of the lead Blackhawk was big enough to have been a football linebacker. It was the newly-commissioned Lieutenant Ben Goldberg. Thirteen others, all dressed in camouflage gear, gathered behind him as they edged to within sight of the compound, about one hundred meters away.

Thirteen men, faces in green and black war camo, crouched around their leader, holding hands like a football team just before the kickoff. Only here in the forest of Germany it was no game.

Goldberg pointed out the various strategic points: the electric fence guarding the perimeter, a single-story farmhouse, a storage shed directly behind the farmhouse, and two bunkhouses.

Goldberg whispered, "Capture any who give up. We need them for interrogation. But, any doubt about your safety, kill first. We need to recover anything that appears to look like chemicals in airtight containers. The chemicals need to be refrigerated and any cooling units will help us locate them. That new wiring strung into the storage shed makes me believe the chemicals are stored there."

One assault team member scanned the four structures with a heat-sensing probe. Six images showed in the farmhouse. Approximately a dozen lifeforms were in each bunkhouse. No image appeared in the storage shed. The only guard outside was at the entrance gate.

Goldberg continued giving orders. "We'll split into three squads. I'll lead Alpha squad and attack the house. I expect the highest-level terrorist to be there. Beta and Gamma, you take out the support personnel in the two bunkhouses. Circle around behind the compound and commence your attack from the rear. Our degree of surprise should equalize the numbers disadvantage. Set your watches for three minutes. Mark."

A sharpshooter from Alpha squad screwed a sound muffler on his rife, took careful aim and fired.

Ping.

The guard grabbed his neck and could only gurgle a warning cry as he fell to the ground, spurting blood from his severed carotid artery.

Another Alpha member disabled the electric fence as Beta and Gamma squads moved into position between the two bunkhouses. They cut openings in the fence and waited. On the mark of their coordinated watches, they moved through their openings into the compound.

One minute.

"Shit. Where'd he come from?" whispered a Beta squad member.

One of the terrorists stepped out of an outhouse near one of the bunkhouses. He spotted the squad and reached for his sidearm.

Gamma squad leader radioed, "Cover is blown. We've been spotted."

Pop. Ping.

Two shots rang out. The first came from the direction of the Gamma squad, the second from the handgun of the terrorist, who instinctively pulled the trigger as he fell.

"Fire at will," yelled the Beta squad leader.

The walls of both bunkhouses splintered into kindling. Fewer and fewer return shots came from them, until only the sounds of the Beta and Gamma squad guns were heard. As the attackers entered the buildings, it was obvious the onslaught was complete. No prisoners.

Alpha squad attacked the farmhouse with full arsenal blazing. Snipers from inside fired back, but their efforts were futile. Then silence. A few seconds later three shots were heard from inside. A white cloth appeared in the window. Three men, hands held high, marched single file onto the porch. Their hands were quickly banded.

One squad member stood guard over the prisoners as Goldberg led the other two into the living room, the main field office of the terrorists. Four men lay dead on the floor. Among them was Alexander Rose, the Shark. A slumped figure wearing an officer's coat was facedown on the small desk. He had three bullet holes that punctured his coat near where his heart was. On the wall behind him was the slogan "TRIUMPH UBER ALLES."

"It looks as if the three prisoners took their leader's life, sir," said one of the men. "They were probably ordered to assassinate their leader and then shoot themselves but chickened out."

"That's the way it seems," answered Goldberg. He leaned into his shoulder mic and said, "Beta, Gamma squads, report."

"Sir, we just entered a storage building. We hit paydirt. There is a large walk-in refrigerator with several metal milk sized canisters inside."

"Good work. Secure them and have them ready for delivery."

"How did your men fare?"

"I sustained one slight injury," said Beta leader. "Gamma squad has two. None of the wounds look serious. We've prepared them for evac."

Goldberg punched his shoulder radio. "This is the Exterminator. The rat's nest is cleared. Bring in the choppers and land inside the compound. We have three winged ducks. Also, we need to load five canisters of nerve virus."

"Roger that, Exterminator. We're on our way."

"Beta leader, stay with the canisters. Be sure they stay good and cold. We don't want any accidents."

Goldberg took out his cell phone and dialed a number. "This is Lieutenant Goldberg, sir. It's all over. We think we got all of them. We've taken three prisoners from the farmhouse. The rest have all been killed. The containers are secure and being handled as instructed. Your agent at the inn has been successfully extracted. Mission complete. We'll be returning tonight."

"Tell me about the head rat," said Danielson.

"Just before we entered the headquarters, we heard three shots. Inside we saw the head terrorist slumped over his desk. He was wearing an officer's tunic. There were three holes in it directed at the heart."

"Are you sure? Dr. Siegal here tells me to be wary of his tricks. This man is not likely to commit suicide. Look at him again. Do you see anything unusual?"

"I'm not sure what you want."

"Just describe what you see."

"Wait, I think I see what you mean. The man at the desk has a peculiar color around his lips."

"What else?"

"Something else. There's no blood around the bullet holes."

"I knew it. He was dead before they shot him, probably by strangulation. He's not the head terrorist. Examine the three prisoners carefully. Is there anything unusual about any of them?"

"The one holding the white flag. His hands seem too soft to be a worker. And his nails are manicured."

"Ben, you just captured the head terrorist alive."

SIXTY-FIVE

THREE DAYS FOLLOWING THE EXTRACTION of Jamie from the German inn and successful raid of the rat's nest, a military dispatcher delivered a thick envelope to Siegal and Danielson at the chalet.

"Pull up a chair, Ross," said Danielson. "Let's see what the fruits of your labor have brought."

Danielson opened the envelope and spread out the contents on the dining room table. The narrative was short, only a few pages. The bulk of the envelope was satellite and ground photographs.

Siegal looked at the first photograph and smiled. "I think I recognize that large man in this picture, even with all that paint on his face. That's Ben, right? Then I suspect the others are more of your special forces men you had stationed around the chalet. Are these your men or part of our government's special guard?"

Danielson smiled back, "A little of both. Originally, they were part of the elite guard that protected the president. But due to the length of this mission, he assigned them to my control and added new Secret Service people for himself."

"These photographs are amazing. It's almost like being there. Their attention to detail amazes me. Even the slogan behind the desk, "Triumph Uber Alles." I suppose you'll now tell me some were taken by Hollywood cinematographers assigned to you from MGM."

"I can't tell you that, but they had hands-on experience in Iraq."

After scanning the pictures, they settled down to the written part of the report, titled "MISSION CODENAME IMMUNIZE."

The first pages, with accompanying photos, were of Jamie, Doug, Kevin and Tim and the initial raids near Saint-Aygulf. None of the photo or descriptions contained the more private moments between Jamie and Alexander Rose.

"I'm glad they left out the intimate details. I wouldn't want Jamie to become fodder for Facebook posts."

The two studied the raid of the rat's nest.

"Do you recognize any of the terrorists from these pictures?" asked Siegal.

"No, but our DNA evidence indicates one was the great-grandson of Reinhardt Heydrick, head of the Gestapo during World War II. Shark's ancestor was Dr. Gerhard Rose, convicted of medical atrocities and sentenced to life imprisonment during the Nuremberg trials. Until recently, both the head rat and Shark were living in Argentina, just waiting for their turn. I suspect others in that farmhouse were also descendants of Nazi despots. We hit one hell of a rats' nest."

"These terrorists were trained and shaped to be exactly as they were, the future of German domination."

"They were more than just terrorists, Ross. They were almost World War III. And your theories stopped them in time."

"Just one more thing. What about the lady innkeeper? Was she part of the rat pack?"

"There is no evidence to indicate this. My team examined the inn's guest register. It seems Jamie was the only American woman ever staying there. Our frau may have been sympathetic to the rat's cause, but all evidence shows she was just curious to know about Jamie and searched her room to find out."

"Then that's it? Case closed?"

"Yep. Your job is over. The terrorist group has been erased and the V-32 virus has been recovered. Tonight, we can celebrate and begin thinking about returning to a normal life."

"Or until the next terrorist surfaces."

"That, too. You can go back to teaching, experimenting or whatever else you want to do. If you want, this chalet can be yours and you can run a consulting business from here. I promise you will get more work than you ever hoped."

Siegal said, "There's still something that needs resolution. What's going to happen to the virus?"

"That's up to the Summit leaders. We appropriated it for them. They can destroy or return it all to China. I only hope they destroy it."

"Me too," agreed Siegal. "Maybe we can destroy it before and give them overheated virus in the containers. We could use the oops technique."

"The oops technique? What the hell is that?"

"It's very technical. We pretend to make a mistake and dispose of the virus by letting it get too warm. There's no reversing the process once it's destroyed."

"Remember, the Chinese developed V-32 once and have the formula to do it again," said Danielson.

"So I guess destroying the stuff isn't the best plan."

"What's bugging you, Ross? I know you as well as any one person can. You have something on your mind. What is it? What's been tweaking you since the last Summit meeting? Out with it, friend."

"I'm not sure we can trust all these SOS guys to stay as diligent about saving the world as they pretend. The SOS members are once again high-powered world leaders. At least now that our head rat has been neutralized."

"I'll agree with you. So…"

"So if we analyze their functioning styles, they are individually self-righteous and crave power. Probably even more power than they have now."

"All right, I give you that."

"For the past month or so, they have allowed us to lead them like bulls with rings in their noses, just as we described our terrorist acting had he been successful. The parallel is just too similar."

"What are you driving at?"

"I don't know. Just a feeling. It's not human nature to behave one way for a long time and be successful at it, and then make a complete turnaround. It just doesn't fit."

"And?"

"These gentlemen are more like our terrorist than they are different from him. Most can handle their style in a positive way. But given the same opportunity to control the world, at least one would jump at it. And it would only take one of them with the virus to set the whole series of events back into motion."

"Who do we worry about most?"

"I've been thinking of the possibilities. Whoever it is will want us out of the way for sure. Our lives won't be worth shit."

"Nevertheless, protocol requires the virus to be delivered to the Summit members. I am calling a meeting for the first of next week."

THE ELECTRONIC MEETING with the SOS went smoothly. Danielson had faxed his report, together with copies of the photographs, to each of the members. Along with the report, Danielson sent the suggestion to split the four virus containers among each of the leaders. He promised to deliver the containers following the meeting, along with technical training of how to contain and control it.

The leaders applauded the work of both Chairman Danielson and Dr. Siegal.

Siegal felt it was an empty victory. Somewhere out there was the next rat terrorist. One who would be after both Danielson and himself. He could sense it in his behavioral bones.

SIXTY-SIX

IT HAD BEEN SIX MONTHS since the rat terrorist organization was eliminated. The nations of the world were back to their status quo, fighting and bickering with each other. Always just short of World War III.

Siegal accepted Danielson's offer to make the chalet a permanent home. The first thing he did was to disconnect the green phone and burn it in the fireplace. His only connection with the outside world was the television, an occasional mail-order catalog, and the situation room equipment used for communication with Danielson.

As Danielson promised, Siegal's consulting business flourished. He made no contact with his former friends, including Simi. He remained a social hermit, drinking too much beer and worrying about the thinning spot on the back of his head.

It was a late day in May when Siegal received a personal dispatch from President Russell:

I am sorry to inform you that an airplane accident claimed the life of our mutual friend, Tom Danielson. He was flying to the Mideast as liaison officer for a public-relations firm. His plane vanished from the radar screen somewhere near the Philippines. An intensive search of the area was made but there were no signs of any remains.

I invite you to the White House to share a moment of re-membrance together for a very good and loyal friend.

Elwin Russell

Siegal chose not to attend. He felt certain the new terrorist activities had begun, just as he predicted.

Am I the next accident? Can I prevent it? Or is it my fate?

It was ten o'clock, time for the evening news. He turned on the television.

The banner story flashed on the screen"

THE UNITED ARAB REPUBLIC LOST A GREAT STATESMAN TODAY

King Ishmere was found dead in his bedchamber early this morning. His medical advisors report that the King died following a short illness.

During the King's illness, the leadership reign of the Republic has been in the hands of Sheikh Ahmad Machim. Sheikh Machim, identified as a hardliner diplomat, has also been serving as military chief of staff. There have been unsubstantiated reports that many small sheikdoms were eliminated during his short tenure as military chief .

I was correct about the nation, only wrong about the man. With Danielson out of the way, they'll be coming for me next. I should be frightened. Instead I feel a certain calmness, similar to the gnu with a lion on his back; there is no sense to struggle against the inevitable.

Siegal walked out to the patio and looked over the serene meadow below. *It was just two years ago, but seems an eternity. I was a research psychologist with two very promising graduate students. We proved theories far beyond what other behavioral researchers had only attempted to postulate, thanks to Danielson and his phony National Research Committee. Then my life went from notoriety to anonymity. All ties with the outside world were severed one by one. Only Danielson, if he was alive, would even be aware of who or what I've become aside from the SOS members. And now I too will disappear without a trace.*

A loud knock on the front door startled Siegal. He closed his eyes for a moment, then opened them, feeling these to be his final moments.

Please let it be quick and painless. He walked inside and opened the door.

"Dr. Siegal?"

"Yes?"

"Registered letter for you, sir."

Siegal signed the receipt and closed the door.

There was no return address on the envelope. He opened the flap and read.

Hey, friend. I know this is a shock, but it is really me. I'm not dead. I had to fake my death to stay out of harm's way and monitor the V-32 virus.

You were right about a new terrorist coming from the ranks of the SOS. They came after me so I ditched my plane in the Pacific and had Ben pick me out of the soup.

I just got intel they are coming after you at the chalet. You don't have much time.

You need to get to the United Airline counter at DIA in Denver. There will be a ticket waiting.

Siegal looked at Tigger still on the wall. "Goodbye, old friend." He finished reading the message.

And if they trap you inside the chalet before you can leave, there is an old gold mine shaft entrance under the floor in the kitchen pantry. Be careful. I don't know how stable the support timbers are. The shaft runs parallel and comes out about a quarter mile away from the house. From there you need to get off the mountain. Central City is about one mile straight downhill. Find transportation there.
I can't help you anymore.
Godspeed, Tom

Siegal looked out over the patio.

He thought he saw movement in the trees at the edge of the meadow. Another wild animal? No. This was not Siegal's imagination playing tricks in his mind.

Four men, faces covered with black masks, carrying rifles emerged from the thicket.

My keys to the car. Where the fuck are they? He searched his pockets. My room. I left them on the dresser.

He recovered the keys and ran out the front door to the parking area.

Too late. Sniper bullets whizzed by him, striking the car and blowing out a tire. He ran back into the chalet.

I'm trapped. No, the mine shaft.

He hurried to the pantry and threw open the door. Bullets started coming in from different directions, breaking windows and slamming into the walls around him.

"Where the hell is that entrance?"

Siegal shoved boxes and other stored items around until he found the trapdoor, stiff from disuse. He finally tugged it open.

The chalet's front door shattered from rifle blasts; the attackers rushed the entryway. Crashing glass told him they were also entering through the dining room patio.

Voices in Arabic came closer. Siegal found a flashlight on one of the shelves and directed the beam down the hole. He eased himself through and dropped to the earthen floor below.

Running and stumbling in the semidarkness with only his small flashlight to guide him, Siegal felt his way through the tunnel. The voices got louder, telling him they found the trapdoor entrance. He tried to negotiate without his light, but only succeeded in bumping his head and bloodying his elbow.

Finally, he saw a dim light a few yards ahead. He sped up.

An Arab yelled and immediately a salvo of shots rang in his direction. A weak timber creaked as it recieved several bullets; it split apart and the ceiling collapsed the portion of tunnel between him and his attackers.

Siegal emerged from the old mine entrance and looked up at the late afternoon sun. He allowed himself a moment to sit on a rock and rest.

Fft, fft, fft. A helicopter that had followed the escape attempt hovered overhead.

Over the loudspeaker, a voice yelled out in broken English, "Do not attempt to run, Dr. Siegal. We will not harm you."

"Bullshit, you bastards."

Siegal ran for a thick grove of aspen out of sight of the sharpshooters. Two Arabs chased after him on foot.

One mile downhill takes me to Central City.

He zigged and zagged among the trees to keep his pursuers from getting a clear shot while remembering to keep going downhill. There was a constant chatter of Arabic over the helicopter loudspeaker, telling the two on the ground where he was.

The hill toward town was steep and covered with shale rock. It was hard for Siegal to keep his balance, but harder for the others in battle gear and holding weapons.

"Aiah!" Siegal heard the cry from one of the pursuers who appeared badly hurt.

Now only one on the ground. Less than a half mile now.

Siegal hid behind a tree, a jagged rock in his hand. The rustle of boots on the slippery shale told Siegal his quarry was near. He hid behind a scrub oak and waited. The man passed just feet away.

Thunk went the hollow sound of the rock as it hit the Arab's skull. He slumped, lifeless.

The buildings of Central City appeared over the next rise.

Another few yards and I can get lost in the crowd.

The gambling town of Central City was always busy with tourists trying their luck at the slot machines. For the moment, Siegal was safe, but the helicopter hovered nearby. He heard a sound from heaven.

"Last call for Denver International Airport. This bus leaves in three minutes."

Siegal stood in line and tried to appear as small as possible. Three minutes felt like an eternity.

Finally, the door closed and the bus began to roll.

THE TICKET WAITED for him at the airline counter as Danielson promised. Siegal had time to buy fresh clothes at one of the shops and discard the ones torn during his escape.

Several hours later he was in Miami and transferring to a float plane headed somewhere south and east.

BY SUNRISE THE next morning, the small plane landed on an un-inhabited island in the Caribbean. The pilot opened the door and let Siegal out.

"Hey. Glad you made it," Tom Danielson said. "Welcome to your new home."